THE KNIFE OF SORROWS

A Blood and Steel Saga Story

E J Doble

ISBN: 9781399976107

Cover art, design and illustration by: @diego_spezzoni

Map illustration and design by: @jogbrogzin

Also by E J Doble:

THE BLOOD AND STEEL SAGA
The Crown of Omens
1: *The Fangs of War*
2: *The Horns of Grief*
The Knife of Sorrows

REALM OF THE PROPHETS
1: *The Crescent Moon*
2: *The Jade Sun*

GRIMDARK FAIRYTALES
Gold, Lock and Key

Dedicated to my readers.

Did you really think I'd kill him off for good?

The Valatuk Hills
J B
2023

CONTENT WARNING

This book contains graphic depictions of violence, dismemberment and bodily mutilation; frequent and heavy profanity; intense scenes of grief, trauma and anger; and the visualisation of apparitions and demons with the intent to physically/emotionally harm people.

This book may be unsuitable for those suffering with schizophrenia or personality/identity disorders.

It is the duty and responsibility of writers to put the reader first, and to keep them appropriately informed of any and all sensitive content described within their work.

"We owe respect to the living;
to the dead, we owe only truth."

Oeuvres, V.1
Virgil

†

Chapter 1

Death Defiant

On a desert plain, in the coursing winds, death approached from the south like a ghost.

Above, in a cloudless sky, the sun made its slow transition overhead and bathed the sands below in light. The harsh breeze rolling off the mountains to the west sent torrents of grit up in spiralling plumes. Rocky outcrops of grey stone – some as large as houses – jutted out from the earth here and there, where tiny desert birds sheltered in their alcoves awaiting the relief of the night.

For few dared venture out into the desert when the sun was at its peak. Few were brave enough – or foolish enough – to go out into the torrid heat, on the thoughtless notion that they could survive. The desert knew no bounds, and offered no mercies. Many who had tried to conquer it had fallen and died, and their bones were returned to the earth without a whisper of prayer to follow.

But death was a fickle creature, and often defied what nature hoped to ordain. As even in the harshness of the desert, with no life for miles around, death made its approach from the south nonetheless.

And they would never even see it coming.

†

Under a large outcrop of blackened stone where the shadows still held out against the sun, three Tarrazi hunters sat pressed against the rock counting their blessings that day.

It was their third day out on the sands since leaving their village in the Valatuk Hills: an area of sandstone cliffs that rose like knuckle-bones to the north-west, swamped in layers of grey trees. It was a hostile place, where only the hardiest souls survived. The Hills had been their home since the dawn of time, and would likely still be there long after their fall. Such was the way of the desert in a sense.

Even when the tree fell, the roots would long remain.

Having set off from their village with meagre supplies and only a handful of spears, the first day had proven largely fruitless for the hunters out on the sands. Despite their prayers to Kal-Vak'tun, and the offerings they had made to the God of the Hunt, their fortunes had been limited at best. They knew Him to be a crafty god, it was true – not that any of them dared usher such heresies – but they had hoped that, in the intense autumn sun, He would prove a touch more forgiving than usual.

So when they then settled down for the second night, stomaching their rations with their spears unbloodied, they did so with heavy hearts and disillusion on their minds, wondering if their prayers would simply go unanswered, and they would be left with nothing to do but starve.

But as they rose on the third day, with Kal-Vak'tun's blessing still wet on their lips, they turned to the south and saw the signs of what they had been looking for at last: depressions in the earth, meandering from side-to-side between the rocks.

Their prey had come at last.

And so they had set off with hoots and jeers, touching the sand to their lips for His blessing, and found the creature nestled in its burrow not far from where they'd made camp. It was a blind serpent, yellow-white in colour, with its tendrils splayed out across the dry earth to detect any dangers while it slept. The poison in its saliva was enough to kill a bear; the electrical pulses in its tendrils could paralyse a man in seconds. But, knowing the creature intimately from generational tales, the hunters had called upon the knowledge of their forefathers and navigated past the tendrils with ease, stepping in close to the creature's flat, exposed head and driving their spears down into the mesh of its brain.

The serpent had died instantaneously. Life left its pale, unseeing eyes. Its wounds had cauterised in the sun before the hunters had even removed it from its burrow, such was the heat that beat down on their backs.

But as they had dragged it back to their camp with jubilant smiles and a warmth in their souls, the hunters knew their struggle had been worth it in the end, and they could feed their village well for days and weeks to come.

Looking on it then from beneath the outcrop of rock – sheltering from the worst of the heat – the hunters studied the serpent's body on the back of their wooden cart, fastened against the panels with thick coils of rope to keep it steady for their long journey ahead. The tendrils along its neck had been flayed off and discarded, and as the serpent lay out in the scolding sun its skin began to slowly petrify, flaking the scales from its back and sealing the fresh meat within. It was still another day's walk until the hunters reached their village, and they knew that letting the creature's skin harden was the safest thing to do before they moved on. That way, less predators would be drawn to the smell as they came out from their subterranean lairs, and the serpent's flesh wouldn't spoil as easily if it all lay sealed inside.

And, if they set a good pace, the hunters knew that they could reach the foot of the Hills before nightfall, avoiding another uneasy sleep out on the sands. But that in itself would require a prodigious amount of luck.

And Kal-Vak'tun was only so forgiving.

Prizing a piece of the serpent's meat from a skewer, one of the hunters with a red mark on his forehead studied it and smiled, grinding it through his teeth to savour the taste. He sat on a natural shelf beneath the huge outcrop of rock, savouring the shadow it produced. The wind diced across his body in waves, prickling his skin with goose-bumps that aggravated the sores on his back. A flask of water sat wedged between his legs, half-empty in an attempt to fight off recurring headaches. One of his fellow hunters lay sleeping at his side, content and still, while another braved the heat in front of him beneath a full-length robe, flaying the last of the beast's tendrils to make ready for transport.

Finishing up and tying the final knot, the robed hunter admired his handiwork and whispered a prayer to the gods. Leaving the body to petrify, he returned to the shadows under the rock and sat next to the others, bearing a harsh look on his face. The red-marked hunter offered his water flask reluctantly: taking three long gulps, the robed man gave his thanks and handed it back, clasping his hands in his lap.

"Az-kabza, Kal-Vak'tun has blessed us today," the robed hunter said in native tongue, gesturing to the serpent before them. "May His greatness be known to all…"

"A mighty beast indeed," the marked one replied, nodding. "I feared that we may not return with anything."

"You doubt the gods' mercy?"

"I doubt nothing." His words were pointed. "But He has blessed us many times before now. Who are we to say when His mercy should come? Or that it shall continue as it always has?"

The robed hunter acknowledged him with a shrug. "Perhaps so."

"As you say though, *va'javesti*, Kal-Vak'tun has indeed blessed us… and blessed the tribe as a whole."

"We shall have to portion it up for the Verlunz and the Gods before we reach camp, as well." He gestured to the skies: imagining the gods there, rubbing their hands together as they awaited their portion of the kill. "I imagine the Verlunz will want the tail meat for their feasts and banquets… it is the most succulent flesh, after all."

"Will the Gods be offered the creature's head, as is normally the case?" the marked one asked.

"It will be as the ceremony dictates: *'that which Their creation has neglected, shall be returned to Them and made right once more'...*"

They both looked over the corpse for a moment and studied the sockets where the eyes should have been. All that remained of them were fleshy lumps of scales and broken skin, so that the beast was completely blind from birth. Using their tendrils to ascertain the world around them – be it to hunt for prey or search for dangers – their eyes had become negligible, and had sealed over with disuse. The Tarrazi knew stories of other species of serpent in the mountains to the far west: similar to the ones of the desert, only they were apparently three times the size and possessed huge eyes the width of shields. Such stories made the dead beast ahead of them seem quaint by comparison – but with their poisoned fangs and paralysing tendrils, the hunters knew better than to second-guess anything they found in the desert.

Especially when death was always so close.

"Dusk should be setting in the next few hours," the marked one exclaimed, looking over to the third hunter sleeping on the rock next to him. "Reckon we should wake her?"

"*Scolgul,* let her rest. She is only young... I imagine this was one of her first successful hunts." The robed hunter kissed two fingers and rubbed a circle on his chest-plate where his heart was. "Let the Gods dance in her dreams in peace."

"Speaking of which... huntresses are more rare in these times, are they not?" The marked one spoke in a hushed tone, as if sharing a secret. "They do not venture out into the wilds with us as often as they used to. Especially since the... well..."

"Since the *Zoltharyya,* yes," the robed figure muttered, unashamed of the term and the hate it brought in his chest. "And as for why there are less of them, well... it is fear that drives the change: we Tarrazi fear for our survival and for our people, even more so when we are faced with the threat of our one *true* enemy." He grimaced. "With the *Zoltha* returning to our lands and attacking our people in the far south, the battlegrounds are not the place for a huntress at this time... especially when the life of the clans is under threat."

"And yet, why is that? Why do they do it?"

"Because of the power they hold within their bodies, and the future they ensure for all of us. They are the bearers of new life in this world, as much as they are the fighters of death…"

The marked hunter frowned. "So… you say that they abandon their ways, to——"

"They take up the *honour* of bearing the next generation of warriors, and *forfeit* their posts as huntresses of the clan, *tarmun*… let us not be *dismissive* of that." The words came out almost as a growl, and the hunter visibly recoiled next to him – but whether that was out of fear or disgust, the robed hunter could not discern. "When faced with existential threats, it is good to maintain our ancient traditions for the good of the clan. There is nothing to *abandon* in that."

The other hunter pursed his lips. "I suppose so, yes," he replied, with a tone suggesting the opposite. "We are creatures of *tradition*, after all."

"Az-Kabza, yes. As all things should be…"

They sat in silence for some time thereafter, squinting out across the sands ahead. The body of the serpent continued to slowly harden in the sun; wind continued to sweep up into their rocky alcove; the delicate snores of the third hunter tickled in their ears. A great, peaceful absence descended on their meagre camp, as the sun drifted slowly to the west and the shadow grew incrementally ahead of them. It would only be a matter of hours until they were returning north again, traversing the grit paths worn down by generations of hunters who had been and gone before them. Returning to the Valatuk Hills; returning to families and homes and friends, with an overwhelming joy at the success of the hunt. Blessings would be given; the tribe would dance all night in honour of Kal-Vak'tun. Things would be right and merry.

Or rather, that was what the hunters thought would happen. That was where their hopes lay, on the long path ahead.

But death was a fickle creature, and often defied what nature hoped to ordain.

And so when the marked hunter looked off to the south, squinting through the haze of impervious heat, he lifted from his seat with a frown plastered to his brow and ushered three fateful words.

"What is *that*—"

†

The spear of lightning launched from his outstretched hand and met its mark in the blink of an eye, ripping through the two Tarrazi men hunkered down in the shade beneath the rock.

The foremost one, covered by a thick robe, seemed to evaporate before his very eyes as the lightning made impact. Smoke streamed from his body, as every sinew and vessel charred and his skin melted like warm butter. A dark shadow of blood splattered up across the rock-face and stained the sand beneath them, throwing them back several feet in a liquidised pile of limbs.

A heartbeat later, and the strike shot through to the second man, staring dumbly at him with a finger extended. He seemed to shudder on the spot, convulsing like a landed fish, before his eyeballs exploded suddenly and his sockets hollowed out, and his finger flayed open like a snapped branch as he quivered and slumped to the floor.

The wanderer lowered his hand.

He thought it was done—

Another scream cried out almost immediately: lifting from behind the two dead hunters, a young woman dashed out into the light completely engulfed in flames, screeching like a banshee pulling up from the depraved abyss of *hellos*. She clawed at her skin in horror, spinning and spiralling as the flames tore across her body.

The third hunter only managed a few more steps before inevitability took hold: before her legs failed her and her body peeled away and her blood boiled in her veins. She swayed and teetered, languishing like a drunk in a pissed-up part of nowhere, when all of a sudden her breathing stopped and she toppled into the dirt as a corpse, never to rise again as the flames exhumed her and she became nothing but cinder and bone.

Three corpses lay in the sand by the rocky alcove. Three Tarrazi hunters, one and all. Death had claimed them all in the end.

And they had never even seen it coming.

Pacing toward the people he had murdered with his teeth grinding in his jaw, the desert wanderer looked to his hand and regarded it for a moment, smirking at just how powerful the lightning blast had been. Static blue energy coursed up his forearm and dissected his fingers, which had blackened like charred wood over the past few days and were numbed to all sensation. Cracks split his skin apart and exposed dirty flesh beneath, powered by this strange electrical current that seemed to quiver over him in waves. His pulse, bulging softly on his wrist, was hardly natural anymore. He felt it in his chest and his skull too. There was a great power there, indomitable, and resistant to all effects. He was neither hot nor cold; aching, nor old. He was just present, approaching the desecration of the Tarrazi camp.

And gods, did he feel *alive*.

Reaching the camp, he looked down and grimaced at the remains of the first hunter – the first victim of the lightning's blast. His spine remained, and a futile section of skull, but all other bones had been dissolved into dust and had merged with the sands below.

Just beyond, the second hunter was in an equally-debauched state, with bruising all over their pale body and empty sockets where their eyes had been. Red stained every inch of the impact zone around them, sizzling already in the hot sun. It stank of flesh and singed hair, like the rind on a roasting pig.

Gazing down upon them carelessly – curling his nose up at the stinking corpse – the wanderer offered no prayers nor sympathies to whichever of their foul gods was listening. Instead, he rolled phlegm along his tongue and spat into the sand at his side, where the mucus hissed and bubbled out of existence in seconds.

Nothing lasts long out here, he thought with a smirk.

Or nothing mortal, that is.

Acknowledging the other body ahead of him – that was now little more than a smouldering carcass spitting fat – he turned to the cart on his right and frowned at the weird, scaly worm that the hunters had trussed to it with thick rope. It was some serpent, was all that he could ascertain, and a large one at that. It was blind, and pale, and possessed no obvious defences on its strange, translucent skin. The hunters had impaled its head several times, and had severed something along its neck with clean, precise cuts. From the butchery marks he could see along its side, it was clear that whoever the hunters were that he had just killed, they were very skilled at their enterprise.

And, at that fact, he allowed himself a smile.

Because where there's skill and technical ability among the native Tarrazi… that usually means a settlement is close by.

Lifting his head, the wanderer shielded his eyes from the sun and looked off to the north-west, away from the unending sands.

And there, about a half-day's walk away, he spied dark shadows and rising mounds pull up from the expanse of the desert, spreading out across the base of the mountains imperiously. He spotted vegetation and life there, with a deceptive mist hanging over everything that one could almost mistake for campfire smoke. With no other signs of life in the vastness all around him, he could only assume the hunters hailed from those same distant hills, and had been planning a return journey there once dusk had started to fall.

Not that they'll be needing to now, he thought facetiously, looking back down to the corpses. *Even so, the presence of Tarrazi in those hills is a good sign. It means I can get out of this gods'-forsaken desert, and reach the Wastelands in the north without suffering so much of this heat.*

He sensed the energy churn in his hand.

That, and I can find out just how powerful this new life has made me.

Reaching down, he prized a small flask from the second hunter's hand and made to take a swig from it – only for the water to have completely evaporated from the lightning strike, so he was left with not even a drop.

He scowled and threw the flask back down into the sand. Stretching his back out, he moved out from the rock's imposing shadow and looked to the distant hills again, sensing a quiet rage turn in his chest.

Traversing those lands, and continuing onwards, puts me a step closer to the truth…

The energy surged in his fingertips; sparks flashed across his palm suddenly.

She's out there somewhere, I know. Out there with bloody hands and hate in her heart, relishing her guilt like lust. Ready to kill, and destroy everything in her path.

She is not the person I once knew; she has become a monster of her own making. And in this new life, with these powers, I am the only one who can stop her evil from spreading.

Closing his palm – subduing the energy that raged within him – Markus started walking.

I'm coming for you, Sav…

†

Chapter 2

The Mud and the Sun

It took one good punch to the head for Xafiri to acknowledge his opponent was better than him, and a second to be absolutely certain he would lose. So when the third punch came, and he managed to duck beneath the meaty fist like a cat, he considered it a blessing of sorts, albeit short-lived.

Stepping back, he wiped a slick of thick mud from his chest and assessed his options, cursing at the heat across his neck. His skull thundered from his opponent's punches: the side of his head felt dented, almost, and an awful ringing chimed in his ears. The cloth wraps woven over his knuckles did little to numb the pain of landing a few good hits. His mother would have told him to mitigate the issue by hitting the soft bits under his arms.

And his father would've told him he was wasting his time, and that he was too feeble to ever win anyway.

Az-Kabza, you're a tough one, Xafiri acknowledged, sizing up his opponent again. He was a lumbering figure, as if he'd been carved from stone but with none of the good graces to go with it. All muscle and knots of flesh, chiselled in place with an ugly perfection. A flash of black-grey hair lined his scalp, curling at the edges in knots, and the black *zaz-gûla* beneath his eyes looked almost like tears. The fact he possessed any facial marks at all meant he must have been over seventeen-winter's old, putting him at least a year older than Xafiri was.

Which also makes this fight invalid, if you refer to the ancient texts, Xafiri considered. *An Unproven like myself should only face another Unproven, if the rite-of-passage is to be deemed legitimate… but, as usual, no-one seems to care for tradition where I'm involved.* He flexed his knuckles and sighed. *Which means I'm left here, dancing in the wind against a Proven man, with the odds entirely stacked against me.*

And my future as a Tarrazi on the line.

He grit his teeth and his opponent advanced again, grappling him across the shoulders as Xafiri reached up to grab the man's collar-bone. He lowered his head like a rutting bull, feeling the man's sweaty scalp brush against his own thin streak of hair. They braced against each other's arms, straining muscles, pressing down with their legs to try and push the other one back. Their feet lay completely submerged in coagulated mud; the sun was impossibly hot and burning overhead. Saliva dripped from their mouths like dogs, baying for blood.

Xafiri felt the brute's left arm dip, and sensed the next attack instinctively. He let go of the man's right arm – twisting away as a punch lunged toward him – and ran through with his own fist. Connecting with the lean muscle under the brute's arm, he heard a grunt somewhere ahead of him and smirked quietly.

Not savouring the moment for too long, however, as the man's stray fist swung through again for another hit far quicker than Xafiri had anticipated. With few options available, the young fighter tensed his stomach and took the blow across the side: the knuckles dug deep into his flank where a bruise was already forming, and Xafiri hissed through his teeth.

A pulse screamed through his head; the training manuals he had memorised like scripture resurfaced suddenly.

Quick attacks, no remorse, back away. Quick attacks, no remorse, back away. Quick attacks, no remorse, back away…

Grumbling, Xafiri shifted backwards and released his grip on the man's shoulder.

Taking the advantage, he swung across and landed a punch in the crook of the man's elbow, feeling the tendons bulge beneath his fingers.

His opponent swayed backwards and growled; they reached across to their elbow——

When Xafiri brought his arm back across suddenly and back-handed the man across the cheek. The percussive *slap* it produced was enough to draw a gasp from the crowd at his back.

And Xafiri found himself gasping too.

Not bad for a skal-thüm, he thought, pulling his arm away and offering up a coy smile. *Perhaps I can last in this fight after——*

The brute charged him suddenly, wrapping his arms around Xafiri's middle and kicking out with his legs.

He was helpless against the man's sheer strength, kicking out desperately to try and stay upright——

Until Xafiri felt his feet slip out beneath him, and he collapsed backwards into the mud with a squeal.

He slapped down on the wet earth with a *thud,* carrying the big man's momentum above him——

The brute's shoulder rammed into his ribs and shuddered against his sternum; Xafiri's entire body buckled, the air exploding from his chest as his opponent let go and flew overhead, turning quickly for the next attack with a crazed glee in his eye.

Coated in mud like layers of paint, Xafiri hauled himself from the ground and turned to face his opponent, who——

Jabbed a fist into his stomach like a spear, forcing him to wheeze and bend double as his abdomen absorbed most of the pain.

You big brute...

Xafiri inhaled sharply and swore in *Zoltha*-tongue, clenching his fist tightly——

Swaying backwards as another punch nearly snapped his jaw open; the man overextended and exposed their flank——

Moving like a pendulum, Xafiri swung back towards his opponent and landed his own punch against the man's collar——

Where his hand crumpled like old paper, his knuckles busting against the man's steel-like collarbone.

Stepping back, Xafiri grabbed at his knuckle and hissed through his teeth, cursing himself for making such a poor choice of attack.

If only I'd ever learn——

Opposite him, like a fighter in the Darbesh pits, the man bucked his leg and kicked out at Xafiri's chest, throwing him back down into the mud again and draining the life from his legs.

Unravelling like a roll of carpet, Xafiri's neck snapped back as he landed and his head crunched on something hard, spinning his eyes in their sockets for a moment as disorientation took hold. High above, the clear sky swam in his vision, streaked with low-lying clouds that shielded away the ferocious heat of the sun. Trying to focus on things, he felt nausea balloon in his stomach, threatening bile in the back of his throat. All around, he heard the jeers and cries of the gathered crowds, glancing off in different directions like the whistling paths of arrows. He seemed to lose track of who he was for a moment – sprawled there stupidly in the mud with contorted limbs and a dim look only a mother could love – as the sky just continued to spin high above.

Az-Kabza, Xafiri thought, almost retching. *So much for solace...*

A heartbeat later, and a shadow passed over the top of him, blotting out the sun like an eclipse. A pair of hands latched onto his shoulders, firm and unruly, and in one motion the brute had braced on top of him and was turning his body into the mud.

Snapped from his trance, Xafiri tried fighting back with what little strength he could conjure: pushing up on his arms; elbowing the man's legs; scrabbling with his feet but finding no purchase any-where.

Sweat leaked from his forehead. He tasted grass and muck, like sour milk on his lips. He spat and coughed and shuddered. The brute continued to turn him, one hand laced through his hair and forcing him into the earth beneath.

Xafiri growled and shifted.

Couldn't move.
His arms flapping; his knees buckling.
Snapping.
Biting.
Sweating.
Earth and muck and shit and——
Sweat——
Blinking——
Consciousness——
Drifting…
On the verge of the unconscious void, with little communication between his head and his limbs, Xafiri's arm stretched out at his side and slapped down on the mud in quick succession——

And then, almost immediately, everything stopped again.

The pressure on his head lifted. Fingers unlatched from the curls of his hair. The pressing weight of a hand on his shoulder slipped away.

Silence followed. The shadows moved around him.

Hardly conscious, and sucking air through his lips like a pipe, Xafiri rolled onto his back and gazed up at the sun again, admiring the vastness of the sky.

Knowing that he'd just conceded defeat.

Knowing that I've just lost.

Slowly, laboriously, Xafiri lifted up onto a shaky arm and prized his body from the mud, which had been slowly fusing him in place like a clay mould. Raising an arm to his head – to distil his headache, as much as to see what was happening – Xafiri let out a long breath and felt the quiet anger simmer in his chest, holding it at bay so he didn't explode as he had done so many times before.

The brute stood before him, little more than a shadow against the sun, with his arms opened wide above his head. Words bellowed from his mouth, pledging the victory to his ancestors and Ras'gandû, God of the Skirmish. He pummelled his chest like a drum, stopping for a moment to place two fingers to his mouth, before circling them over his heart. Performing the victor's ritual.

Even though he's no victor.

Xafiri scowled, as the brute ignored the clear heresy of his act, and the disrespect he invoked on his family name. To enter into a fight illegally, and violate the rite-of-passage for an Unproven of the clan, was enough to be flogged in most places. It was enough to be exiled in others. The brute's ancestors, looking down on the display of violence, would have likely been appalled.

Xafiri scoffed. *Then again, I dread to think what they'd make of me, just for existing...*

Lifting to a stand — swaying, with crusted mud caked across his back and arms — Xafiri looked past the brute and shook his head in disbelief, cursing whoever was listening.

Beyond the man, about six rows of spectators stood on a raised platform, applauding and jeering their newest victor. There were elders there, awash with *zaz-gûla* and the sanded marks of war paint; there were matrons of the town, blushing with joy and slapping their arms; there were hunters and guardsmen, gathered for a spot of entertainment between their shifts. There were even a number of children Xafiri recognised who would not be far off their own rites-of-passage, clapping along with the rest of them and ignoring the traditions that had been broken. They all admired the fight and admired the victor in equal measure, it seemed.

This is another farce...

He lifted his hands in disgust, almost challenging the crowds — but the longer he stood there alone, the more he realised his own insignificance, as no-one even acknowledged him or took a moment to spare him a thought. Not a single pair of eyes met his own; not even the children dared look at him.

Because they don't see what they don't want to know.

And he could see it there himself, behind their pupils: that they knew he was there, and what he was, but chose to ignore him all the same. They refused to mark him out against the victor; they declared him as an 'other' — as a *mantugo* — just by averting their gaze. Even though he bore the same blood, belonging to the very same clan, he was beyond their interests at every turn.

I am abandoned by my own people… for choices that were never mine to make in the first place. Xafiri ground his teeth and sighed, turning his back on them and leaving the mud pit without a word spoken. *They will never see it. They will never let me be Proven, or treat me as one of their own. I'll never see what lies beyond this accursed arena.*

He tightened his fist, stifling the energy, and disappeared from sight.

I will never be Tarrazi to them.

†

Chapter 3

Mark of the Ancients

With the sun dipping below the western mountains, and the desert growing suddenly cold and empty, Markus reached the base of the Tarrazi hills and set down for the night amongst the trees, looking out on the sands at his back. The darkness had come thick and fast as dusk descended, turning the sands from a gritty yellow to a dour, iridescent blue. The rocky outcrops – that had become far sparser as he approached the hills – were marked along the horizon only by the dim glow of the moon.

Around him, weird, tube-branched bushes speared out from the sand along the desert's border, reaching out like fingers in the dark. Blankets of dry moss coated the earth like natural cushions, their fine hairs sensing the air with minute twitches. The dead trees he now sheltered amongst stood solemnly in their hundreds, as if they had not birthed leaves for generations at least.

But, despite the dramatic shift in his environment, Markus' eyes had adjusted quickly as he had approached the Tarrazi foothills, allowing him a deeper perception of the world than most others were granted. He wasn't sure if it was the power cavorting through him that offered him such enhancements, or whether several long days traversing the deserts had acclimatised him to desert life – but either way, the transition from day to night had proven effortless out on the sands, and for that the old wanderer was grateful.

Perhaps their gods are blessing me after all, and granting me safe passage, Markus had scoffed, kicking the sand at his feet with dusty, cracked boots. *Perhaps they're taking mercy on my poor, angered soul. I mean, that'd be quite something, considering everything I've been through.*

And, while they're at it, they could do me a favour and do something about this damn wind too.

And the judgement was not without reason, either: as night had claimed the desert, the coursing winds that had previously offered him great relief now froze him to his core, coiling across his skin like river leeches. With no protection from the elements until the foothills, Markus had trudged on slowly as the wind battered his side and sent shivers racketing up his spine. His fingers had grown numb; his ears had often ceased to function. He had been seized by spasms several times, as the energy in his system seemed to relent against the cold – and in the end, it was only by the warmth of his adrenaline that he made it to the tree-line at all, sheltering behind a knotted tree trunk and rubbing his hands furiously.

Never gets this cold in Provenci, he had growled, sliding down the trunk and settling amongst its roots. *And in a desert, of all places…*

Looking out across the sands then – having spent almost an hour setting a measly fire at his feet – Markus wrapped his cloth blanket tighter about his chest and cursed under his breath. Despite the protection the tree offered against the worst of the wind, the night air itself was still undeniably cold, and the sand beneath his toes was almost icy to the touch. The small fire he had built and ignited with his lightning did little to stem the chills of the open air – but it remained preferable, he knew, to lighting a big fire and warming himself through, only to have his throat cut in his sleep by some Tarrazi hunter with a particularly keen eye.

Not that I believe that's the biggest threat here, however…

Squinting at the desert horizon, he spied the twisting, undulating shapes of massive creatures out there burrowing through the sands in the dark. They were colossal, some the size of buildings, navigating through the dark. Undeniable horrors, with fleshy skin and sightless eyes and meshing vortexes of teeth, sharing their nocturnal world with other creatures that seemed to be plucked from Tarrazi folk tales: beasts with spearing arms and twitching fangs lying in wait in their burrows, alongside needly, bug-like monsters the size of one's arm that laid eggs in people's ears while they slept. They were the denizens of absent gods who had long abandoned the world they once loved; things best left in people's nightmares, out on the distant sands. After several days wandering out there, sleeping on the desolate tops of rock-faces, Markus considered how lucky he had been not to become one of their victims. His survival in the wastes had been an oblivious game of chance, acknowledging how any one of those creatures, in any foul measure, could've torn him to shreds or dragged him into its lair. The desert would've swallowed him whole, and he'd have had no way of stopping it in time.

Well… perhaps the gods have blessed me after all…

Markus turned his nose up at the thought and grunted, plucking a skewer from the fire and shoving a chunk of meat in his mouth. He had taken it from the Tarrazi hunters' packs, which they had in turn taken from the flesh of the blind desert serpent that they had killed earlier that day. Markus had taken enough to last him a couple of days if he rationed – and, as he ground through the coarse meat with sharp incisors, he found the serpent's flesh to be rather appetising.

Best bit of food I've had in days, he acknowledged, wedging another chunk on the end and leaving it to cook in the flames. *Probably the best bit of food I've had since I… well…*

Markus looked up to the stars, inhaling deeply.

Since I died.

For many long, gruelling, arduous miles – crossing sand plains and rocky plateaus and open expanses of nothingness – Markus had trudged on almost in a trance, lost in the echoes of being alive with no other thought to occupy him.

Because he accepted that he was alive, without a doubt: he wasn't a reanimated corpse, or some alchemist's experiment gone wrong. He continued to move and sleep and eat and shit as any mortal being did; emotions conjured in his chest, and hazy memories surfaced now and again to remind him of what had once been. He still ached in places, and still wore the scars of his previous encounters. The stump where his arm had been still twitched absently whenever he thought to use it.

But then there are also things I don't have an explanation for, he thought, sliding a hand beneath the folds of his blanket and touching a knot of flesh just below his ribcage.

Some things that no man should ever survive...

Placing his hand flat against the wound, tiny electric pulses spurred across his palm and ignited in his stomach, drawing sensation back into his body again. His fingers seemed to warm softly, being close to the mark on his stomach. Almost like it was home.

When he had inspected it at first, the wound had looked far older than it actually was: the skin had completely sealed over, and there had been no infection nor oozing. And, considering how prior to that he had been decaying in a cesspit for several weeks, it should have been an outright impossibility that the wound could heal at all.

And yet here I am, more than alive in so many ways, when I should be so utterly dead. And I was dead, for a time...

On the fire, the wedge of meat dripped with fat and fed the flames beneath it. Markus blinked.

What's happened to me?

He tried to think back to the arena, and the events that had unfolded once he'd entered Val Darbesh: being guided through the underbelly of the city in chains; witnessing the auction of fighters, flogged off like prize-winning cows; entering his cell and awaiting the judgement of his handler. Nothing had stood out to him as unusual about the whole process: in fact, in a morbid part of his mind, he imagined that his experience had been one of the more accommodating examples of fighters entering the arena. He knew of several horror stories, taken from illegal pits in the Provenci highlands, where fighters gnawed off their own fingers for sustenance if rations got slim, or smothered other competitors in their sleep when things got tough. By comparison, Markus admitted he had got off lightly.

But that still doesn't explain why I'm like this, he thought, placing his electrified hand flat on the floor. *It still doesn't explain how I'm alive, and none of the other poor bastards are.*

Returning his thoughts to Val Darbesh, he recalled the first lot of fighting he had endured, and the injuries he had sustained combating the massive Titan creature. After the skirmish, he had been dragged out of the arena in a horrific state and had moved into a far nicer room, where Tarrazi medical staff had tended to his wounds while he led unconscious on the old bed. They had clearly given him something to numb his senses and keep him in the sleeping realm, and had also applied a thick, oily coating to his numerous grisly wounds.

But none of that explained why he had come to possess such strange and volatile powers in the aftermath. It certainly didn't explain how, after lying dormant in the Darbesh cesspit for several weeks, he had managed to not only return from the dead, but also walk amongst the living once more with lightning coursing through his veins. The Tarrazi officers in the fighting pits would have had rudimentary medical knowledge at best. They couldn't have been responsible for lending him otherworldly powers, especially ones almost verging on the definition of *magic*—

Markus stopped; a scoff escaped his lips.

Magic? Really? he laughed, looking over the trees before him. *Gods, I must've been dead a while to start considering all that shit...*

And yet, as he pried through his memories for answers to satisfy his multitude of questions, Markus found he had no other way of describing how he felt. He possessed otherworldly powers, the likes of which no other person in known history had exhibited. He could conjure lightning from the sky; ignite it from his hand; draw it up from the very earth at his feet, and tear holes in the world at his whim. The possession of such abilities, and his utilisation of them, could only be described as magical. There were few other terms that fitted the mark.

And something in Markus' heart just didn't like that.

I've never wanted anything to do with magic. I like the realm that I know. Herbal remedies; flint and steel; water vapour and cold stores and salting meats. He eyed the chunk of serpent meat on the fire and licked his lips. *I live within the natural bounds of this world, and the laws that dictate it. I've never been one for corrupting that, and getting in its way.* He nodded, proclaiming his truths to the world.

And that's how I've always been, especially since——

He stopped, drawing the thought still in his mind.

Something rumbled inside him; like a loose bolt on a trebuchet, he felt part of him slip away.

His heart started thundering in his chest.

Since... I...

The pounding in his head grew louder. He started trembling.

The air was so thin.

It was all so thin...

I, just...

His hand clawed at the earth; the lightning pulsed between his fingers. He was gasping, he realised. His shoulders shuddered in the dark.

Connecting life and death; her treachery with her act.

She...

It was all so thin and dark and bright and open and——

Sav...

A memory struck out in his head suddenly, erupting over his eyes and consuming the copse of trees around him. Flashing lights and colours and numb echoes quivered through his body like tremors——

There was a clear blue sky. There were sandstone walls and tiny dots of colour. There were sounds: people shouting and cheering and gasping, leaning over sides to see——

A body stood over him, a sword glinting in the sun over their head.

There was blood on their skin and on their armour. And in their heart. In *her* heart. Stood over him, watching. A sheer, resolute emptiness in her eyes. No remorse. No guilt. No mercy.

Death and death and death and——

Markus blinked once, his vision tunnelling, shuddering with the body looming above. The walls seemed to close in. The woman opened her mouth.

"I'm sorry, Markus," she said, as the blade plunged down into his chest——

He screamed; the world screamed.

Air rushed into his lungs.

His eyes felt like they were exploding——

Lightning detonated in his hand.

The shockwaves tore the ground apart all around him. The tiny fire at his feet exploded with furious, unrelenting flames, torching the meat nestled at its base and scolding the earth around it. Blue strikes of energy speared off over the sands and fizzed like trailing comets. Several strands erupted up the trunk of the tree at his back and scorched lines through the bark, igniting over the broken buds that hissed out of existence in seconds.

Markus heaved breaths into his body, clenching his hand in fear as the lightning extinguished and the fire went out in a pile of ash. His entire arm seized up: the blue veins snaking across his skin pulsed and flushed with power, ripping his skin apart like tributaries. His vision swam, tunnelling, hardly focusing on anything. The vast expanse of the night sky coiled above his head like serpent tails.

He tried to move, kicking away from the scorched earth surrounding his straggled body, but the power in his legs gave in almost immediately.

Gasping for air, Markus collapsed on his side and let the sudden exhaustion claim his body. Closing his eyes, he fell back into the unconscious void, fateful words ringing in his ears.

I'm sorry, Markus.

I'm sorry...

†

Chapter 4

Tarrazi

So, Xafi, how was… fight… you do… today?"

Xafiri lowered his spoon back into his bowl of broth and sighed, before looking up to his mother again, smiling as pleasantly as he could. She looked very youthful in the light, he acknowledged: soft-featured, with a crop of greying hair coiled into a bun and held together with long needles atop her head. Her flowing gown was quaint, with the tiny woven accents of ivy up one side. Plying with the bronze-coil rings laced around her wrists, she seemed keen to make conversation with him. At least she was trying, he supposed.

No-one else does, he admitted.

"It did not go well… I lost, sad to say," he explained plainly, trying to not overload her with *Zoltha* words. His understanding of his own language was shaky at best, so he knew how difficult it was to bridge the gap from the other side. "The man I fight, had *zaz-qûla* under his eye… fight no good. Bad for… for tradition." He winced at using the word '*tradition*', but his mother seemed to understand its meaning nonetheless, as she frowned and set her spoon down.

"Man older, fight you?" she asked.

"Yes. Man older."

"Fight… he fight good?"

"Yes, he fight good. He was a Proven man."

"P… *proven?*"

"Ah, um…" Xafiri grappled for the word, trying to dissect his vocabulary. "*Desgundy… paraba?*"

His mother's eyes alighted. "Yes!" she exclaimed. "*Desgundy paraba!* Proven, yes!" Then her frown returned. "That very bad. Not good. Lacking fair. Big shame, no fair."

Her mother smiled, proud that she had understood his meaning; Xafiri looked down into his broth and scowled.

Yea… it is not fair.

He had returned home after the fight in a fit of fury, storming into his mother's domed house with venom on his tongue and fire at his heels. He was caked in mud, with purple bruising up his side and across his arms, blossoming there like algae. He hardly remembered the walk from the arena to his home, such was the rage that had burned inside of him.

Pushing through the heavy drapes into the entranceway of the house, he was immediately buffeted with the alluring smells of his mother's cooking and found his anger suddenly disarmed. The smoke filled the vaulted ceiling and spouted out the hole at the apex of the roof; the scent of ginger and chasetine root snaked over the partition walls that dissected the room, catching in his nose whimsically like the embrace of a loved one. Memories blossomed in his mind, and a tiredness crept into his body that he hadn't realised was there. His fury dissolved, so that when he finally stepped into the kitchen quarter and his mother turned to him with the same big, glowing eyes that she always had, all he could do was smile and shrug.

What's done is done, he had considered.

At least I'm home now.

Xafiri spooned more broth out of the bowl and enjoyed the smell for a moment, before he gulped it down and savoured the heat in his stomach. "Thank you for food… and for letting me use rain-holder outside," he said, pointing to the drape across the rear opening of the house and imitating water over his head. "Feels good to be clean.

Very cold, though… very cold evening."

And that's something of an understatement, he thought, spooning more broth into his mouth. As he had started washing, the sun had dipped below the western mountains and a chill wind had swept up from the desert, freezing him to the bone. The trees around them seemed to shudder, bristling along their thick roots; wrapped in several heavy robes, Xafiri had not lingered outside for very long, welcoming the warmth of the kitchen and his mother's delicious cooking.

"You are… okay, Xafi," his mother said, unsure of the word '*welcome*'. "You've had hard day."

Xafiri laughed. "Yea, well… that's true."

"Lots of m… mud."

"Yes, lots of mud."

"And your… your…" Slightly frustrated, she pointed at her sides and arms, trying to find the word.

Xafiri gestured to his ribs. "My bruises?"

"Yes! Them… they hurt?"

"A little, yes. A little hurt. Not too bad, though."

"Need oils. Need health. Rub better. Clean, so no bad gets in." She imitated rubbing ointment on her hands.

"Yes, it does… but not yet," Xafiri explained. "In a few days… I have more fights yet."

"What you have got… left of *Fendûrii?* How hard is next bit?" Again, his mother's eyes glowed like shimmering moons, waiting expectantly for his response.

Xafiri smiled, appreciating her concern for his health, but part of him could sense her hollowness even from there. That something was missing between them, lost in the sunset gloom: something imperceptible, that only he could see after spending so long in her presence.

You're putting all of this on, he acknowledged, rolling his tongue over his teeth. *I know you're showing such interest and trying so hard because it's what I need to hear, but that doesn't mean that it's necessarily what you feel.* Because he knew the truth of their relationship, mother and son: that her real feelings about who he was — and all the nuances that possessed — would never leave her lips. That every smile hid away a thousand words that would forever remain unspoken. That the reality would always be sealed, locked away by a guilt she could never relinquish, and a language barrier she could never overcome.

I appreciate you trying, ma, but I know deep down you're tired of this. Tired of hearing me talk like a Zoltha. *Tired of the same stories of failure, over and over. Tired of the fact we can understand each other with a look, but never with our words. Because I do honestly appreciate that you still try and make all of this work, despite how much it must eat you up inside and never let you go. But I'm just wondering when the day will come when you'll finally give up on that.*

And I'll have nowhere left to go.

"What of *Fendûrii* is left?" she repeated, thinking he hadn't understood.

"Quite a bit to go yet." He paused. "And by the way, to say *Fendûrii*, is '*rite… of… passage*'… okay?"

His mother blinked, forcing a smile. "Okay."

Xafiri breathed noisily. *You didn't get that then… never mind.* "Okay, so, I have a *fire* trial…" – he pointed to the fire-blasted cooking pot suspended behind him – "…then an *endurance* test…" – swinging his arms up and down beside him, he imitated running and heavy breathing – "… and then I am done. Then *Fendûrii* done."

"Okay… so, two more test?"

"Yes. Two days, two tests."

"Then you *Desgundy paraba?*"

Xafiri felt his expression slip, and nodded noncommittally. "As an idea… yes."

"As an… idea?" his mother asked.

"I mean… I hope so."

Her expression grew cold and stony, struggling to understand him.

He sighed, pointing at his head. "Sorry, no understand word for it. Cannot explain."

"Oh… right. Okay." Although she had limited grasp on *Zoltha-tongue*, his mother seemed to have mastered expressions of disappointment perfectly. "I… sorry."

"Is not your fault. No worries. All… it's okay."

She smiled at him, relieved that their mutual understanding had returned even if – *once again* – it had led nowhere. Spooning another mouthful of broth into her mouth, his mother held a hand to her lips and swallowed uneasily, the liquid evidently still a touch hot. Xafiri took a spoonful himself, embracing the silence and collecting his thoughts.

"Xafi?" she asked suddenly, her pitch slightly higher.

"Yes, *marzedna?*"

"Do you… you want to become p… Proven? Do you want to?"

Xafiri frowned, leaving the spoon in his bowl. A sense of dread clawed at his stomach. "What… do you mean by that?"

"Do you want to be part of tribe, like us?" She spoke with such perfect innocence that it made his heart rip into pieces. "Do you want to be… us? You have tried, done it so many times… and yet you have nothing. You still have hard day. Why? Do you not want it anymore?"

With the silent expanse of the table between them, and the orange glow of evening pulling through the hole in the ceiling above, Xafiri sat there in silence, hardly able to speak.

Do I… not want it anymore?

Lifting a hand to his face, he wiped a tiny tear from the corner of his eye, and clenched his other hand into a fist under the table. For a few desperate moments, his heart sat weeping in his chest, and every insular emotion within his body bubbled and flushed through him. First came guilt, then shame and sorrow and then, rising once more from the embarrassment he had endured in the mud pits, anger came in full force, pushing back against the homely smells around him and his innocent mother sat opposite, threatening to consume his soul entirely.

You're so ignorant to my struggles, he longed to scream. *You're so ignorant to my pain and my hate. You have nothing to offer, and I have nothing to show for it, and we're sat here walking in circles, wondering who should be fucking blamed for the* Zoltha *taking me in——*

Xafiri blinked once, inhaling deeply, and sighed through his nostrils. The fist in his lap — with his knuckles tense and white — unravelled and lay flat against his thigh. He looked up into the perfect rounds of his mother's eyes.

It's not worth it... not to cause her pain.

"I do want it, ma," he said softly, tiredly. "I want it more than anything in this world. I want it until I bleed and sing and cry. I've wanted it every day since I was a young boy, watching the first fights with my da. I want to be a part of this tribe. I want to be a member of these people: to wear my *zaz-gûla* with pride, and to kill a beast on the Triumph Hunts in the summer suns. I want to join the Verlunz's host, and dine at his table, and bring riches to this place from our ancestral grounds in the north. I want to provide for you, ma; to provide for all of us, even. It's what I've always wanted... but it's also something I can never have."

He rubbed his fingers together on the table-top. "Because I'm *mantugo*, ma. I'm 'other', to them. When the imperial forces came, and the occupation began, and they sent their Educators to our homes to teach us their 'civilised ways'... I became a *mantugo*, just for breathing. Because I did the one thing that no-one else dared to; the one thing that felt right at the time..."

He ground his jaw, fighting the tears that rose within him. "I did as they asked. I listened, and I learned. I never rebelled. I translated, and I understood them, better than I've ever understood anyone in this clan. They taught me their ways... and while doing so, I never abandoned my principles, and our traditions as a people. Never once did I claim to be anything other than Tarrazi. It was my whole heart, and my heritage, and my future. It was everything to me." He sighed. "But it didn't matter in the end: because no-one cares to know the difference. It was the enemy that educated me, and so it is the enemy that I now bear the name of. I may as well be a *Zoltha,* for all they care. They all damn-well treat me like one. And because of *that*, I will never be Proven. They will never *let me* be Proven. Because I am a corruption on this tribe, so they say. I am an outcast. Even if we are of the same blood, and the same people... it doesn't matter in the end. Because I made a choice, that I was too young to realise I was making..."

A single tear rolled down his cheek.

And I will wear it as a black mark, for the rest of my life.

Looking up into his mother's eyes, with his face curled up in despair, Xafiri saw deep into her emptiness and confusion, and longed for it to swallow him up. The distance between them was vast, despite the metre that separated them at the table. The tangible emotions he bled, were just reams of thread in her hands. She saw the ruin marked on his face, and although their kinship meant she felt it too, she could never begin to grasp why.

Because she hadn't understood a word he'd just said, Xafiri knew. As much as she wanted to – and as much as she *tried* – the words ultimately fell on deaf ears. She could never make sense of him.

She never has.

Xafiri pushed his bowl away and rose to a stand, hiding the shakes in his hand as his mother looked on so perfectly, trying her best to smile.

"I love you, ma, I hope you know... and I hope you understand one day," he said softly, trying in his own way to smile.

His mother said nothing in response, lost in their shared feeling and the echoey expanse it contained. Instead, she lifted two fingers to her lips, and tapped them on her heart.

I love you too.

Another tear fell down Xafiri's cheek, tracing down his jaw and dropping into his palm. He turned from the table and left.

He did not sleep for a long time thereafter.

✝

Chapter 5

Murmurs

Dawn rose the next day, sharp as a knife edge, and after a troubled night with little chance to coalesce, Markus was on the hunt.

To his right, a deer sat in a small grove between the dead trees, sheltered amongst the dense vegetation that dominated the base of the Hills. From his ambush point, Markus could see the tiny, three-pronged antlers over the mass of pastel-green plants, accompanied by a pair of ears that twitched and curled with the wind. The sun shone down on it through a gap in the canopy, bathing it in a warm, radiant light.

The deer was most certainly awake, Markus observed, and from his limited knowledge of the animal he also knew that they were very perceptive of sound. He had hunted many over his four dozen years, and had utilised both a knife and a bow in that time to maintain his stealth – but it had always been the ground underfoot that had ended up deciding his success, where one snapped branch could send the deer running long before he'd even readied his arrow.

To his luck, however, the ground he had encountered on the foothills thus far was so dry and compact from a lack of rainfall that any footsteps he made were indistinguishable from the rustle of the trees above. Every noise he made was masked by the sounds of nature. He could move silently, effortlessly. The conditions were almost perfect.

Or they would've been, that was, had a whispering noise not been plaguing his every thought with a persistent, infuriating rhythm, making it impossible to listen out for any sounds, let alone to hunt a deer.

It had started as soon as he'd woken up, when the heat from the desert drew him out of a shaky slumber. At first, he'd thought it was the start of some headache he had obtained from too little water and too much time in the sun: a dull knocking sound like the drum of horse hooves, rattling through his brain. He had tried to dispel it by eating a small, sweet-tasting snack that he had scavenged from the Tarrazi in the desert, and that seemed to work for a while. But as soon as he set off into the trees and began his tedious ascent up the first hill, the drumbeats had grown louder and louder again, until they consumed his every sense and made no sign of stopping.

So, sat there amongst the tube-branched bushes with lightning scattered between his fingers, Markus rubbed against his temple with his palm and scowled at the petulant noise, trying to keep track of the deer just ahead.

It's all in my head… it's all in my head, he thought, wondering for the life of him where the space was in his head to make that judge-ment in the first place. *Nothing in this godforsaken place could produce such an annoying fucking noise for this length of time.*

And yet here I am stuck with it, and with no means of making it go away…

For a time, when he had been searching for a suitable path through the undergrowth, Markus had started deciphering the noise echoing through his head, and part of him almost believed that there was a voice somewhere lost within it, as if whispering through glass. It was faint, and uncomfortably tuneful, and had the distinct inflections of a native Provencian. That, and it seemed to be calling his name near-constantly, like it wanted to grab his attention.

But what it was – or, more unnervingly, *who* it was – Markus could hardly fathom. And, as the sound intensified into a deafening thunder the higher he climbed into the Hills, he failed to find reason to care either, as his only intention became to dispel it by any means possible.

I've had the blissful silence of the desert for three long, beautiful days, Markus recalled, resting a hand on the trunk of a gnarled tree. *And now I have constant chatter, like rattling pans, deceiving my every thought.* He scoffed.

I should be more grateful for the little things, ay?

Keeping his eye on the deer ahead of him, Markus shifted from his position and circled it slowly, hoping to get behind it and make use of its blind-spot without being detected. Edging through the trees, he kept his steps light and his breathing shallow, avoiding the bushes and their brittle branches as much as he could. If he kept low to the ground, and used the undergrowth as cover, he would almost be at the deer's throat without issue——

"Markus..."

His heels ground into the soil, dislodging rocks where tiny, multi-legged creatures scurried for the nearest cover.

The bushes bristled around him; one of the deer's ears twitched suddenly, but its overall body language remained unchanged.

And, like a wayward cloud, Markus felt the voice pass through one ear and out the other, being carried off by the wind as if it had never been at all.

The fuck was that?

He looked around the copse of trees with a frustrated glare – imagining some impish wretch out there playing tricks on him – picking apart the shadows with studious precision. It took several moments before he consigned defeat and snarled, setting his sights on the deer again just ahead.

It's all in your head, he deduced, holding branches still as he shifted between two bushes. *It's all in your head, and it isn't real. None of it is. Just focus on the hunt, and claiming your kill.* He paused, clamping his teeth together.

But that was a woman's *voice that said my name...*

Passing between another set of bushes, fixed on the target ahead, he kept his steps low to the ground tentatively, embracing the silence of the foothills, placing his foot down gently on the uneven ground…

And took far too long to realise, as his heel snapped one of the tube branches and the sound ricocheted out over the air.

Shivers shot over his skin; he cursed—

The deer twigged, its head turning sharply—

Markus bent low, using the vegetation to hide—

"*Markus…*"

Shut the fuck up!

In the unsettling silence that followed, with the glow of the sun passing through the broken canopies above, the deer rose to its feet like unfolding a tent and surveyed its surroundings frightfully.

It flared its nostrils; it sensed danger.

Its ears twitched slowly.

The copse lay still and unassuming.

Gonna have to make a move before it bolts, Markus hissed. Keeping in a low stoop that wreaked havoc on his knees, he adjusted his angle to keep downwind of the deer and squared his shoulders between the bushes. He found a suitable ambush point after several nerve-wrenching steps, the deer's white-grey tail just visible between the undergrowth.

At his side, the lightning conjured at his fingertips, ready to exact its kill. Perfectly balanced; perfectly lethal. All it would take was a touch of patience, and a bit of time—

"*Markus…*"

And for this voice in my head to fuck off for just a moment.

Rolling his finger-tips together as the energy channelled through his system, he tightened his hand against his side and kept his thumb and index finger tightly locked. He knew the action he needed to make his kill, having practiced it several times out on the sands against the local flocks of birds. All he needed was a single blast: one bolt of energy, straight through the back of the deer's skull. Enough to kill it outright, but not enough to burn it to ash and spoil the meat he desperately craved. He was already out of the serpent's meat.

And by my estimation, venison sounds like an excellent replacement.

Breathing slowly – letting a numbness claim his mind – Markus took in a lungful of air and stood upright sharply, aiming his pinched fingers out toward the deer—

The creature turned, its nostrils flaring, studying him with a chilling wonder—

The energy snapped across his hand; his fingers opened—

"Markus!"

The bolt shuddered skyward and clipped the deer across the antler, impacting a tree trunk several paces behind it.

Startled, and perhaps amazed it was still alive, the deer wasted no time in hurtling off between the trees and disappearing from sight, tearing through the undergrowth at an impressive speed. It was lost to the shadows in seconds, kicking up a trail of dust.

Gone without a whisper.

Markus closed his eyes slowly and looked up to the sky above, letting a despairing breath funnel through his lips as the energy dispersed once again.

Unbelievable…

Opening his mind out once more, he found that the murmurs had all but dispersed, leaving only a quiet tapping in the back of his head like the scurrying feet of a mouse. There was no clatter; there were no voices anymore, calling out his name. The rancour that had plagued him since sunrise finally ceased to be, and all he was left with was the distant twittering of birds and the gentle rustle of old leaves.

And now, of course, comes the silence, he scoffed, eyes closed tightly, burying the anger that had risen swiftly in his chest. *Now that the deer has bolted, and my food is gone… now it offers me silence.*

Markus opened his eyes again, sighing softly. His tongue wrinkles in his mouth, wanting to condemn the world and its vagrant gods and the powers within him for their commitment to making his life an unequivocal bloody misery—

When he spied something above him, drifting through the air, that made all the damning thoughts slide away.

Is that... smoke?

Tracing the effortless blue skies above him, beyond the thin, misty clouds of the morning, he noted a thicker trail of yellowing smoke rising from somewhere just north of him, catching on the winds high above. It didn't have the chaotic, black smudging of a wildfire like he was used to in the dry Provenci summers: it was a clean, deliberate mark. One made by human hands.

Which means somewhere ahead must be that Tarrazi village where the hunter's hailed from, he thought, looking off through the trees to the north. *And that means that there's food and supplies nearby, too. Probably a bounty of them.*

He smiled, watching the lightning dance across his palm like a spider's-web, playful like a whore's hips.

Best go pay them a visit, ay?

†

Chapter 6

Unproven

Xafiri had awoken stiffly with his mouth parched and his skull thumping, as if he'd been beaten by a hundred sticks and left out to dry in the sun. Which in many ways he had been: his skin crawled, and the bruises from the previous day's fighting had begun to show properly, swelling across his skin in thick purple knots. Moving out of bed had been arduous; walking across his partition room to the cabinet of tinctures had been excruciating. As he applied the various balms and ointments his mother had left out for him, Xafiri studied his pale skin and the scrapes that seemed to decorate it like badges. He looked like he had been dragged from a funeral pyre – he *felt* like he had been dragged from a funeral pyre. All stiffness and dryness and pain. His back was in pieces. His shoulders hung on threads. His hands were on fire.

Although not really on fire, he acknowledged, donning a robe and a pair of breeches before exiting into the kitchen space to his left.

That fun comes later.

Xafiri had then sat for breakfast with his mother, enjoying a bowl of rolled oats with a sprinkle of cannelza flower, used to ease the tension in his joints. It tasted good, and his mother had clearly put a lot of soul into its making, but Xafiri could sense beyond that that the mood was still off between them, carrying over from the previous night. Xafiri saw how his mother wore the usual signs of a

38

restless night, fretting about things she couldn't control: she had dark circles under her eyes, and fidgety hands that busied themselves on meagre, repetitive tasks. Whenever she drifted past him, she always stroked his shoulder or planted a kiss on his scalp, not caring much if her own bowl of oats got cold in the meantime. Xafiri knew what she was trying to do with the gestures, as he had done something similar many times himself: when words failed, and the language barrier was too great, physical touch became the best expression of love to bridge the gap. So whenever his mother came to embrace him gently in her fragile arms, wearing the warm, delicate smile she always carried, Xafiri knew a thousand words lay behind that single gesture and he wished for a second that she would never let go.

"Heart with you, Xafi," she had said, touching two fingers to her breast.

"Heart with you too, ma," he replied.

"Was thinking, can you... me do... a favour?" She had stepped back and looked at him softly, almost ashamed to ask.

"Of course, ma... what do you need?"

"You have fire test today... yes?"

Xafiri nodded.

"So we need balms for... fire," she had explained, rubbing her skin. "Balms to stop the... the..."

"The burning?"

"Yes! Yes, burning, yes. No flame pain. Balms make it better. I make for you, I show you. But I need things first."

Xafiri smiled, seeing the sweet concern in her eyes. "Of course. I will get them for you, ma, don't worry. Now... what do you need?"

She had listed off a number of ingredients in short succession, some of which he knew from his training under the Imperial medicine branch, while others were entirely unknown to him and required some explaining. There was a red root that was said to sizzle on a person's fingertips; a droplet-shaped berry that changed colour when it popped; and brush-grasses, too, with succulent-sweet stems and prickly, poisonous leaves. He noted them all down on a piece of parchment, fussing over the spellings and pronunciations several times, until his mother seemed satisfied at last and handed over a small cloth bag.

"Go to Temusceh," she told him, nodding. "He will have all."

Taking the bag from her, Xafiri's expression had remained un-readable, betraying his true feelings with a casual smile and a well-wishing hug goodbye. He wouldn't disappoint his mother again, and certainly not over something as trivial as a meeting with Temusceh. His dread and curdling anxieties would remain securely under wraps.

I mean, it's not like his eldest son bested me in a rite-of-passage fight yesterday, or anything ridiculous like that, Xafiri had mused as he departed shortly after, looking up to the open skies outside his front door and wondering what he had done to anger the gods so. *It's not like his son buried my face in the mud and stood jeering to the crowds over my body. Of course not.*

Which god would ever allow that?

And stood there then – several hundred regretful steps later – staring into the dead, discontented eyes of *Hajiin* Temusceh, Xafiri wished more than anything that he'd watch his tongue more, and show the gods a bit of damn respect.

Too late for that now, I guess.

"Par ton'turi, *tarmun?*" the herbalist growled, placing a venomous-looking knife down on his chopping block and folding his arms like two huge gates. He stood under a canopy attached to the side of his dwelling, with a table at his waist displaying a vast array of colourful plants and objects. The sheer number of them was mesmerising to Xafiri, who had only ever dabbled with the few plants the Educators allowed young Tarrazi boys to use in their classes.

Not that I would ever dare mention that in front of Temusceh, he thought, breathing through the shame and embarrassment that ate away in his chest. *They think little of me as it is... best not remind them that I was once a student of the* Zoltha, *too.*

Glancing over the arrangement of plants laid out beneath him, the sheer abundance of them almost made Xafiri blush with ignorance, seeing how little the *Zoltha* Educators had really shown him in their camps. But, under the stern gaze of Temusceh, Xafiri remained as studious and upright as he could manage, betraying none of the anxieties that rallied through his system nor the embarrassment that bubbled in his chest.

Now, anyway… what do I want from all of this? he thought, turning his attention back to the question the herbalist had asked. Pulling the scrawl of paper from his side — which in of itself made the huge man before him scowl with suspicion — Xafiri scanned over the notes and studied the arrangement beneath him, picking out any mentions of colours or plant types.

Spying one he recognised, Xafiri rolled his tongue across the roof of his mouth and whispered a quiet prayer. "*Thäntun'tul-cûlii,*" he said with a false and incredibly-betraying confidence, pointing to a red flower on the left with tiny, iridescent petals.

Temusceh stared him down for some time thereafter, like a bear trying to work out if something was worth killing, before Xafiri opened out his hand and gestured to the quantity he required.

And, mercifully, the herbalist slid a handful into his small cloth bag, and placed it down on the block beneath him.

Okay, there's one.

Bolstered by his success, Xafiri gestured to two other plants next to the red flower: a knot of root the colour of bruises, and a finely-ground powder piled opposite. For the purple root, he made the same open-palmed gesture to the herbalist as he had done before — and for the powder, he pinched his fingers together, indicating he only needed a little.

Looking between the two plants, Temusceh sucked his cheeks in and sighed; Xafiri — trying his best at being pleasant and cordial — sensed the dread continue to build in his stomach. He had taken one look at the pronunciations scrawled over the diagrams on his paper, and opted against any attempt at saying them aloud. His mother had named them with such ease and fluency when she had explained it earlier, meeting linguistic standards that he could hardly understand, let alone replicate. Xafiri squirmed on the spot thinking about it; his skull pounded, meeting the big man's eyes and smiling meekly.

Come on, come on, please don't ask anymore ques——

Without another word, Temusceh scooped up the purple root and a pinch of brown powder in his huge hands. Placing them in another bag and sealing it shut, the herbalist dropped it down next to the red flowers and crossed his arms again.

Oh… okay. Xafiri blinked slowly, lost in a sense of shock, and studied his notes again. *That was easier than expected.*

Perhaps I misjudged him after all.

Looking between the table and his diagrams, Xafiri spied another of his mother's herbs on the far side: a blue leaf the colour of sea-water, with a relatively simple name.

Hasvent, he recited, nodding with a smug joy. *That shouldn't be too hard.*

"*Hajiin* Temusceh, *Hasvent*——"

The herbalist held out his hand. "*Nedu.*"

Xafiri frowned. *No?* "Wait——"

"*Nedu, tarmun,*" he said, firmer, before gesturing to the bags already on his chopping block. "*Bujanti.*"

Enough? Xafiri puzzled over what the herbalist was trying to say to him, or what he meant by saying the three bags were 'enough'. *Is there some sort of rationing in place? Are we low on medical supplies? Surely mother would've told me by now if there was. She wouldn't have sent me out here uninformed.*

Grounding his teeth together, Xafiri showed Temusceh the list of herbs and plants he required, and pointed to a few that he could see on the table before him. Part of him believed it was just a difference in their understanding, and that it could be resolved by a simple explanation of what he was after——

When Temusceh reached over the table and took the note from his hands, snatching it away like a clawing cat.

Xafiri gasped. "Wait——"

Without even breaking eye contact, the herbalist scrunched the paper between the meat of his fingers, and planted his thumb back down on the chopping block next to the bags.

"Bujanti… *Desgundy nedu-paraba,*" he growled.

Hearing the *Hajiin's* reply, Xafiri bristled. A fire bellowed in his chest, his anger and anxiety crashing into each other like storm-clouds. He clenched his fist behind his back.

'Unproven'… so that's what this is, then, he grumbled, staring deep into Temusceh's uncaring eyes. *I am only allowed a quota of plants and herbs… because I am unworthy of holding any more. Because I am not Proven like the rest of them.*

Not Proven like your feckless fucking son is, who beat me to a fucking pulp today and disrespected his own ancestors——

Xafiri took in a deep breath and let it rasp through his nostrils, quelling the tide that rose in his throat and threatened to explode like dragon's fire. His fist unclenched at his back.

There's no point starting a fight here… especially one I can't win.

He reached into his jacket pocket slowly, and felt the cold metallic rounds of coins between his fingers.

Anger solves nothing. My hatred, solves nothing.

Withdrawing a half-dozen of them, Xafiri placed the bronze coins down on the tabletop and opened his palm calmly, looking between Temusceh and the three bags sat innocently beneath him.

The herbalist did nothing for some time, letting the moments tick by absently with the tension taut like a bowstring. Xafiri watched his massive arms twitch and bulge in the sun; the huge man's forehead furrowed deeper and deeper under the cooling shadow of his canopy.

Sometime later – when it was clear Xafiri wouldn't bite back as he had hoped – Temusceh scoffed and muttered a curse under his breath: something about the gods and their misgivings to idle fools and traitors.

Reaching out for the coins opposite him, the herbalist dragged them up and shoved them in his pocket, before depositing the three bags in Xafiri's open palm with a sneer of tangible disgust.

Offering only a nod in return – with his legs reduced to nervous stilts – Xafiri turned sharply and left the scene, salvaging what dignity he had left as his heart thundered in his chest.

Thank the gods that that's over.

He navigated down the narrow street, struggling to put one foot in front of the other. The sun lay hot and heavy across his scalp; sweat and fear lay slick across his fingers. He had achieved something in the end, even if it wasn't as much as his mother had wanted—

Somewhere behind him, he heard Temusceh's voice garble out a furious command, just above the din of the sprawling market square.

Looking back, he saw the herbalist stood addressing three young men, gesturing wildly for a moment before pointing off towards—

Wait.

His heart stuttered; his mouth was suddenly dry.

He's pointing at me.

Spooking like a horse ready to bolt, Xafiri locked eyes with one of the men stood opposite Temusceh and gasped.

That's his son… the bastard who bested me in the fight yesterday. He saw the teardrop-marks under his eyes, and the purpling bruise under his right arm. *That's him, without a doubt.*

And it looks like he's ready for round two.

As the thought claimed his mind, the three men left Temusceh's side and started pursuing him down the street, gaining on him quickly. One veered off and disappeared between the houses to Xafiri's left; the other slipped behind some fishing poles and out towards the tree-line to his right.

And the third – Temusceh's son – continued his direct approach down the street, grinning wildly at Xafiri with the joy of the hunt in his eyes.

Xafiri swallowed a lump in his throat.

Oh gods, no…

He slipped the bags into his breech pockets and picked up the pace suddenly, drifting past his fellow tribesmen like a river through stone. Part of him thought to run: that maybe he could reach his mother's door before they reached his throat, and he could shelter there like a lost cub until they gave up and went on their way. It was only one direct assailant, after all, and Xafiri was known for his endurance.

But I don't know where those other two have gone, he assessed, sliding between another group of people who glared his way as he passed. *For all I know, they could be planning for me to make a run for it: to catch me out on a tight corner, and land me flat on my face. I wouldn't know any different.*

And by then it'd be too late anyway.

Xafiri bristled at the thought, as people drifted out onto the street from the paths next to him, woven between the domed houses like lengths of twine. Each structure was moulded using thick clay and reinforced with tree resin, which made it impervious to the fragile winters and belting summers of the Valatuk Hills. They were organised in neat patterns, bordering the main streets like sentries.

Hiding away any approaching threats, hunting through the village like Hounds.

Trying to keep his bearings – knowing his time was running out, and his assailants were approaching fast – he felt a sudden wash of relief come over him as he followed the curve of the street ahead and saw it open out onto the main village square. It was a ceremonial space, used for dances, initiations and feasts during the high-sun months. People navigated across it in small clusters, going about their business, while some stood deep in discussion, hoping the gods would overhear their conversations and grant them their small mercies from above. It was an important place for any Tarrazi, for its history and ceremony, but in that moment that was hardly on Xafiri's mind: because he knew that, if he followed the descending path on the western tip of the square, he would reach his mother's house in a matter of moments and that would be the end of the pursuit. All he had to do, was get there in one piece.

And pray I'm not caught in the process.

Assessing his options, Xafiri heard the footsteps at his back accelerate suddenly, as Temusceh's son realised that they were about to enter open ground. Evidently, the brute's plan relied on corralling him somewhere before they reached the village square – and, now that they were both hurtling towards it at an impressive pace, it seemed their plan was falling apart.

Xafiri moved between another group of people – whispering half-garbled apologies to any who bothered to listen – and looked out over the sun-drenched square ahead, with light glancing off the polished stones and——

One of the men who had broken off from the pursuit earlier emerged from between the houses just ahead of him, smirking at him with a clear and calculated menace.

Xafiri's heart caught in his chest.

Shit.

He adjusted his stride, turning away from them——

To spy the other assailant duck under a line of hanging clothes and cross the street to his left, approaching his friend opposite and closing the doors on Xafiri's exit route.

Shit!

Xafiri stopped; his heels ground against the dirt and stone. Turning back suddenly, Temusceh's son stood a few paces away with his arms crossed, smiling with a smugness that made Xafiri's blood boil. Bystanders around them turned to assess the scene, but made clear it was not in their interest when they looked away and walked on as if nothing had happened. A number of parents grabbed their children and steered them down the side-paths, averting their wandering eyes.

Hunkering down and curling his fists up, Xafiri looked deep into the brute's eyes and shook his head.

"I don't want to do this," he said quietly, fatally.

Temusceh's son spat on the floor at his feet and sneered.

"Az-Kabza, *Zoltha,*" he growled.

Then all three approached at once.

Xafiri blinked slowly and let sensation take over——

A fist circled round toward his left side; he knocked it away with his forearm and planted his own punch across the man's cheek—

A knuckle connected with his other arm; Xafiri hissed and twisted on his heels—

The scrape of dirt and stone sounded behind him; Temusceh's son swung across and missed Xafiri by a hair's-breadth as he adjusted and kicked out at the brute's shin, watching him stumble away—

A hand grabbed his shoulder—

Xafiri turned and backhanded them, with a force like a thunder-clap against their cheek—

A punch landed in the small of his back; another caught across his chest, just below the collarbone. Xafiri lurched sideways and cursed under his breath, shoving the man in front of him and—

A kick against the back of his leg nearly popped his knee from its socket; a hiss escaped his lips—

Another punch came in from the left, which Xafiri caught with an outstretched arm—

But he didn't have time to see, let alone register, the right-hand swing coming toward his face, as it snapped across his cheek-bone and stunned him for a second.

Time seemed to stop altogether, as Xafiri blinked and tried desperately to see. Black dots circled his vision like crows. Pain ate through his body again like an old friend.

His fate seemed all but certain.

'*You are never... given... opportunities, Xafi,*' his mother had said that morning, talking of the fire trials he was due to start at high-sun. She had held his shoulders tight, the deep wells of her eyes had spoken volumes. '*Opportunity is false.*'

Stood swaying in the street, power echoed through his bones suddenly; vibrations rippled up his spine.

'*It is never given, Xafi,*' his mother had said.

'*Now, you must take it.*'

Pressing down on his feet, Xafiri launched forward and tackled the nearest assailant to the ground, wedging his shoulder into their chest and throwing them down onto their back—

They landed against the stone with a *thud* of limbs; Xafiri charged over them and ran—

As Temusceh's son bellowed, his dignity wounded, and went to make some feigned attempt at a pursuit—

But Xafiri was already gone. Kicking out, accelerating across the village square, ignoring the pains in his chest and the looks of the other villagers as he passed them by. Ignoring the angry shouts at his back, clouded by anger and ignorance. Ignoring everything in a blur of motion, as he made for the western-most tip of the square where the path to his mother's house lay, her words still echoing in his mind.

Leaving the assailants to collect themselves, with tails tucked between their legs...

He crashed through the entrance to his mother's house and stood swaying like a drunkard, heaving air into his lungs to counteract the adrenaline flooding his system. His skin crawled with sweat and dust; pain pulsed through his calves and up into his back, where the bruises expressed their anger in wrenching spasms. Putting a hand out, Xafiri supported himself against the partition wall and exhaled weightily.

That was close...

Alerted by his abrupt entrance, his mother poked her head around the side of the wooden partition and her eyes seemed to swell with concern.

"Xafi!" she said, bustling in and looking to give him a hug – thinking twice about it, as she noted how sweaty he was. "What happen, what happen!"

"Is okay... is okay," he replied.

"No! What happen?"

"Just got stuck."

"Stuck? What stuck?"

Xafiri said nothing in response: instead, he reached into the folds of his jacket and pulled the three bags free, handing them to her with a tired expression.

"Here you go," he rasped. "Like you asked for."

His mother took them from him cautiously and opened the bags up one at a time, studying the contents within. Several expressions crossed her face as she looked over the herbs he had collected: at first, there came a look of joy; then, a quiet confusion; then, her brow furrowed, almost with concern.

And then — as bitter to his soul as it had always been — was one expression Xafiri knew all too well, that wormed its way into him like a parasite.

Disappointment.

"Where the rest?" his mother said, scowling furiously at the bags and then at Xafiri. "Where the rest? You not listen? I give you a list! You have everything… I show you!"

Xafiri shuddered, looking deep into her eyes. He went to open his mouth and conjure something in reply, but his lips fell shut like a trapdoor. His mind — and his *heart* — couldn't bear to try and explain it. He didn't have the words for her; he didn't *know* the words for her. There was nothing he could say, he knew, that would make his mother actually *understand* what had happened to him, and why he had come back nearly empty-handed.

So there's no point saying anything at all, Xafiri sighed.

There never has been.

Without a word spoken, he shifted past her in silence and moved across the kitchen toward his room, where not even the joy of his mother's cooking pot could draw him out of his own mind. He rolled his fingers together, wincing at the bruises that coated his body. As much as he had been expecting his mother's disappointment, it never seemed to get any easier when he heard it spoken aloud. He wondered if it *would* ever get easier, as he grew up and grew older, or if he was doomed to feel her confused spite for the rest of his life——

"Xafi!"

He stopped suddenly, and let a rasp of air escape through his nostrils.

Turning, he looked over to his mother propped next to the partition wall, tapping her hand against the woven wood with an anxious repetition. She stared at him intensely – almost looking through him, in the sombre light coming through the opening in the roof – and pursed her lips.

Then, like a meek little mouse, she placed two fingers on her chest and circled them around her heart, attempting a smile.

"Love… you, Xafi," she said, softly.

Xafiri circled his own heart and nodded.

"Love you too," he whispered, before turning to his room and slipping from sight.

†

Chapter 7

The Feast

Markus could smell it long before he saw it. It was oddly captivating in its own way. Salted meats left to sizzle on an open fire; ground fruits, mashed into a paste; the hints of skeletia and the mellowness of honey left to stew in the open air. It was an intense mixture of delicacies, which left his month salivating and his eyes glowing with hunger. Swimming through the air along with the ashen smell of incense, it bombarded his senses at all angles. If it was poisonous, he didn't care; if it was drugged, he could hardly complain. Sat at the edge of the tree-line, with a rocky crag and several streaks of smoke lacing over the midday sky ahead, Markus let it all wash over him and savoured every breath that came.

Say what you want about the Tarrazi, he thought with a deep inhale, *they sure are masters of the senses.*

Checking his blade was still fastened at his side, Markus tightened his belt and surveyed the open land ahead of him, scowling into the sun. Exposed to the heat, the beige rock seemed to vibrate before him, and the distant rising hills were lost in a haze of shapes and colours. The trees around him seemed to fall away in a natural horseshoe, their gnarled boughs hanging over at odd angles with bare, rotten branches. The earth that remained where the trees did not was parched and broken, jutting up in splintery crags much like the Kazbak Hills further south. Tiny bushels of spiny plants struck up between the cracks like fingers; here and there, he saw the tiny, twisting shapes of lizards skitter over the rocks into the shade.

But beyond that — over the lip of the crags a few dozen steps ahead of him — Markus spied something far more intriguing than any scenery could offer.

There were domes, or the tops of domes at least, littering the space beyond. They were shaped like teardrops, with their points chiselled off to act as rudimentary chimneys, gushing thin plumes of smoke that filled the air with aromatic smells. On some of the taller ones, he spied coloured bands around the upper portion, varying in number and colour with a symbolism that was entirely lost on him. From a distance, assessing studiously where he could, Markus looked them over them with a furrowed brow and came to a single conclusion.

This isn't just some primitive village, he mused, shifting on the balls of his feet.

This is a whole fuckin' town.

Markus counted at least seven large domes that were tall enough to clear the crags ahead of him, each of which must have been about twelve feet high at their peaks. And, with how spaced out they were, he assumed on a conservative mark that there were at least three dozen smaller dwellings out of sight just beneath them, making the village almost as big as a Provenci town.

I didn't realise they built permanent structures like this so far north, beyond the big metal cities that survived the occupation, Markus thought, stepping out into the sun and feeling the heat smack him in the face. *I thought they were all nomadic out here, moving with the seasons and that. I never imagined anything like this.*

Perhaps there's more to these savages than us southerners give credit for.

Keeping low to the ground, with his feet sliding over the soft dirt that layered the rocks, Markus wiped sweat from his brow and located a split between two rocks just ahead. Skittering over like a prowling cat and lying flat on his stomach, he peered down into the Tarrazi settlement below and held his breath.

A celebration of some sort was occurring, it seemed, with a massive congregation of Tarrazi villagers flooding the main square, adorned in striking robes. Each dress he saw was remarkably dyed, and sewn into beautiful rolling shapes with tiny depictions of trees and plants. Children wore headbands of tiny gemstones; the women had bronze rings snaking up their calves and thighs. Those in red – who were predominantly young men, Markus found – also had the dried skin of animals draped across their shoulders, and wore ornaments on their chests of tiny teeth and claws.

Looking upon them from his vantage point, Markus found himself impressed by the character and culture on display. There was a clear link between the impressive robes and the delightful smell of food that caught in his nostrils, as he saw a vast number of those in the square below tearing through hunks of meat and delighting in tiny leaf-bowls of berries. What purpose it served, and what they were celebrating in particular, Markus has no idea: all he could work out was that, before they took the first bite of their food, they spoke the words *'Ful-Vankyra'* and a few cheers went up from those around them.

Perhaps this is a celebration of one of their gods, Markus thought, tensing his stomach as it growled angrily. *They certainly seem to have a lot of food on offer.*

A twitch of a smile caught at the corner of his mouth.

So I'm sure they wouldn't mind if some went missing...

Glancing to his left, he saw how the crags beneath him formed a natural overlook to the village, and that the village itself lay on a large plateau that joined the tree-line just beyond. If he was able to get down from the rocky outcrop he was on and reach the village's perimeter, he could find a good entry point that didn't involve abseiling off the cliff ahead of him.

And with one arm, I wouldn't fancy my chances with that.

Rolling his tongue over the roof of his mouth, he lifted off of his stomach and stooped low to the ground, moving left over the dry earth with small, nimble steps.

This may be my last chance at getting decent food before I hit the Waste-lands in the far north, he thought, working through the path ahead. *I'll still be able to scavenge in the undergrowth and hunt sometimes, but with how bleak it is and how open the landscape gets, I won't have much hope of landing any larger prey.*

Or, none that won't eat me first, that is.

Approaching a ledge ahead of him, he recalled the campfire stories shared between his old mercenary company, about those who had gone into the Wastelands of the far north for work during the Occupation. They had described it as a desolation, above all else: a foul, foreboding place where nothing grew and no rain fell and very few animals could survive. According to them, it was a place of black earth and dark chasms deeper than the sea, with pools of acrid water that could melt the boots from one's feet if they stood in it for too long. It was a place of spectres and ghosts, where the wind carried its own screams; a place where leeches rose from the ground and sucked the life from one's body while they slept, leaving nothing but an empty husk when sunrise finally came.

The mercenaries had been bold in their descriptions, eliciting tall tales of horror and fear, but as far as Markus could tell none of it had evaded the truth, and the land north of the deserts and hills was just as awful as they had described.

And that isn't even the half of it, Markus thought with a shiver, reaching the edge of the crag. *I know there's far worse out there, in the desolation beyond. Things that would make any hardy war veteran shit themselves. Vast creatures; monsters from the bowels of* hellos. *Things with massive wings...*

And lungs of scolding fire.

Turning his attention back to the task at hand, Markus found that the village was surrounded by a wall of twisted logs, interlocking like rows of teeth and lashed together with twine. The land around it had been cleared, and jagged rocks had been embedded in the earth to deter any creature from getting too close. A few stray guardsmen in hide and chitin armour paced along the tree-line, too, prodding at bushes with their spears and scowling up into the sun.

Looking down over the ledge beneath him — hiding his presence from the stray guards — Markus spied one of the strange tubular bushes at the intersection between the wall and the crag, twitching delicately in the wind. It lay bathed in shadow from the rock-face above, and had sprouted yellow flowers like tiny suns.

Markus frowned — *why have they not cleared you out?* — and puzzled at it for a while, trying to decipher why it hadn't been removed like the rest——

When a gust of wind shifted the branches aside and he saw a tiny opening in the tree wall, hiding an access point where two large roots intertwined.

Markus smirked to himself, looking out to the nearest guard who had turned on their heel and started their long walk back along the tree-line. With them gone, there were no other Tarrazi around, and his path into the village was clear.

Well… must be my lucky day.

Taking a shallow breath, he slid down over the edge of the crag and landed in the bush, bending his knees gently to break his fall and keep low amongst the branches.

The cold air of the shade diced up his back. Sweat and dust prickled over his scalp. The electrical waves in his hands pulsed with delight.

Go in, grab food and clothes, and get out again, he thought, turning to the opening under the tree wall.

How hard can it be?

†

Chapter 8

The Plight of the Dead

With a final wash of clay paint under his left eye, Xafiri's death mask was complete, and the fate of the fire trial was sealed across his skin.

The red-orange marks that coated his pale face looked like burns in the low light of his room. Crushed red flowers traced over his brow and coiled across the left side of his face, imitating blood. The smudges of charcoal coiled around his ear canals like tiny river springs.

It was a mask to embody the passage from one life to the next. An imitation of the end of days, from which all Tarrazi were born from and would return to one day. For death was a ghost, he knew, lying above all things.

And, for a short spell with the gods as his witness, Xafiri would become its shadow.

Looking into the basin of water beneath him, he doused his hands and rubbed the last of the clay from his fingertips, whispering a quiet prayer to Ras'gandû and whoever else was listening. With what he had experienced of the fire trial before, he knew he would need Their blessings more than ever.

Because this isn't my first outing in the arena, conjuring fire with my hands, he admitted, pursing his lips. He had undergone the rite-of-passage before, at the height of the Scorching Season the previous year. He had been fifteen-winter's old, full of vigour and guile with the truth about his *Zoltha* education largely under wraps, although even then it was slowly unravelling with rumours amongst his peers. Xafiri had made the bold and ultimately-fatal decision to tell a number of his friends that he had been visited by the Imperial Educators shortly before the trials were due to commence. They had kept it to themselves for some time – long enough for Xafiri to be confirmed by the Verlunz as a contender for the next round of the *Fendûrii* – but, even as the trials started properly, there were mur-murs among his peers and their parents of the truth. Of the Educators, and the *Zoltha,* and the steep slope that followed any accusations concerning their sworn enemy. Xafiri's decision to be open about his past proved to be an incredibly damaging mistake.

And it's a mistake that I'm still reeling from now, nearly a year and a half later.

Xafiri had remained largely ignorant of his fate at the time, enjoying the rigmarole of the rite-of-passage instead while the rumours churned on in the background. He had bested his opponent in the mud fight first, and went on to the fire trials with an inflated confidence typical of a boy his age. But he had approached it clinically nonetheless, focusing on his mind and keeping the flame alight at the end of his weapon. His opponent couldn't seem to keep their flame going by comparison, he recalled, fumbling with the powder like a trainee cook in an army camp. They were hopeless; Xafiri was ready and grinning with pride. With such decisive odds stacked in his favour, the fight was Xafiri's to lose.

And then the sun started beating down against my back, and the pains started in my head...

He sighed at the recollection, shaking his hands free of water and gripping the edge of the basin.

...and then it all came crashing down on top of me, as if the gods had planned it all along.

With his opponent moments from submitting, covered in ashen burns, Xafiri had succumbed to the effects of the scorching heat and collapsed into the dust suddenly, knocking himself unconscious in the process.

In the aftermath, Xafiri had been dragged from the scene and sent to the village healer, where he spent several long days in a partial coma with his skin radiating heat. It was almost feverish at times; his skin seemed to glow like fire. His mother had remained at his bedside like a haunting spectre, monitoring his pulse as if it were keeping her alive too. When she had asked the healer what had caused the effects, the healer thought it was some sort of omen. Then, after a day had passed, there were concerns about the effects of the sun.

But on the second day, when word had finally broke about Xafiri's time with the Imperial Educators, it was agreed by all parties of the tribe that it was neither of those things at all. What it was, so they said, was the wrath of the gods. Their wrath, and their disgust.

Condemning Xafiri to death.

In shame and horror, they had sent him home and placed a black mark on the entrance to their house, declaring him as good as dead and forsaken by the tribe. His mother had wept over his incapacitated body for another whole day, propped up in his bed, watching him shake and tremble in fits, waiting for something to happen. Waiting for *anything* to happen. Waiting… to the point where Xafiri couldn't believe he *hadn't* died, for how long he'd gone without food or water.

And then, on the third night, some miracle occurred. He had awoken suddenly in sweats and shakes, swaying from his bed like a drunk, and had proceeded to raid the pantry for food in the depths of the night wondering what in *hellos* had gone on.

His mother had appeared moments later, wondering what all the noise was about, and had screamed her prayers to the gods like a pilgrim as she looked upon her living son. She had embraced him tightly, refusing to let go like bound clay, until Xafiri finally prized her arms from his back and demanded she explain what was going on.

And you couldn't have made it up if you tried, Xafiri recalled, thinking back to that hallowed night.

I was approaching death… and then I was alive again.

The following morning — after a night of feasting and resuscitating his limbs — Xafiri had emerged from his house once more with a healthy glow across his skin, and every person he laid eyes upon had made their ambivalence clear almost immediately. No-one could look at him directly as he passed; no-one could believe he was still alive at all. The Verlunz, upon hearing the news, was apoplectic. Something had come over Xafiri that night and provided him with a miracle, saving him from the precipice so he could walk amongst them once more.

And it was that — the mercy of the gods in my brush with death — that gave them enough reason not to spear me dead, just for being alive. It was the gods mercy, which allowed me to live on even as an outsider as I do now. I still have my life, because of Them.

Touching two fingers to the side of his head, he looked through the hole in the ceiling and whistled.

And I shall never forget it, I promise.

Draining the sink, he turned from the wash space and paced through to the kitchen, drawing deep breaths into his lungs.

Sat at the end of the table, his mother was eating from a bowl of dried fruits with orange hoops laced through her hair. At the sight of him, she leapt up from her seat with a scrape of stone and hurried over, studying his death mask with a tiny smile of pride.

"Az-kabza, *marzedna*," Xafiri said softly, smiling to her.

"Az-kabza, Xafi," she replied, squeezing his shoulders. "You look strong."

"I *feel* strong."

"This" — she tapped his face — "good."

"Thank you."

"Is just like *he* show you, all those years ago…"

Xafiri swallowed, surprised by his reaction to her words; his mother pulled her hair behind her ears and seemed to shake away the thought awkwardly, almost regretting the fact she had said it at all.

"You look ready," she said instead, offering up a pleasant smile.

"I am ready," Xafiri proclaimed. "Always ready."

"Know what must do?"

"I know. Don't worry."

She nodded, her eyes like glowing stars, before holding a finger up to him.

"Ah! Before you go…"

She stepped back over to the table and plucked a tiny sachet from the top, tucking it into his waistband and ensuring it was securely in place.

"I… made some-thing… with things you get," she mumbled, gesturing to the sachet at his belt. "Is not much, but… when you put—"

"*Hasvent* and *Thäntun'tul-cûlii* together, it makes a balm to save my head from the sun…" he explained, imitating sunlight hitting his scalp. "To stop what happened last time. I know… I remembered."

The smile she produced at his response was one that could've drawn flowers from their buds, it was so radiant. Placing his head in her hands, she planted a kiss on his cheek.

"Proud… of you," she said.

Xafiri placed her hands in his own and squeezed them.

"Love you, ma."

"Love you too, Xafi."

He left her by the table and drifted toward the entrance, adjusting his waistband and shifting his feet in his boots. The weight of what came next washed over him like the rolling waves of the sea, settled by a long breath that streamed out through his lips.

This is the moment, he thought, nodding his head. *Time to make up for the loss in the mud pit, and show them you are worthy of this tribe.*

Smiling to his mother again, Xafiri pulled the drape away from the doorway and entered out into the sun.

Let's do this.

*

The heat. The soul. Living. Dying. Every inch of me becomes one with the world.

I am here. I am present. The gods are present with me.

Show to me Your prowess.

Stepping out onto the village square through crowds of jeering people, Xafiri took in a deep breath and shielded his eyes from the sun.

This is my time; this is my place.

Redemption… shall come.

The village square had been transformed in preparation for the *Fendûrii*, with areas sectioned off and demarked to make ready for the upcoming event. A rope had been laid out in a rough circle to form an arena, behind which the spectators stood in their formal robes surveying the enclosed space beyond. Several openings had been left for the fighters to enter, and as Xafiri stepped over the rope threshold he spied his three other competitors do likewise, assessing each other with a snarl. There was a scrawny lad with a tuft of black chest hair and a spiralling birth-mark on his arm; a young woman with a face like chipped stone and a mean looking scar down one leg; and an older boy – older than Xafiri, he acknowledged – who appeared the most confident of them all, striding into the light with a clear, self-effacing bravado. His face was unblemished, and his sandstone skin seemed almost translucent in the light. He stood amongst the crowds for a moment scratching at his braid of hair, muttering to someone just hidden from sight. Xafiri wondered what they were conspiring about, trying to see past the jostling spectators to locate the source – when the heads parted like the sea suddenly and the big, brutish face of Temusceh appeared, looking between the man and Xafiri with a grin.

So we're still playing games, are we? he thought with a sigh, clenching his fists. *I outsmarted your boy and his cronies yesterday… and now you're back for revenge.*

Looking more closely at the man Temusceh was speaking to, Xafiri released under the harsh light that the fighter's face was covered in a fine powder, and concealed the three dots of *zaz-gûla* under his left eye.

Xafiri scoffed, shaking his head. *And you've even entered another illegal fighter into the Fendûrii, to take me out and ensure I don't win the trials. As if my current task wasn't hard enough.* Looking up to the clear blue skies above, he whispered a quiet prayer to Ras'gandû and kissed his fingers.

I hope you're watching this, wherever you are…

Feeling down at his side, he removed the items he'd been given by the trial-masters before entering the arena, holding them up to the light: there was a bag of *felgul,* or ignition powder, used to coat objects with a flammable dust, and a rough-piece of rock known as a striking stone that assisted with creating sparks. Both were very prevalent in the Valatuk Hills, where a millennia of heat, wind and erosion had allowed perfect conditions for them to form. To work properly, all they needed was something dry to ignite, and everything would go up in flames in an instant.

Which meant that, looking down to the stones at his feet, the weapon Xafiri had been left by the trial-masters was perfectly designed for such conditions. It was a bronze pole with a leather handle and an opening at one end, which had been stuffed to the brim with thick knots of dried grass and thatch. Like some primitive broom, Xafiri knew that the intention was to ignite the thatch and use the burning end to attack one's opponents, literally beating them with flames until they yielded and a victor was crowned. It was the most brutal and exacting trial of the *Fendûrii,* Xafiri knew, and although he had dropped out of the previous fight in a heat-induced coma, he had become accustomed to the fighting style quite quickly. Part of him hoped the skills would return almost like second nature.

But I also know that Ras'gandû is as cunning as He is clever… and that this fight will be a test of my faith as much as my skill.

Touching his forehead and rubbing the paste of his death-mask between his fingers, Xafiri whispered another prayer and hefted the fire-pole from the ground, testing it with a few deft spins before setting it against his shoulder.

And it seems it won't just be the gods that watch over our fight this day, Xafiri thought, looking across the arena ahead to watch a canopy being erected, with guards stationing themselves at its edges like solemn statues. As the poles were set between the stones and the canopy stood aloft, a chair was then carried into the shade, covered in gilded blue fabrics with embroidered animals across its back.

At the sight of it, the villagers all around him clasped their forearms and closed their eyes suddenly, chanting rhythmically like a heartbeat and invoking the gods with every breath. He heard a thousand names of a thousand deities ripple through the crowds; their stamping feet sent shivers up his spine. The sun seemed to burn even brighter overhead, until the blue of the sky lay consumed in its unwieldly splendour. Xafiri took it all in and felt his breath quiver in his lungs.

Until he saw a robust figure emerge from the right hand side of the canopy, wearing a head-crest of bronze and glistening gemstones that shimmered over their scalp. Adorning blue robes with gold trim and an impervious coil of animal teeth around their neck, their face was measured and austere as they approached the canopy, with several different patterns of *zaz-gûla* tracing around their eyes and over their chest. Through the pulsing haze, Xafiri watched as they regarded the fighters and the crowds in turn, stopping at the edge of the shade with an aura that captivated one's very soul.

May we all bear witness, Xafiri mouthed.

The Verlunz, has come…

"*Vas-gal, dügër'ma!*" the Verlunz bellowed — and, with a deafening silence, the crowds on either side drew still suddenly, opening their eyes and looking to their leader with adoration and awe.

"Az-kabza, my people," the Verlunz exclaimed in Tarrazi, lowering their hands and kissing their fingers. "Welcome to a most… and grand occasion, to celebrate the *Fendûrii* and Our God, Ras'gandû." Xafiri focused in on their words intently, but his limited vocabulary struggled to conjure some of the terms that they spoke. "May the gods bless His soul, and reveal the truth for us. For today, four of our *skal* shall fight with weapons of flame, and use their … to crown a victor. We are … to welcome them to this arena, and witness their skill in combat. May they serve and mark our greatness in this time!"

A cheer went up among the spectators. The other fighters jeered and clapped their hands. The Verlunz looked out upon them in joy.

And Xafiri, who had felt his brain melt trying to interpret the last of their chief's words, just stared dumbly at the canopy and the guards stood at its edges. The sky darkened above him as an absent cloud passed overhead.

I am so out of my depth here, with all of this, Xafiri thought, tightening his grip on the fire-pole. *I hardly understand my place in this world. I hardly understand the language of my own people, and their many, many customs. I was never taught these things — and to be ask to be taught now, at my age, will only bring greater shame than not knowing. Because I am Unproven in this life; an unformed part of the clan… but I am also more than that. I am uneducated. Perverse. Corrupted. Faithful and yet so faithless. Stood here, awaiting my trial, with the Verlunz watching over us. This is but one fight.*

But the battle from here remains so long.

"*Ready!*" the Verlunz bellowed in Tarrazi, pounding a fist against their chest.

Around him, the other fighters hefted their weapons and prepared their ignition powder. Striking stones lay taut on their fingertips, with coy smiles gracing their faces.

Xafiri let his muscle-memory take hold, dousing the end of the bronze pole and readying his stone in his other hand. He did not acknowledge the other fighters, nor the expectant crowds, nor the Verlunz rubbing his hands together, ready to announce the trial had begun. He didn't acknowledge the *Fendûrii* at all, in that moment. He was lost to the world; lost to his own mind too.

Redemption… shall come.

The Verlunz opened their palms out and slapped them together with a percussive *thud*. Xafiri hefted the weapon in his hand, striking the stone against the bronze pole, and watched a dash of sparks ignite the thatch end and set the whole thing aflame. It roared to life in seconds, flaring like a firebird.

The Verlunz opened their arms.

"BEGIN!"

†

Chapter 9

A Savage Encounter

Markus snuck up behind the Tarrazi guard and wrapped his hand around their mouth, silencing their scream as a pulse of electric quivered through his palm. He braced against the man's writhing body, as they tried to reach down to their side and grapple for their sword. Lightning fizzed at Markus' fingertips like a thousand tiny nettles, as a shockwave rattled through the guard's skull and siphoned off down his neck.

In the end, it took less than a heartbeat — silent, beyond the scraping of the man's boots on the dirt — for the Tarrazi's body to seize up and go limp in his arms, the fight evaporating from their body as the conscious light left their eyes.

One less threat to deal with, Markus rasped, slipping his hand from the guard's drooling mouth. He let them drop to the ground before rolling them to one side, using a ream of fabric against the nearest building's wall to hide their body away in a cocoon. There, the guard stirred quietly in his strange, electrified slumber, muttering to himself beneath the old carpet about dreams and old friends. The lightning blast would leave him incapacitated for several hours, Markus hoped.

Which gives me plenty of time to get what I came here for.

Pinning himself to the clay wall opposite as the sun beat down overhead, Markus navigated between the next row of dwellings and kept low to the ground, skittering between them quickly like a cockroach. He peered around corners with an air of caution; the skittering sounds of bugs and lizards kept him light on his feet. The noise from the feast continued to echo out at his back and made no sign of stopping. It almost gave him a sense of confidence, as misguided as it was, that he would remain undiscovered and escape the village without anyone knowing he'd been there at all. The guard had been the first person he had encountered thus-far — maybe they would be the last, too.

But he knew better than to second-guess the Tarrazi, in truth: because as soon as the feast was over, and they went back to their duties, the game would be up, and they'd hunt him down like a filthy rodent until his blood washed every wall of their village.

And that is not an eventuality that I want to entertain, especially with so much still ahead of me.

Studying the structures around him, Markus gritted his teeth and sighed, wiping a sheen of sweat from his brow. His frustration, mixed with the unrelenting heat of the midday sun, proved a rather venomous concoction.

Where the fuck do they keep their supplies? he growled, looking up to the coloured bands around the upper-reaches of their dwellings — hoping on some whim that one of the colours would scream 'armoury' or 'storehouse' to him, and he could go about his thievery in peace. His understanding of Tarrazi customs had been piecemeal at best before he had crossed the fateful border several months before, but now that he was in the bear's den his ignorance seemed to plague his every move. All he had managed to discern thus-far was that the red bands meant 'hunter', and he knew that purely because every red-banded dwelling he had encountered so far had an excessive assortment of spears just outside the door. And that knowledge came as both a blessing and a fear: that they seemed to possess no swords or killing blades gave Markus cause for relief.

That there seem to be dozens of hunters here, all armed to the teeth and ready to kill, is less than ideal, however...

Spitting a globule of phlegm into the dirt, Markus skirted down another side-path on his left and looked up to the next building he encountered – where he spied a new coloured band along the upper edge that he hadn't seen yet: a sage green, like the colour of old grass. It was the only band on the building, and the only one with that colour in the vicinity, which told him that the owner of the dwelling possessed some kind of specialism among the tribe.

And hopefully it's one befitting a thief like me, so I can be on my merry fucking way.

With ample curiosity, Markus darted over to it and checked the surrounding paths, constantly aware of the enemy who could've been lurking nearby. Upon finding no threats – and with no noise emanating from the green-banded building ahead of him – Markus pulled the cloth drape away from the door and peered inside, studying the pallid interior under the half-light of the roof.

Hm… interesting.

The room was open and stuffy, with the aromas of spice tempting him closer like a kitchen in a Provenci longhouse. Despite being largely empty, the domed walls were lined with tiny bronze hooks, wedged into the clay in neat lines from the floor to the ceiling. Hanging from each hook were an assortment of grasses, herbs and roots that were entirely foreign to Markus, producing a number of exotic, pervasive scents. There were sheafs of dried stems with wilted flowers at their ends; dissected pieces of root that looked like pale bones; several netted bags of aromatic spices that both made his head spin and his stomach churn. A few wicker baskets lay at the edges of the room, too, full of shells, stones and other precious gems that glinted and winked in the low light.

It was a storehouse of some sort, Markus gathered, although that was about all he could ascertain from the room laid out before him. Some of the grasses he saw across the walls he recognised from his time foraging with the company back in Provenci: cooking spices that complimented venison and other fresh meats, as well as roots used for sealing wounds. But as for the rest of them – hypnotic red flowers and thorny vines and powders that looked like stardust — Markus could only imagine what purpose they served. He assumed it was all medicinal in some way.

Meaning this is the storehouse for the village healer, he deduced, sealing the drape back across the opening. *And once upon a time, stumbling upon a place like this, I would've taken the lot and not thought twice.*

But now…

He looked down to his charred hand, which spat and fizzed with electrical glee.

Now I have other means of salvation.

Stepping back and sealing the entranceway, Markus turned away from the herbalist's dome and made off toward the next set of dwellings, studying a lone cloud drifting sightlessly overhead as he considered his next move—

When the sound of footsteps suddenly echoed out on his right, moving away from the feast toward him—

Forcing him to hide behind a cluster of wicker baskets arranged outside the nearest house, pulling his grey, straggled hair out of sight.

They haven't finished the feast yet… have they? he gasped, tensing his hand. He held his breath, peering up above the lip of the basket—

Ducking down again sharply as two armoured guards sauntered past him, muttering between themselves in native tongue. With their bronze spears pointing up as if ready to impale the sun, they strode between the dwellings and disappeared from sight without a second thought to their surroundings — not registering the intruder a couple of feet to their left, tucked away neatly under cover. It was only when they had slipped from view that Markus realised he was holding his breath, clutching the lip of the wicker basket in a white-knuckle grasp.

Need to be more careful. He exhaled at length and cursed, checking that no other surprises awaited him around the next corner.

Now where the fuck is the armoury?

Markus rolled his tongue across the roof of his mouth, glaring at the sun. He knew there was a touch of ignorance in assuming the

Tarrazi possessed anything like an '*armoury*' in the first place. It was, he understood, a very 'imperial' concept: back in Provenci, every village bigger than a few huts had a soldier's storehouse nearby, usually adjacent to a blacksmith's or a cobbler's. There, they stowed weapons and armaments to allow for resupply in the event of a rebellion, using it as a deterrent to monitor such a vast land.

It was not a shared custom, however, in what many Provencians regarded as the 'savage' Tarrazi north. It was true that some Tarrazi villages just over the southern border had adopted the use of storehouses during the Occupation, as a means of showing their compliance to imperial logistical demands — *but then those same storehouses ended up being rebel hideouts right under the Governors' noses, giving the Tarrazi the means to make war while they talked of everlasting peace.* But regardless of that, in the middle- and northern-regions of Tarraz where Imperial control had been limited at best, Markus admitted the adoption of a weapon's store remained highly unlikely.

And that makes my job a hell of a lot harder in finding decent supplies, he grunted, peering over the baskets again to find the coast was clear. Taking a shallow breath, he lifted from his stoop and made to move on—

When he stopped suddenly and frowned, clamping his jaw.
Wait...
Looking up to the building next to him, he assessed the coloured bands at its peak: two red, and one yellow. A hunter's dwelling.

If they're all at the feast, and have guards on patrol already... then surely they would've left their armour and supplies at home? Markus puzzled for a moment, running through his options, before his mouth twisted into a covetous grin. *And if that's the case, then I don't need to worry about finding a storehouse at all...*

Not when every dwelling has a mini-armoury of its own.
Checking once more that he was alone, Markus skirted the edge of the hunter's house and prized the cloth drape away from the door, peering inside inquisitively. With no sign of movement and no noise emanating from within, he slid inside without a whisper and sealed

it shut at his back.

Stepping into the half-light, Markus studied the interior of the dwelling and produced a discerning frown, creasing his face up like old paper left out in the sun too long. The room was partitioned through the middle with woven wicker walls and sticks, offering communal and private spaces for the family that called it home. From the entrance, he had stepped into the living and cooking space, where feather cushions lined one corner under thick reams of dyed cloth. The other corner was occupied by a long wood counter covered in various dried foods, and an intricate stand of three cauldrons suspended over a fire-pit. The cauldrons looked like some alchemist's workshop to Markus, who had never seen anything like it before: three pots connected by sections of brass, stood at different heights to allow for various methods of cooking. It was not quite like the kindle-stoves fitted into kitchens back in Provenci, but it was a feat of technical engineering that he hadn't expected nonetheless.

How about that...

Markus approached the fire-pit first, cocking his leg out and knocking the charred logs with the end of his foot. With no embers burning when the wood broke, he safely assumed the hunters had been out for some time, and the house was empty.

Good, he mused with satisfaction.

Time to get to work then.

Approaching the countertop against the wicker partition, Markus smirked at the bounty available and started shovelling items under his arm: a pheasant looking creature that had been plucked, salted and roasted; a knotted coil of soft bread, burnt on the bottom where the bronze had heated too quickly; and a rush of reed-like plants, with red polyps encased in their leaves. There were several other smaller items that he stashed in his breech pockets, but he left the rest for the sake of not being overburdened.

I'll have to find a bag for this stuff... maybe there'll be one in the next room over.

Markus turned from the countertop and slipped around the

partition into the next 'room', which as it turned out was the bedroom. A wooden frame against the back wall held a large cloth mattress stuffed with straw, alongside more of the dyed fabrics and plump, feather-filled cushions. Several ornaments had been woven into the head-board to give the impression of stained glass, which caught the light every so often and glistened with beautiful colours. An assortment of boxes and baskets had been wedged beneath the outer wall, too, which contained a number of clothing items spilling over the edges like a flagon of booze.

But none of that drew Markus' attention for any length of time in reality: his eyes had wandered elsewhere instead, and landed on the bed to his right.

Where a suit of chitin-and-bronze armour lay perfectly arranged over the cushions, almost inviting him over.

Luck ventures here, it seems…

He paced over to it and looked it over more closely: each piece of the armour consisted of bronze plates with woven leather straps, and had clearly been crafted by studious, deft hands. As with the guards he had seen patrolling the walls outside, each part was also covered by a piece of a monster's carapace, which was dusky-grey in colour and covered in brown pock-marks. From the array of chitin pieces in front of him, it was clear that the monster they had killed for the armour was quite large in size – and, considering the number of guards and hunters they had in the village with the same armour, the creatures were also quite prevalent in the area.

Wonder if I'll bump into them at some point on my travels, Markus thought, before shivering.

Actually, best not give their gods any ideas…

Turning back to the bed, he got to work with putting the armour on, assessing which parts fitted best and which of the bindings would withstand the rigorous path ahead. The boots and shin-plates were a touch tight but would keep secure on the journey into the hills; the leg-braces against his thighs were far too wide, so Markus kept his heavy breeches on reluctantly in their place; the huge chitin plate across his back and stomach fit across him like a corset, but the breast-plate was far too wide by comparison; the forearm guard was too intricate to put on properly, and the shoulder pads had to be discarded.

Fitting the last of it on – wrestling with the bindings and cursing the stump that made up his right arm – Markus tightened the last strap and rolled his shoulder, nodding to himself with a quiet satisfaction. The sensation of being back in armour was a comforting one, he found, having spent so much of his life kitted up as a mercenary.

Feels like a lifetime ago, he thought, reaching across the bed to unravel a beige robe led there. *Little over six weeks ago I was a mercenary out on the Provenci plains, hunting bandits for a living along the border.* He slipped the robe on, and found it fitted nicely over the armour he'd adorned. *Now I'm a one-armed nobody with unfathomable powers, brought back from the dead in the depths of Tarraz with only one goal in mind.*

His eye spasmed; he scratched at his neck like a noose was growing tighter. The thoughts resurfaced like ugly boils.

To end that which has forsaken me.

He exhaled; a condemnation.

To cut the head from the true serpent of these lands.

He gritted his teeth, conveying his vengeance to the gods above who were no doubt listening, and made to turn back to the wider room beyond——

When a noise caught in his ear, almost like the fractious shuffling of feet, and Markus stopped in his tracks.

Wide-eyed and suddenly fearful, he reached down to his side slowly and withdrew the blade from its sheath——

Spinning on his heel, ready to carve the newcomer down the middle in one strike——

Stopping, with a gasp escaping his lips, as he looked deep into the eyes of a child, no older than eight-winter's old.

The world stopped. Markus watched the child bristle, freezing up on the spot. The child in turn looked between his gnarled face and the blade in his hand, thinking of the sheer wrath Markus could inflict with just a sweep of his weapon. The child's life could be snuffed out in one strike.

Just one…

Stood there, lost in the depths of their eyes, Markus felt a wrenching pain contract in his lungs, spearing up his neck like a serpent. He blinked and twitched, shaking his head loose——

As a conflation of memories streamed through his skull suddenly: ones that were of his mind but not his own. Memories of a child's face and their fleeing body; a knife in his hand——

A knife in her hand, stabbing down into his back. Slitting the child's throat. Exacting death——

A camp, in the hills. In search of sustenance for the journey ahead.

Smoke rising nearby. Tents. People.

Tarrazi.

A boy's blood on my hands.

On her *hands.*

He opened his mouth to speak, but found no words could follow. The blade trembled in his hand. He saw——

I see death, wrought by another's blade… by another's choice. A poisoned hand — prayers escaping poisoned lips. Afflicted by a hate in the soul that corrupts all things.

Death and death and death——

Markus lowered his blade and gasped.

Savanta…

The boy turned from him and screamed, bolting from the room and disappearing off to his right to hide somewhere therein.

Markus gawked dumbly at the open space ahead, swaying away from the bed and out toward the living space, leaving the child to cower away.

He sheathed his blade. His skin was impossibly cold. The child continued to whimper and cry in the other room.

He forgot how to breathe and forgot how to think.

Death and death and death——

He stumbled toward the entrance to the house and pulled the cloth drape aside, stepping out into the light beyond with the blood of a child behind his eyelids.

Memories circled like crows. The sky was so impossibly bright overhead.

He took one step, drawing a breath in through his nostrils—

To be grabbed by the throat, and drawn toward a huge Tarrazi figure stood just outside, snarling at him with red marks on his face and a busted nose like old rock. His eyes seemed to bulge in their sockets as he laid eyes on the grey-haired wanderer.

"*Zoltha!*" he roared, with more figures arriving at his back.

Markus blinked.

Wait...

He hardly registered – *could* hardly register – before he was thrown against the side of the house and snapped back to reality, slapping across the dirt in a pile of tangled limbs.

Pushing up on his hand with a hiss of breath, he looked up into the light and saw figures approaching at all angles: Tarrazi men and women strapped up in armour, their faces like knotted bark hewn from a twisted tree. All hate and malice. All death and hell.

The feast was over, it seemed; their knives and spears were drawn.

Markus rose to his feet and reached for his sword.

Death and death and death and death and—

†

Chapter 10

Trial by Fire

Xafiri ground his heels and spat a gobbet of ashy phlegm into the dirt, the colour of wet stone. Looking out across the bright arena, he clenched his jaw as his opponent made another pass, the fire-pole looming dangerously in their hands. It swept across towards his neck; Xafiri ducked low and let the burning thatch sail above him, wincing at the intensity of heat inches from his scalp. The man's unruly gaze ahead of him unveiled feelings of frustration, as Xafiri reasserted himself with his own weapon and squared his jaw.

A second attack followed the first in quick succession: Xafiri brought his weapon across his body and bent low on one knee, smashing the two bronze poles together with an echoey chime of metal. The vibrations rattled up his arms; he shied away as a shower of ash and ignition powder coated his skin. The Proven man opposite seemed impressed with himself and flashed his teeth with glee.

Game on.

Shoving his opponent away again, Xafiri regained his stance and levelled the fire-pole across his chest. His opponent — the illegal fighter with the powdered face — smirked childishly and diced his own weapon back and forth in reply, so the flames seemed to draw circles in the air between them. Ash hailed across the stone underfoot; the silhouette of the flames were impossible to follow. It was mesmerising, almost. There was a certain showmanship—

As the scrape of dirt caught in Xafiri's left ear, and he instinctively ducked out the way—

To watch another fire-pole streak through the air where his head had just been, in the hands of the only other fighter still left standing.

Forgot there were two of them, Xafiri acknowledged, catching sight of the fourth fighter — the scrawny man with the chest of hair — as he was dragged unconscious from the arena with a ferocious scorch-mark lining his face. *She made short work of him.*

And if I'm not careful, I'll be next.

Snarling, Xafiri swung his fire-pole across and forced the woman to teeter backwards, using the momentum to lunge forward and lash her stomach with flames. The burning thatch diced across her exposed skin and singed the underside of her breast-plate; with a hiss, she planted her feet and circled off to the right, reconsidering her method of attack.

Xafiri exhaled softly. *Dealing with you is fine, so long as I'm careful,* he acknowledged, returning his gaze to the fore.

It's the other one I have to worry about.

Stepping back, he looked between his two opponents and the wider arena beyond. The sun was ferocious overhead: the stones seemed to sizzle and bite under his feet, so he could hardly stand in any place for very long. Sweat leaked from every pore over his body, as a sheen coated his scalp like the surface of a lake. Sunburn plastered across his back and his scalp, where even the heat resistant balm failed to protect him from the malcontents of the midday sun.

The other two fighters looked much the same: the woman with the harsh face trembled under the sun's intensity, and the Proven brute heaved great torrents of air through his chest just to keep steady. The onlookers around them had been chastised of their excitement, and looked out upon the three remaining fighters with a desperation and tiredness. Children huddled in their mothers' robes; the hunters slung drapes of cloth over their heads. The Verlunz at the far end, out of the sun under his canopy, was tended to by a fan-bearer and looked visibly distressed.

This is going on longer than they wanted, Xafiri thought, keeping an eye on his weapon as a sweep of cool air crossed the arena. *Which is no surprise, really, considering one of us is too experienced to be here anyway. They expected him to take me out by now.*

How wrong you are...

Xafiri looked between them both and pummelled a fist against his chest. Adrenaline washed over him, igniting in his bones.

Come on then you bastards!

The woman stood back and flashed her teeth, keeping her weapon balanced and still...

But the Proven man, clutching the fire-pole in both hands, was more than happy to oblige in her place.

Xafiri engaged as he did, clashing poles with embers showering the dry ground beneath them. One strike resounded – then another – and another – and a fourth, sending shockwaves up through his elbow with the force of it.

The Proven man speared down like a hunter, the fire-coated thatch surging across Xafiri's vision; he back-stepped and snapped his own pole up, batting the attack to one side.

A heartbeat later, and Xafiri made his counter, bellowing with fury. Lacking the mobility to parry, the Proven man opened his hands out wide and let Xafiri's weapon scrape against his stomach, leaving tiny red burns across his skin like the raking claws of a Hound.

A hiss escaped his lips. Xafiri watched his face tense.

But, regardless of his small victory, the Proven man seemed unchanged by Xafiri's attack: seconds later, he was gritting his teeth again and going in for another lunge.

Squatting low this time, the man pushed his fire-pole up like a joust straight toward Xafiri's chest.

Xafiri bristled in response, dragging his weapon up at an awkward angle to intercept the attack—

Forcing the flames to connect suddenly, interwoven like vines with a crackle of anger.

A hail of embers and ash splattered across Xafiri's abdomen and breeches, singing the fabric and embedding against his skin like shrapnel. Hissing agony ripped across his stomach, as if he'd been stung by insects. The heat that swam through the air in that moment was enough to daze him, as he stumbled backwards and wiped his face with a sweaty palm. The Proven man did likewise, shifting back and scowling furiously, shaking his fire-pole to try and keep it alight.

I was... wondering when we'd start to have problems... with the flames going out, Xafiri gasped, blinking the dust from his eyes. *Because if it isn't the wind that takes the flame, then... it's the dust...*

Absently trying to focus his energies back into the fight ahead, his eyes drifted down to the pole swaying delicately at his side—

And the smouldering thatch at its end, producing a miserable trail of smoke.

Xafiri held his breath.

Shit!

Reaching for the powder at his side, he looked up to find the Proven man had also lost his flame, fumbling for his own ignition powder hanging loosely from his belt.

Time... of the essence...

Prying the knot open, Xafiri reached into the bag and felt the dusty substance against his fingertips, looking up to his left—

Where the woman was closing in on him again, grinning from ear-to-ear with her fire-pole still spitting with life.

Xafiri cursed; his eyes bulged.

And I'm all out of time.

He twisted out the way as the flaming thatch slapped across the earth where he'd been standing, feeling the rawness of its heat lancing up his calf. Twisting on his heel, another attack came in almost immediately after, forcing him to duck out the way and swing his extinguished weapon around to block. It still proved to be an effective counter-measure, as the woman's third attack skittered off the bronze pole and she hissed with frustration.

This is getting ridiculous, Xafiri rasped, wishing for a moment's reprieve – but he had little time to gather himself in the end as the woman made her next onslaught, thrashing her fire-pole back and forth, ever intent on his demise.

The first strike he was able to bat away without issue, sweeping lazily across his side. The second attack came just as mercifully, with Xafiri grappling the bronze pole in both hands to shove the woman's weapon from his face. The third lunged in toward his stomach, which he spun away from like a dancer as he readied his own weapon for a counter. For a second, he almost thought she was going easy on him, or that she had bitten off more than she could chew——

When her weapon lowered suddenly, and she stepped into his circle with a snarl.

What——

A fist curled up and caught Xafiri in the stomach, crunching up under his ribs with the force of a cannon-blast.

Air rasped through his mouth as he keeled over, the woman's hot breath in his ear.

The pain was ferocious. Immeasurable. The bruises on his side went off like alarms.

He looked up into the light——

And he could do nothing, in the end, as the woman stepped back and swung the fire-pole across her body, aiming straight for Xafiri's head.

He flinched away, turning his face from the sudden explosion of heat that suddenly eclipsed his senses. Ash splattered across his skin embers and sparks bristled across his cheek and eyelid. The thatch fronds lashed across his scalp like tiny whips, burning deep grooves across his head that would never fully heal.

The agony was incredible. His entire skull seemed to explode. Consciousness dimmed in his mind, as the fire licked across his skin and slipped away again just as fast.

Around them, the crowd gasped and jeered.

The Verlunz leaned forward in his seat with quizzical eyes.

Over on the opposite side, *Hajiin* Temusceh lifted his hands and roared in triumph.

And stumbling backwards, feeling the skin hiss around his right eye, Xafiri pressed his feet against the base of his boots and struggled to stay aloft. Numbness swept his legs; to give up, seemed an inevitable path. He propped himself up on his bronze pole and sighed——

When a power coursed through his chest suddenly, engulfing all thought. A confluence of emotion, cracking up his spine and swirling through his head. A great vengeance, rising to the fore. Pain. Hate. Disgust.

Anger.

Sensing the fury ignite in his veins, Xafiri hefted the bronze pole and flared his nostrils, looking defiantly out on the crowds and the woman stood smugly opposite him.

"*Bujanti, Zoltha?*" the woman mocked.

In reply, Xafiri found it in him to smile.

Not even close, my dear... not even close.

The woman advanced, oozing confidence; holding his pole against his shoulder, Xafiri crouched down and waited.

She stepped in and swung up with her weapon, watching the burning thatch sizzle through the air toward him. Xafiri swung across his body with staggering momentum and smacked the fire-pole away, shrugging at the reverberations that trembled through his arm.

Caught off-guard, the woman started to teeter——

Lifting his foot, Xafiri kicked out at the woman's knee that had locked trying to keep her balance——

And the joint popped out of its socket, bulging against the skin like a parasite crawling through her leg.

The woman exploded with screams, toppling forward slowly as the leg gave way——

Xafiri brought his weapon up, sensing an opening, gritting his teeth like a mad dog——

When the woman screeched——

And the bronze pole clattered against her cheek, snapping her head to the side with a string of teeth and phlegm as the crowd behind stood in awe and horror facing the brutality first-hand.

Sliding forwards, the woman clattered down across the hot stone floor in a crumpled mess, alive still but lost to the world in a void of pain and stars.

Xafiri rose to a stand again, as the emotions ebbed in his soul. He rolled his shoulders and looked down on the body with a sigh.

You did try, he acknowledged, tightening the pole in his hand, *and you failed, in the end.*

Looking up to the arena, he took in a great length of air and winced at the pain bubbling across his scalp.

I'll have to get that checked over soon——

Running feet sounded on his right; the bellow of anger and the hiss of flame followed——

Xafiri turned sharply and brought his weapon up in both hands, stopping an overhead strike from the Proven man who's fire-pole seemed to seethe with flames, far brighter than usual. His face looked demented in the fractured light, like staring into the eye of a dead-god.

"You... *die,*" the man spat.

Xafiri threw him off and lowered into a fighter's stance. Exhaustion wracked his body.

Just give up already...

Without missing a beat, the Proven man levelled his weapon and looked ready to make his advance regardless——

When a strong gust of wind swept up across the square, and his fire-pole was snuffed out in an instant.

The crowd gasped around him; the Verlunz lifted from his seat.

The brute studied the end of it, perplexed, and frowned at Xafiri as if it were his fault.

What's going on? Xafiri wondered, with a growing sense of dread lifting in his chest. A moment later, he watched the man glance behind him suddenly and shrug at the crowds, gesturing to the end of his fire-pole as if it were a toy he had broken in a tantrum.

And there, within the goggling faces of the spectators, he watched Temusceh lift a vial in his hand and imitate using a striking stone, glaring at the extinguished fire-pole that lay smouldering in the man's grasp.

Except, it wasn't smouldering: it wasn't even burnt at all.

Because he's been given oil to douse the thatch with, Xafiri realised, clenching his own weapon tighter in his hand. *Because he's run out of ignition powder, which would crown me the victor by default...*

Turning back to Xafiri, the man slid the striking stone from his waistband and held it aloft in the air. Lifting his weapon in the other hand, he scraped the stone down the pole in one long stroke, and watched as the flames roared back to life with a menacing, powerful glow.

The brute's face opened up with a grin; he lowered his weapon for a charge.

And all the while Xafiri stood in shock, not believing what he saw.

Even if I had prevailed... I was always destined to lose.

Coated in sweat, with pain throbbing across his skull, he lifted his fire-pole and looked up over the sky, wondering where the gods were when he needed them.

I need something... anything, from you. I just need to survive.

Xafiri gulped.

The Proven man charged.

Or I'll probably be dead come morning...

†

Chapter 11

Zazkan Stor'oma

hat a fucking mess.

WMarkus lashed his blade down and sent a spear of lightning out from his fingertips, directed at the nearest pursuer like an arrow in flight. It connected with a woman's stomach as she attempted a dodge: impacting against her bronze corset, the woman squirmed like she'd pissed herself, as one leg collapsed and she spewed brown vomit across the dirt at her feet. Markus' face knotted up in disgust.

She doubled over and wretched again.

Behind her, three other villagers emerged armed with spears and chitin cuirasses, growling towards Markus with the word '*Zoltha*' on their tongues. Markus hadn't a clue what it meant: some insult or derogative term, he expected. And part of him didn't blame them for the accusations.

It's not every day you see a southerner in your village, wearing your armour with a bag of your food on his back.

He allowed himself a smile.

I'd be pretty pissed too.

Hunkering down into a fighter's stance, Markus edged slowly backwards as more fighters appeared – including the massive Tarrazi who had thrown him against the clay wall when he'd first been discovered.

He's my biggest concern, Markus admitted, snarling toward them with his robes billowing in the breeze. The six other Tarrazi – or seven, if he was counting the woman who was still throwing up – were average fighters of inconsistent skill, trained for stealthy ambush kills out among the trees rather than any hand-to-hand combat. But, comparatively, the huge Tarrazi in the chitin plates wore the scars of an entirely different fighter: one who revelled in snapping their enemies in two and watching the blood drain from their bodies, like a fire-drake toying with its prey. A fighter that struck fear into their opponents with a look.

Best keep out of your fighting circle, Markus assessed, taking a few more steps back – but even as he did so, he heard the sound of running in his right ear as more enemies approached.

I need to get out, and fast.

An anger rose and fell in his chest, like a dragon dozing in its eternal slumber.

I don't want to kill all these people. They're just angry and don't understand. They're innocents in all this.

And I am no monster.

Markus turned on his heel and bolted off to his left, vaulting over wicker baskets and throwing their contents over the path behind him, his breath caught in his throat.

Like a stampede, Tarrazi boots thudded all around him suddenly, either taking off in pursuit or hoping to close him down in one of the many winding paths nearby. Shouts continued to rise up alongside the sounds of running: garbled orders and commands, dutiful and resolute, directing the hunters to their prey. There was no fear in their voices. There was no call for retreat. The tribe was mobilised and everyone was armed.

And Markus was running out of options.

He slipped past another circle of buildings, his vision buzzing with activity. The grey threads of his hair seemed to sizzle on his head. He scoured the path ahead, rounding the next building on the left—

And ground to a sudden, fearful halt, as a pair of Tarrazi guards lurched into view with spears raised, more of them mobilising just behind.

Markus pivoted suddenly to dodge an incoming attack – a spear aiming down toward his gut – and kicked out like a horse to bruise the man's shin. The guard hissed under the sudden pressure and stumbled back——

Not wasting any time, Markus accelerated away with a wild freneticism, following the curve of the tree wall as it meandered slowly north. His legs pumped and his calves burned beneath him, kicking out and spitting curses to whichever Tarrazi gods were listening.

Well that's my initial plan down the fuckin' drain, he grumbled, as the two guards started their pursuit and closed off his path to escape. By his estimation, he'd been less than twenty strides from the concealed entrance behind the bushes that he'd used to get in.

And with it, twenty strides from his freedom, too.

They must've assumed that's how I snuck in, and closed it off so I couldn't return that way. Corralling me within the walls so I panic and get stuck somewhere.

Clever bastards.

Opening his stride out, Markus followed the wall as it banked slowly right, matching the natural horseshoe of the tree-line just beyond. The swollen sun remained impervious in the sky above; reaching up to his head, Markus wiped a line of sweat from his scalp and exhaled heavily. A general fatigue had started to take hold of his muscles, and he knew his dexterity was starting to dwindle. But, despite that, he remained completely astute in his mind, lending his power to the electrical pulse in his hand and the adrenaline biting through his veins. It seemed to possess him, driving his legs forward as if they were bolted together with steel rods, uncaring of the strain that was slowly consuming every muscle. He was powered by it – no, *fuelled* by it. A furnace in his soul, exacting its toll for a wish. The wish being to press on, and keep running as fast as he could.

The wish being to survive, and see the ordeal through to its end.

As the thought came, Markus rounded another corner and ducked sharply as a Tarrazi spear arrowed across his path, thudding into a dwelling's wall right next to his shoulder. A number of shouts followed – angry ones, filled with frustration – and the padding of feet picked up again like a stampede to his right.

This is getting close, Markus thought with a hiss, his eyes darting ahead. *This is getting way too close*——

Shadows crossed his gaze: A Tarrazi lunged into his path with a bronze knife tucked neatly in their hand.

Markus ground his heels into the dirt, hurtling towards the fighter at speed——

The Tarrazi thrust the knife——

And with a sudden reflex, Markus grabbed the knife-hand and pushed against it, the blade of the weapon hovering a mere few inches from his chest.

The Tarrazi opposite growled, reaching his other hand across to punch Markus in the side. Markus took it with a grunt, before the enemy recoiled and aimed another one at his head——

Markus froze——

Energy engulfed his arm——

An electrical pulse snapped from his fingers and ignited through the Tarrazi man's wrist——

As their entire forearm tore open like a breach, spewing blood and bone and shrapnel over their clothes.

The Tarrazi screeched and let go immediately, collapsing against the nearest house, holding their arm in horror.

Behind them, more screams and terrified gasps echoed out from the pursuers at the barbarity of what they had just witnessed.

Markus – with flecks of blood against his cheek – looked down at his fizzing hand and the unrefined energy it contained, and found it hard to breathe.

What the fuck is this thing...

A whistling sound caught in his left ear suddenly, as a spear narrowly missed his head and skittered off a dwelling wall next to him.

Snapping from his trance again, Markus kicked out and started running fast with the enemy closing in on all sides. As he did so, the power in his arm tensed and seemed to take on a mind of its own, cavorting over his ribs like prying hands and up around his neck. His pulse seemed to expand, with his heart swelling beyond the usual constraints of a mortal organ. The drumming beats snapped across his skull and nearly threw him to the ground with the force of it. Looking ahead, with blue energy staining his pupils, Markus shivered at the force of the power that seemed to be slowly consuming him.

What is all this? How can this be happening to me? he spluttered, staggering forward. *This power... this* hate *in my system, I can feel it eating away at me. I feel so alive, and so powered, and yet so... close...*

To death...

He rounded another house – struggling to maintain his grip on the world – and found himself out in the open suddenly, with patch-work-stone underfoot and the tree-wall jutting up just ahead––

Where there was an opening, about ten-feet across, leading out into the trees to the north.

His escape route.

At last...

Markus picked up the pace, ignoring the shouts and bellows at his back. Ignoring the death that haunted him with pale faces and black marks. There was just a single path, and his pumping legs beneath him, and the opening into the trees just ahead.

His vision tunnelled; the wall expanded across his periphery. Within moments, he was out of the village altogether, passing the gnarled tree wall and scrabbling across open rock––

When a searing pain lanced across his unprotected shoulder, biting deep and tearing through the sinews––

As a bloody spear-head appeared at his side, driven straight through his shoulder, carrying him forward with its momentum––

And he didn't have time to scream in the end, let alone comprehend the pain that suddenly enveloped his body, as he was thrown to the ground in a tumbling mass and the spear dislodged from the wound, clattering over the rock next to him in several shattered pieces.

Warmth spilled over the stump of his arm. Red stained the beige robe he wore like wine. He reached over to the wound and felt blood spurt between his fingers.

Dark dots scattered over his eyes. The sun above dimmed slightly, and the sky seemed less blue. Blood pooled across the stone at his back, taking his life-force with it.

Looking behind, he spied the Tarrazi approaching with their weapons raised, grinning and hooting like dogs. Among them, he saw the one who had thrown the spear stop a few feet away and cup their hands over their mouth.

"So… close, *Zoltha*," they bellowed, to the jeers and laughter of the other fighters. Markus could hardly make any of them out beyond the shadows of the sun. "And so… *far*."

Markus tried lifting up from the ground – tried to do *anything* – but the adrenaline had already left his system. He could offer nothing in response, as death made its slow approach. All that remained for him was a great numbness, eating away at his tired limbs.

Somewhere in the sky above, Markus swore he heard laughing.

"Now… death," the Tarrazi exclaimed, rubbing the skin around the holes of their ears. "Now… *death*."

As the words fell from their mouth, the other hunters lifted their hands and beat them against their forearms, producing a dull, percussive sound like charging horses.

Above Markus, the sky swam in viscous colours, bleeding into oranges and deep greys over the distant mountains. From somewhere nearby, the *thud* of feet closed in around him, baying for his blood like wolves. He didn't have the strength to fight them; he didn't have the power in his soul to drag his body away, just to live those few moments longer.

So much for my comeuppance, and righting the wrongs inflicted on me, he thought, feeling his life drip away. *So much for revenge, and ridding the world of another rotten soul. Death remains a cruel mistress as ever, and my task shall remain undone.*

Blinking delicately, on the edge of the unconscious, Markus saw a tiny glint of light dart between his fingertips again, before disappearing into a haze of nothing. It was microscopic, and hardly distinguishable in the light. Like the flash of a firefly over a dark swamp. He didn't understand what it meant, or just where the power had come from. He had no life left to give, after all; his body had long abandoned him.

And yet, in an act of sheer defiance, Markus lifted his hand to the sky all the same, as the Tarrazi drummed and the spearman approached and the blood slowly wept from his body.

Death may come for me in this godforsaken place…

A prayer escaped his lips; a fizz of electric left the end of his fingers.

…but I will not die today, you bastards.

The spearman bellowed.

Markus closed his eyes.

And the last thing he knew before he slipped into the void, was his body being thrown into the trees, as the world was consumed by dazzling, horrifying light…

INTERLUDE

I've lost connection with him… I'm not too sure what's happened. I could sense his physical strain through the Rapture: it increased exponentially, and then… nothing. Almost like he's disappeared from the world."

"Is there anything left of him?"

"There is, but its fractious… dormant, almost. I can't really tell. It's like the rumbles before a landslide."

"Then he still lives at least… this is good."

"How can you tell?"

"The low level vibrations you're experiencing are another Ascendant's heartbeat. All those present in the Rapture experience them. And this person — this Markus — can probably feel your heartbeat, too, almost like a drum in their head transmitting across the Rapture."

"So they know I'm here? That I exist?"

"Not quite… he knows something is different, or perhaps wrong, but he doesn't seem to know what it is exactly. There's a block in his comprehension that we cannot get past at the moment. It's as if you're shouting through a pane of glass, and he's not quite close enough to hear you."

"But I've nearly got through to him before, is the frustration." She sighed. "I was so close, I could… I could feel him drawing into the Rapture at last, and then… he just disappeared again, almost shutting me out. He must see this numbness that the Rapture causes as a threat or an irritation, that he just swats away whenever it bothers him."

"I understand it is frustrating, but do remember just how much strain this person must be under. He has woken up with a strange connection to the world *and no clear way of explaining it… I expect the presence of a voice in his head does little to help with his discomfort."*

"But I have to try and get through to him still. I have to try and bridge that gap and draw him into the Rapture, and let him know that he's in serious danger. He probably has no idea what kind of threat is currently seeking him. I mean, as soon as the Mother's soul entered him… I expect the Iron Queen started sharpening her knives, sending her assassins out to find him."

"Perhaps so… but if I may, I do not believe that the Iron Queen even knows that he exists, or what power he now possesses."

She frowned. "How are you sure?"

"Because of your connection to the Ascendant Soul, and the certain benefits that power carries."

"Like the fact I can feel this Markus person through the Rapture, and can attempt communication with him whenever I want."

"Precisely so… and you can be safe in the knowledge that, possessing the All-Mother's soul, you are the only person capable of such a feat."

"So the Iron Queen can't feel their presence at all, even though she possesses a soul herself?"

"In a way, yes. Under usual circumstances, the All-Mother uses the other Mothers as conduits to communicate with the mortal world: She can see all of Them and speak to Them, but They cannot see each other. And, in that same way, you can see this Markus person, but they cannot see anyone else… including the Iron Queen."

"Because even though she's powerful, in the Rapture she's still just a conduit to me…"

"So the only way that the Iron Queen can learn of Mother Katastro's successor… is by finding him herself. And the sheer unlikelihood of this Markus person walking up to the walls of Val Azbann and demanding an audience with her Highness … is beyond comprehension."

"There's no chance he would even think of doing something that stupid."

"Not if he was expecting to survive it, that is for certain."

She paused. "So, what do we do now? What's the next step?"

"There is little we can do now, until Katastro's heir has come to terms with the power he possesses, and starts to push the boundaries of the Rapture on

his own accord," they replied. "Although, with that being said, we must also be cautious of just how much *power this newcomer has, and how he intends to use it..."*

She looked up, her eyes widening. "So... you can feel it too? That... fracturing, in the void."

"I can, yes."

"What is it?"

"It's an energy, Successor. The power emanating through the Rapture from Katastro's heir is... like nothing I've ever witnessed before. It defies the normal — mortal — limits of energy within a person's soul. And that either means that this newcomer is an incredibly powerful being with untapped potential the likes of which we've never seen... or is a gunpowder keg waiting to explode the moment it lights." They pursed their lips. "Either way, we must keep a close eye on him, and as you have rightly said we must continue with our attempts to establish contact with him. It may be the difference between life and death... and not just for Markus.*"*

"I understand..." she said softly. She closed her eyes and sensed the numbness close in. "I guess we just have to pray he doesn't explode before we get to him..."

†

Chapter 12

The Omen

Xafiri lunged forwards, entering up into the Proven man's circle and ramming his fist into their chest.

The brute took it with a hiss of disgust; Xafiri stepped back again and raised his pole, anticipating a harsh counter.

His anticipation proved correct: with the flames roaring at the end of their weapon, the Proven man swung down toward Xafiri's head in a white-knuckle rage. Xafiri dodged backwards and batted the weapon aside, directing the fire away from his skull. His head still throbbed from the previous encounter, where the woman had scarred his head and nearly ripped his cheek open, and he was hardly in the mood for repeating mistakes.

But, as the Proven man adjusted his grip and swung the fire-pole back across, Xafiri wondered just how easy that would be.

I just need to outlast him, he thought, deflecting the next two blows and parrying the third. *The heat from the flames will tire him out eventually, and I'm a far more agile fighter. It's only a matter of time.*

Ras'gandû protect me...

Invoking the God of the Skirmish, Xafiri went on the offensive suddenly, to the muted surprise of the crowds around them and the very-audible surprise of his opponent opposite.

Wielding the bronze pole with lethal intent, Xafiri struck out several times using both ends of his weapon, striking across his body like a pendulum. The Proven man flailed about in response, negotiating with his weapon as he tried to counter the onslaught of attacks. Xafiri managed to land two of them – both across the man's exposed torso – but he also received a meaty punch in the stomach for his efforts, angering the bruises there.

Once his attacks subsided, Xafiri stepped backwards and gritted his teeth, crunching the bones in his neck. Looking up, the clouds seemed to swirl and gyrate in the skies above, matching the natural ebb and flow of the adrenaline in his veins. It tempered him: challenging him to do better, beckoning him on with all of its natural might. He breathed it in and swallowed it, abandoning his restraint in degrees.

With wind pulling against his back, Xafiri closed his mind, and channelled his energy towards one final attack .

He struck out like a battering ram first, forcing the Proven man to step back and stumble over his own feet.

His second attack rounded in from the left, forcing a defensive block from the brute, showering him in ash and sparks.

The third attack then came through on the right, which the man couldn't adjust to fast enough——

And Xafiri's bronze pole smacked into his flank, with the power of a godly hammer.

The Proven man howled and crumpled like paper, his entire leg giving way in a quivering, mangled mess. He sprawled out across the stone in a heap, the bronze pole rattling over the dry earth as the flames became choked with dust, extinguishing any chance the brute had of pressing on with the fight.

An audible gasp rippled through the crowds. The Verlunz lifted away from his seat, squinting at the scene before him. A shout bellowed out from Xafiri's left: the garbled voice of Temusceh, witnessing his treachery unravel before his very eyes.

Meanwhile, Xafiri stood over the Proven man's lame body, watching them writhe and retch as he adjusted the bronze pole in his grasp. The man was the colour of fatty blood, his hands twitching like a corpse, not a morsel of pride or strength left in his body as he lay there and groaned and cried. It had been so simple in the end; Xafiri's patience had paid off at last.

The skies churned violently overhead.

This is the day, at last, that the gods favour me, Xafiri thought, steadying his heart. *This is the day I become Proven, and finish what I started.*

Looking up with a whimper, the cheating brute begged for his mercy.

Redemption has come for me.

Lifting the pole above his head, Xafiri grit his teeth and aimed down at the man's skull——

When a flash of light eclipsed his vision to the left, and the world seemed to explode.

From the skies in the south, where clouds had gathered to do battle, a swirling vortex emerged from the darkness and speared down into the trees, the terrifying glow of lightning rippling through its mass like a vein of molten ore. The blue haze of mid-afternoon disappeared in its wake, consumed by a black-grey nightmare that swallowed the landscape whole.

Xafiri blinked once, and that was all he could manage. The lightning took less than a heartbeat to strike, connecting with the ground somewhere in the south, birthing a carnage the likes of which Xafiri had never seen.

What the——

The lightning detonated in the valley with a blast of raw power, seizing across the sky in all directions. The air rippled; the vortex lurched. The impact point exploded in a hail of rock and trees. A mushroom cloud of smoke rose several dozen feet into the air, consuming everything in its maw.

He was the only one who saw it. The only one who witnessed its terrifying destruction.

No noise emanated from the blast. There was only the wind and muttering voices. The spectators goggled at him dumbly, wondering what he was looking at—

BANG.

The detonation tore at his ears. A blast of air roared up the hillside and broke across the arena. The very earth seemed to tremble at his feet—

Hunkering down, Xafiri watched as the spectators before him were swept off their feet and clattered on top of each other in great piles—

The air hit him a fraction later: his entire body shuddered in spasms, railing against the strike—

Screams went up. Terror swept the arena around him. An intense ringing claimed his ears, drowning out all other thought.

Children started crying; mothers clung to them desperately. Hunters cried out and trembled on hands and knees, invoking the gods above. On his right, the royal canopy toppled sidelong and collapsed with the snap of wooden struts; the guards struggled to their feet and rushed over to assist the Verlunz, caught beneath the cloth drapery with his hands waving frantically.

Xafiri let the air wash over him and blinked the dust out of his eyes. His ears were ringing, drowning out all other noise. Rubbing his face, he rose to his full height again on shaky legs, looking out on the massive cloud of smoke in the distance that continued to explode with light.

The spectators, once they had recovered from their falls, looked out on the devastation and gasped. No-one dared speak. No-one dared look to the skies for answers. There could be no belief in what they'd just witnessed.

What's... happened? Xafiri thought, sucking air through his teeth. Above, the black clouds continued to crackle, their booming voices like thunder.

What have the gods done?

"Listen, my people!" the Verlunz bellowed, as they were lifted to their feet by the guards and gasped at the mushroom cloud off to the south. The chief seemed unable to collect their thoughts for several moments, gazing out on the devastation in horror. "The... the *Fendûrii* is suspended... until further notice. Gather your loved ones, please... go home, stay... you shall be summoned soon, once the... are secure." They muttered breathlessly, before turning to face their people. "Dal-Guzud has come for us this day... let us pray that we emerge with our *lives*..."

The Verlunz turned from the arena and left without a word more. The villagers looked on in shock, trembling and weeping softly.

Xafiri gulped, wiping dust from his eyes, taking the scene in.

Dal-Guzud... the God of Omens, came the whispers in his mind.

The end times really have come.

All around him, the citizens of the village gathered in each other's arms and ambled slowly away from the square, returning to their homes to take shelter until the threat had been ascertained. Xafiri watched them go in silence, feeling a great weight in his chest. He knew his mother would be afraid, too, wondering where he was or if he was even alive.

And she isn't the only one who's scared, he admitted, trying to breathe through the tremors in his heart. As the thought came, lightning fizzed in the sky high above between the dark smudges of clouds.

What have we done?

Returning to his house as instructed, Xafiri had not been there long before a guard arrived at their door and explained that the tribe was amassing in the square, where the Verlunz hoped to settle their concerns and forge a path ahead. The entire village had been asked to attend, and the guard passed over his assurances that things were safe: the outer reaches of their land had been secured, and the warriors had been mobilised to the south in preparation for any potential attack. Not that they truly believed there would be one: the impact of the lightning had been some distance away, and an entire forest lay between that place and their village. It would take a good day or two of hiking for anyone to reach their high-altitude home, and even then an attack would've taken hours to plan.

Or so they hoped.

When he had first arrived home – still shaking from the blast with ringing in his ears – Xafiri's mother had been all over him like a rash, asking questions and inspecting wounds as she tried to apply her various balms. Massaging a lotion over the damaged half of his skull, Xafiri had tried his best to explain to his mother what had happened in a way that she could understand – and in a way that made sense to him, at that. What he had witnessed had never happened in his or his mother's lifetime, he knew. It had probably never happened in the history of the Valatuk Hills. Lightning storms were fairly common at that time of year, and thunder often came down over the distant mountains during the rainy season. But to experience a single blast, on a clear day, with enough force to tear the earth apart where it impacted… was beyond anything Xafiri could comprehend, and had left his mother speechless.

"So, what… happen now?" his mother asked sometime later as they followed the path up to the village square, alongside several other villagers with equally-perplexed stares.

"I don't know, ma… but someone will, I'm sure," Xafiri replied, attempting reassurance. He had bathed in the short time he had spent at home, watching the paint of his death-mask wash away as well as the grey-white dust kicked up from the blast. Neither offered him much comfort or solace in the end – and as he watched the colours merge and trickle off down the hillside from their rain-holder, he wondered if the marks of both events would ever really wash off his skin, or if they'd remain stained to his body and haunt his mind forever, testament to the omen he'd seen.

"The Verlunz will help, though… they will know," he continued quietly. "They will help us. Tell us what to do."

"They have answers?" her mother asked, still fussing with tiny wounds on his arms.

"As far as I'm aware, yes."

"But what if… what if they not know?"

Xafiri rolled his tongue across the roof of his mouth and sighed.

Yea… that's what I'm worried about too.

They reached the plateau of the square and saw it flooded with Tarrazi villagers, jostling between each other to get a look at the stone podium to the north. There were hundreds of people there – more than Xafiri had ever seen at one time – all wearing dark or muted robes to mark the occasion, with a sombre mood that seemed to eclipse their collective minds. Smoke continued to rise in several wide columns to the south, and despite the disappearance of the freak storm clouds, tiny shards of lightning still danced over the skies above.

Xafiri looked over it all and winced.

What have we done to deserve this?

"I see the rising," his mother said, looking south and gesturing to the smoke. "That where it happen?"

"Yes, there," Xafiri replied. "During my fight. I saw it, no-one else… then wave came, knocked everyone over."

"Wave?"

"Air and sound." He imitated waves and tapped his ears – which, on closer inspection, still produced a numb ringing sound even then. "Came from explosion."

"Very scary."

"It was, yes."

"Came from sky?"

"What did?"

She lifted her hand and pushed it down to her side. "The anger… it came from the sky?"

"Anger is *'lightning'*, ma. *Zazkan*. And yes, it did. From the sky."

"Ah, *zazkan*… yes. Okay. Very powerful." She frowned suddenly. "But sky is clear now? Why light…ning?"

"I am not sure," he admitted, looking back over the crowds to the podium where guards had started to appear. "I don't think any of us are."

"Is it because Dal-Guzud… angry?"

Xafiri shot her a look, sensing his heart tense in his chest.

I hope not, ma… or a little lightning will be the very least of our problems.

To the north, over the heads of the crowd, the Verlunz appeared suddenly and shifted onto the podium with the assistance of their guards. They had changed out of their ceremonial robes and adorned muted pastel sashes instead, the colours of old bark and wet sand. They moved with a great exertion, too, Xafiri noticed: there was a visible limp on one side, likely caused by the fall they had suffered when the blast swept through.

The Tarrazi villagers who had gathered drew silent and still, as the Verlunz lifted their wrinkled hand to address them.

"Az-kabza, *dügër'ma*… my people," the Verlunz began in native tongue, placing their outstretched hand against their chest. "I have gathered you here, because a great fear has… us, and I know that many of you are scared by the events that have occurred. During the *Fendûrii*, a great strike of *zazkan* fell from the sky in the south, and… the land where it hit. The power was strong, and I fear what this means — as I'm sure you all do as well. We know that *zazkan* does not strike without the Gods' warning first… and as there came no warning when it hit, we can assume this was either a sleight by the gods… or the wrath of *another*."

A ripple of discontent wormed its way through the crowds; next to Xafiri, his mother put a hand to her mouth.

"We have been good to our gods, and they in turn have been…" — Xafiri assumed the word '*merciful*' — "… to us. We understand each other… good to us all. But… this is where we go wrong. Where we are less, to them. We settle in our ways too much: we show our praise to them, and perform our *omura*, and they in turn offer us solace. But that is not… to them: it is *laziness*. We lose sight of our belief; our *omura* becomes empty. And now, they may not have forsaken us… but they believe we have forsaken *them*." The Verlunz paused, looking out across the crowd. "I do not believe it is our…

that have caused this to happen. I do not believe our *mercies* have caused their wrath…"

Scouring over the many faces before him, Xafiri watched as the Verlunz landed squarely on him and a twitch caught in their eye. They were joined by several other people around him, who looked at Xafiri and sneered.

They think I'm the cause of this, by entering the Fendûrii, he assessed, keeping his face level. *They all think it. And even if they say otherwise, I know the Verlunz feels I've invoked the wrath of the gods today. Me: the* mantugo *of the village.*

Always with a chip on his shoulder…

"So, it is my belief, with the Gods, that we must right this wrong and appease Dal-Guzud," the Verlunz bellowed. The use of the God of Omen's name sent a shudder through the crowd, and the winds swept up with an icy coldness. "Because if this is an *ubentü,* and we as a tribe have done wrong under their watch… then the… will be very bad indeed."

The Verlunz opened their hand out to one side, and a number of hunters took a stand alongside them suddenly, filtering up onto the podium with purposeful strides. There were streaks of red war paint lashed over their cheeks and brows, and their bronze spears glinted in the dozing sun. They had already been outfitted in hunting gear, which offered something of a hint as to what the Verlunz would say next.

"We should not gamble with our Gods, my people, as they do not gamble with us in return," the Verlunz thundered. "There is too much at risk here to let things go… and be wasted. So, the…" – *dozen?* – "…hunters here next to me shall depart shortly through the south gates, and will… through the forests to see what they can find. A village lies in the… there, and they may have been attacked." They paused, breathing deeply. "For we do not know if this *zazkan* was caused by the gods' hands, or by the hands of a dangerous mortal soul. We cannot let this… and pass us idly by. Because if this was an attack, and there is an enemy approaching from the south… we should not rely on Ras'gandû to protect us when they arrive. The Gods do not appreciate idle fools… and neither should we."

The Verlunz lifted a hand and beat it against their forearm twice, signalling that the announcement was over and the villagers could return to their homes.

As the crowds turned away and muttered amongst themselves, Xafiri watched the Verlunz shake their head and turn away from the crowds dismissively.

As if they don't really believe we will survive this ordeal, against this potential threat approaching from the south, Xafiri deduced, hissing at the pains scattering over his face. *The Verlunz has already consigned our fate in their mind.*

And perhaps they aren't wrong for doing so.

"They go off to fight," his mother echoed softly, nodding her head. "Hope they find nothing… then we safe."

"Yea… hopefully."

But Xafiri was distracted, and the response was automatic. What he was actually focusing on – in the active, deciphering part of his mind – were the hunters and huntresses stepping down from the podium, adjusting their straps and receiving a number of blessings from the villagers passing by. Xafiri saw that a number of the hunters were only a year or two older than him, and had probably undergone their rite-of-passage in the last few seasons.

It could've been me, he thought, as a coil of jealousy knotted about his heart like a serpent. *I could be the one doing my part, and displaying my honour to the Gods and the tribe, going out and facing this potential foe. I could be rising to the challenge for my people. It could be me…*

He looked between them with flitting eyes, wiping the sweat from his brow – when he noted something in particular that caught his attention quite acutely.

They're only wearing light armour. They don't have any heavy pieces, or hunter's marks. To the common eye, they look like any other Tarrazi in uniform…

Xafiri felt a gust of wind lash across his face; he produced a wicked smiled.

I have an idea…

"We best go… I have lots to do," his mother said, pulling him by the arm.

"Yea… we go now, ma," Xafiri muttered, turning to her. "Uh, once… once we're home, I may go out for a while."

"Oh." She frowned. "To do?"

"Some work. Do not worry… I won't be gone long."

"Okay, okay, just… safe. Please."

"I will. Do not worry."

Xafiri followed her toward the path leading to their house, and managed to steal one final glance at the hunters before he left. He looked over their armour and their weapons – at their posture and their smiles and their assuredness – and nodded his head slightly.

I have an old suit of armour from my father in a case back home, and these hunters don't seem to care who they're with and what their business is, so long as they can follow orders. They just want to see the job done.

Xafiri allowed himself a smirk, looking up to the Gods.

So I'm sure one tag-along wouldn't hurt…

†

Chapter 13

The Skin of One's Teeth

*M**erry are we who come; condemned are we to die…*
Sing the song of blood and sacrament; to blood and steel we fly…
Prisoners and slaves, ye rotten souls, broken bones do come…
These are the songs of the fighting pits…
"To death, a deed is done…"

Markus' eyes snapped open and he took in the world around him, staring up at the hazy sky where the orange of dusk began to set in. Ash had fused his eyelids together, so every blink came with a sharp pain as something dug into his sockets. A stinging sensation twinged across his brow, where a nasty cut continued to weep quietly. Wood shrapnel coated his face and embedded in his sweaty skin, where dried blood lined his cheeks like trenches formed in the pits of war.

Looking up, the sky was impossibly bright overhead, despite the encroachment of dusk. The quiet rasps of wind licked at Markus' ears, tentative like a cat. He felt the sleeping void draw in close once more, putting an arm across his shoulder like an old friend as the drowsiness set in…

Or rather, that would have been the case, had something not been trying to gnaw his finger off at the same time.

Despite how unresponsive the rest of his body proved to be, led there in the copse of trees staring dumbly at the sky, Markus felt every sharp pain lancing up his arm with an acuteness that made his head throb. Like two prying knives, something dug into the end of his index finger with slow, deliberate bites, testing how soft his charred skin was – and probably how tasty the flesh was underneath. He would have moved his leg and kicked whatever it was away, or swatted it aside with a turn of his wrist, but all sensation in his body seemed to betray him in that moment, as it recovered from the blast that had him thrown him into the trees in the first place.

And, if he was honest, part of him couldn't believe he wasn't already dead——

Another bite against his finger, and Markus flared his nostrils, flashing his porcelain teeth with disgust. His neck muscles tensed, bunching up on his nape like the heckles of a dog, but it came to no avail. Impossibly heavy, his head lay planted in the ground and refused to budge——

When a third bite burst the skin on his fingertip and a shiver snapped up his spine, reconnecting certain components in his body that had been otherwise-unresponsive.

A torrent of pain crawled over his skin suddenly, forcing Markus to clench his jaw as aches and cuts and deep bruises alighted in expansively-painful ways. The skin over his back lay in pieces; the sword-scar under his sternum throbbed like a clenched fist. He still couldn't move, or really connect his feet with his legs, but the acknowledgement of pain came with the good graces that he wasn't paralysed at least.

Not to say this is any better, though——
Ow! You bitch!

Markus craned his neck up like a door-hinge and looked down to his arm with a grunt, which lay upturned in a patch of dried leaves and was coated in a layer of mud. He could feel very little of his arm, or the hand it was connected to – but at the end of his fingers, squat down in the earth, he spied the bulky, twitching shape of a rat licking its feet. It was a big creature – a good foot long, Markus deduced – with deep black eyes and fluttering whiskers that one could almost describe as cute. It studied his hand absently, pressing its nose against his fingertip where a tiny column of blood trickled from a wound.

A bite mark wound, Markus snarled, ignoring the pain in his head.

You'll pay for that, you little shit.

Intent on the rat's untimely demise, Markus focused in on the blue haze coiling about his hand and felt a connection ripple through his skull. Even then, with the rest of his body in a numb stupor, he could still feel the electrical energy lying dormant, ready to strike at a moment's notice.

Perfect.

With the pain in his finger as a guide – and tiny sparks darting across his skin – Markus stuck his fingertip in the rat's face and waited for a response.

At first, the small rodent pulled back and rubbed its nose with a foot, studying the bloody fingertip with dumb, senseless eyes. After a moment of being still, however, it leaned forward slowly to investigate—

When a column of electric shot through its body and killed it outright, charring its corpse and bursting its eyeballs like a pair of overripe cherries. The squeak it made as it was burnt alive put a tiny smile on Markus' face.

That's what you get, you bastard.

With sensation recovering across his body, Markus gripped the earth in his charred fingers and hauled himself onto his side, looking down on his stained robe covered in burn marks and dirt. He grimaced at the damages to his clothes, and the pain rifling through his system.

But as he looked ahead through the trees, as if peering through the eye of the storm, Markus saw there an unrequited destruction that took the breath from his lungs.

The tree wall that had marked the northern entrance to the village had been obliterated, with a crater the size of a small lake dominating the land where it had been. Columns of ashen smoke consumed the air above, coating the orange sky. A number of the clay dwellings to either side had caved in, or had been wiped clear of their foundations altogether.

And bodies, numbering at least a dozen, lay sprawled around the crater in pieces, their mouths stood ajar like wooden chests staring at him in disbelief.

Markus looked out on the destruction with despair, and felt a tiny piece of his heart shatter at the sight of it. Propped up on his arm, he trembled under the weight of his body — and the bodies of the many dead slain by his hand, staring back at him from the other side.

All of this… done by my hand?

He looked down to the blackened stubs of his fingers and flexed them slowly, watching the blue energy flash across them and circle over his palm like a web. It was unrelenting and fleeting, shivering across his skin. It was directionless and volatile, hungry for more violence.

As the thought crossed his mind, a stabbing pain ignited in his opposite shoulder, and when Markus looked there he saw the wound where the spear had impaled him was entirely sealed over, covered in blue-pink knots of skin. It pulsed angrily, similar to the scar that lined his abdomen. Considering no more than an hour had passed since the injury had happened, the speed of recovery should have been impossible.

So much of this should be impossible, he thought solemnly, lifting to a stand and tensing the muscles in his legs. *My recovery. My powers. My sheer being alive, after everything I've been through.*

Markus gritted his teeth; the drumbeats rose in his head again, vibrating around his skull.

I need to get out of here, I… I need to get away from this.

Turning his back on the village, and the haunting faces of those he had killed, Markus strode off into the trees with the power lurching through his system, wondering what the gods made of him.

Wondering what happens now…

*

"*Markuss.*"

Markus lifted his hand and swat a bug against his ear, feeling its tiny body crush beneath his palm with a satisfying dissolution of life. Looking at his fingers afterwards, he saw the spindly shape of a mosquito-creature squat against his thumb, with tiny purple tendrils extending out from its carapace. Its long limbs twitched in the throes of death and its wings seem to tremble in the breeze – as another mosquito buzzed across his vision and inspected his hand hungrily.

Markus bared his teeth and grumbled.

Didn't think I'd be contending with this shit out here.

In the sparse landscape around him – dotted with the same gnarled trees and finger-like bushes as before – a dramatic shift had occurred in the environment, likely in response to the lightning blast that had torn a hole in the village further south. The air around Markus felt lighter than it had before; despite the heat, his lungs could fill without any strain and exhale with energy to spare. Gentle winds swept down from the distant mountains and aggravated the sunburn under his robes. The weird bushes that struck up from the rocks had lifted their slumbering heads, and now pointed skyward like strange arboreal funnels. Even the trees – devoid of any signs of life – produced tiny pockets of leaves on their ends, with a beautiful green colour that wouldn't have looked out of place on the Provenci plains.

And then there are the flies, of course, Markus thought, swatting another tiny bug away from his face. *Can't forget the flies.*

In the dry heat of the desert hills, he found that flying insects were nearly non-existent, and that the invertebrate world was dominated by roving beetles and the menacing pincers of scorpions. But, beyond that – and the numerous species of lizard that seemed to cling to every rock he found – the hills were largely devoid of small creatures and bugs.

Until the lightning had ruptured the sky and cleared the air of its ungodly weight, that was, and then from every possible crevasse in the landscape ahead, flying insects had emerged in their droves to scour the world. There were millions them, coating the air like smoke trails as they searched for their next meal: be it dead flesh or leaf-litter, or the leaves of the local flora.

Or blood, as Markus had come to understand, watching another mosquito land on his shoulder, which he promptly executed before it could lance his skin with its nasty needle mouth. All around him, tiny swarms of them dived through the air, with their strange purple tendrils twitching like fine hairs. And they weren't alone, either: there were big, boggle-eyed insects flying about with two sets of wings; laborious, loud bugs with heavy bodies and silver claws; tiny fizzing creatures with pronged tails—

"Markusssssss..."

The voice came and went like the flame of a candle, snuffed from existence the moment it had been lit. Sliding through one ear and out the other; trembling for a moment in his mind, so the vibrations haunted his thoughts long after they'd gone.

Ever since he'd dragged himself up from the dirt outside the ruined village, the numbness from before had started to pulse through his mind again, accompanied by the tiny, near-indescribable echo of a voice. The sensation had nearly knocked him off-balance at first: fearing a seizure of some sort, Markus had grabbed for the nearest tree and steadied his breathing, waiting for the tide to pass. But, after a good while trekking through the arid undergrowth of the Tarrazi hills with the numbness as his only company, the fear of a seizure had become little more than a casual irritation. So much so, that the numbness in his head and the flies buzzing around him like he was a crock of shit were now inseparable from one other: both were annoyances that he wanted nothing more than to swat away and be rid of at once. Anything to let him think straight for just a moment—

"Markus."

The fucking voice is getting clearer, he noted, plugging a finger in his ear and rattling it about to try and dispel some of the numbness. It worked temporarily, and came as a pleasant release — or that was, until the droning of the bugs filled the gap, and dispelled all notions of silence.

This robe seems to be saving me from the worst of the bugs' attacks, he admitted, pulling it tighter at his collar. *I just hope it's enough to——*

"*Markussss.*"

His head snapped to the left, looking out past the three trees that dotted the dry earth there.

That… was nearby…

But nothing moved between the trees. Nothing moved in his periphery, either. A stillness – beyond the clouds of flies buzzing around his head – descended around him.

That was odd, he thought, swatting another bug next to his ear. *Could've sworn that was right next to——*

"*Markusss.*"

He twisted to his right, the electrical energy pulsing up and down his arm in shockwaves.

Sweat pulled across his skin. He stared out into the trees——

But there was nothing there. Nothing but gnarled boughs and shadows. Nothing but rocks and dirt and dust and flies and plants.

Nothing but silence, again.

Markus curled his nose up and spat at his feet, his hand lingering tentatively at his sword. It was madness he knew; caused by a knock to the head, he expected.

I mean, come on, what the fuck does it even want with me——

"*Markus.*"

His ears went numb; all senses ceased to exist.

He held his breath.

"*Behind you…*"

A scraping sound at his back; Markus gasped and ducked, reality rattling back through his body.

A spear whistled through the air above him and skittered across the dirt several feet ahead, twisting like a snake off into the trees and disappearing just beyond.

Markus pressed up on his toes and pivoted, reaching for the weapon at his side——

Slinging it up in front of his face, just before a bronze knife could carve it open.

Markus gritted his teeth and pushed against the knife, shoving his opponent back a few steps where he could get a better look at them. The flies above seemed to flee the scene, as the branches rustled nearby.

Markus looked across to his opponent, and scoffed in disbelief.

You've got to be shitting me...

The massive Tarrazi fighter who had first discovered him in the village stood swaying opposite him, an unrelenting hate painted clear across their eyes for all to see. It was clear that they had suffered badly from Markus' lightning strike: their body lay coated in scorch marks and bruises, and one of their knees twisted inwards at an awkward angle that must have been excruciating to walk on. But even that wasn't the worst of the damage they had sustained: clutching at their side, the Tarrazi fighter had been impaled by a huge shard of wood from the village wall, which had eviscerated the organs within and still lay embedded in their stomach.

Markus felt sick just looking at him. He could see the life being drained from the man's body with each second that passed, as blood leaked down their leg and splattered over the dry ground below. The paleness of their skin – accompanied by the porcelain tones of a native Tarrazi – made him almost translucent in the dusky light.

This bastard should be dead... more than dead, Markus grumbled, tightening the knife in his hand. *He should've died in the blast. Should've died from his wounds.*

Then again, so should've I.

The Tarrazi gritted his bloody teeth and took a painful step forward.

I could just run, he considered. *I could outrun him and let the wounds do the work. He won't survive much longer: definitely not long enough to return to his village. He's come out here with one intention, and one goal: to kill me for what I've done to him.*

To have his revenge.

The fighter took another step forward; Markus shook his head.

I had a friend once like you, y'know? So bitter, and embattled by her lust for revenge. So lost to the world and her own senses. It consumed her, in the end. Ate away at her until she had nothing left. And whereas you will succumb to your wounds and never see your vengeance come to fruition... she did not.

Facing little other choice, Markus approached the huge Tarrazi warrior, his sword coiling in his hand.

And perhaps she still lives, y'know: somewhere to the north, in the depths of that tyrant's palace, awaiting her chance at vengeance. Perhaps her story continues. Perhaps she's alluded death once again... and ruined everything in her path to get there.

But she will succumb to it in the end. Everyone will in their own way. Death waits for no-one...

The Tarrazi's knife flashed across his vision; Markus grabbed their hand and twisted their wrist away, before letting go and stepping in and driving his sword up into the man's chest.

A shudder went through them; the bronze knife slipped from their grasp.

Markus leaned in to their ear.

"*...and neither do I.*"

He stepped back and withdrew the knife, letting the Tarrazi fall to the ground and lie still in a crumpled heap, finally succumbing to their wounds.

Wiping his weapon clean – with swarms of flies circling above his head and the numb voice still echoing between his ears – Markus thought of vengeance and sighed.

To death, a deed is done.

†

Chapter 14

Deception

Xafiri adjusted his ill-fitting armour and muttered a quiet apology to Kand'u, God of the Warrior, as he approached the southern gates with hasty strides and his head held low. He knew Kand'u would be frowning at him from His gilded home high above, wondering what the little warrior-pretender was thinking going out into the trees in search of an omen. Xafiri's armour hardly stayed on his torso; his boots clunked and clattered, with the leather straps already as tight as they could go; the spear trussed against his back was three-sizes too large, designed for a much larger man and a much more able hunter. He looked out of place, in many ways — he looked like a fool, in every respect of the word. Somewhere above, Kand'u was probably wondering whether it was more appropriate to scold Xafiri, or mock him for how stupid he looked.

And, as one of the leg-plates started sliding down Xafiri's thigh and nearly dragged his cloth breeches down with them, the warrior-pretender could hazard a guess at which one Kand'u would pick.

I'm taking a massive risk doing this… and not a very logical one at that, Xafiri acknowledged with a grimace, tightening his chest-plate against the scars he had sustained in the fire trial. *Kand'u blessed my father in this armour long ago, during his battles with the Darbesh slavers in the south. The entire hunting party received His blessing, and they carried it through to victories for many battles to follow. My father hung his armour up several years ago now, following his long service to the tribe… and the suit has remained there ever since.* Xafiri sighed.

Even though he did not.

He drew a hand over the chitin plates protecting his forearms, and shook his head. *And who knows? Perhaps the armour still yields Kand'u's blessing after so many years. Perhaps Kand'u will come to my aid, when facing whatever evil cast that lightning earlier today. Because I know I will need every ounce of luck if I'm to do this and come out of it alive…*

Looking skyward, Xafiri kissed two fingers and placed them on his chest.

Deserving or not… I need every chance I can get.

As the thought came, a fly buzzed past his face and drifted very close to his left eye: lifting a hand to swat it against his cheek, Xafiri stopped himself and shook his head, deterring the insect from coming any closer and spoiling the marks on his face.

Spoiling the sins I've committed, he remarked, letting loose a long and painful breath.

Before he had left home, Xafiri had filled the water basin in his room and stared down at his reflection on the surface, considering his fate and the path that lay ahead. He knew what had to be done to follow the hunters out into the trees, and the shame he had to bring on himself to do so.

For a long while he had looked at the clay powder, and the vial of black liquid on the counter at his side. He considered his fate as he did so, and the consequences of his actions. He knew there would be no going back once he did the condemnable thing; but in the same breath, he also felt he had little other option.

So, squaring his jaw with a muttered prayer, he dipped his feather quill into the black liquid in the vial, and placed its end beneath his eye like a piercing knife through the throat.

He had been tentative about it — shutting all the drapes in his room in the hope that the gods weren't watching — and had guided the feather under his eye with deft strokes. Following the curves of his skin; balancing the weight against his thumb. It had taken a good hour, and the final product had been amateur at best in the end, but he knew it would serve its purpose well enough as he stared down into the basin once more.

To spy his *zaz-gûla* of a tiny bronze knife, with a single tiny teardrop dripping down from its end…

What had made Xafiri choose a knife as his Proven mark was beyond him even then. Perhaps it was subconsciously sentimental, or was a sign of his endurance against the odds. But in many ways it didn't matter. He made no plans of being idle long enough for people to question it: its entire purpose was to get him through the gates in one piece, and to imitate the warriors long enough to investigate what had happened in the south. After that – should he survive to return to the village – Xafiri intended to wipe it off and make his apologies to Kand'u then, finding it far easier to ask for forgiveness than try and fail for permission.

Because this is in no way permissible, by any stretch of the imagination, Xafiri admitted, clamping his jaw. *Not by Kand'u's judgement, and certainly not by the tribe's. To mark myself as Proven without completing my* Fendûrii… *is enough to have me lanced to death on a burning pyre. That's not an eventuality I want to entertain.*

I have to keep my wits about me.

Ahead, the southern gate honed into view, looming large on its wooden struts with bronze panels to either side. It stood slightly ajar, with a congregation of guards and Tarrazi warriors lined up outside. They were deep in conversation, assessing gear and trading stories, with some of the younger hunters stood at the back chattering excitedly amongst themselves.

This is good so far… I'm glad I'm not late for their departure.

Approaching at speed, Xafiri saw the young warriors look off down the street toward him. They all clasped their forearms one after another, a gesture which Xafiri returned and promptly bowed his head.

Well, the ruse seems to be holding at the moment. They clearly don't know how many warriors have been assigned to the expedition, and just assume any person in armour is with them. That makes my life a lot easier.

Approaching at speed, Xafiri slowed his pace and caught his breath, watching the first few warriors nod to the guards and filter through the gates beyond. He wanted to avoid having any inter-actions with them for as long as he could, as he knew the powder marks that covered his burns would give him away eventually.

Best stay back and stay quiet, he considered.

And not tempt fate with stupid mistakes.

Xafiri watched the warriors slowly disperse out of the gate, slipping between the wooden pillars and out into the trees beyond. The younger warriors – who had stood expectantly awaiting his arrival – turned their attention back to the task at hand and followed their compatriots through the gap.

Xafiri smirked and picked up the pace again.

Now's my time.

Catching up with them as the last two warriors slipped away, Xafiri felt his heart in his throat and crossed the empty space toward the guards. He whispered a quiet prayer as he did so, passing between the first two guards without question, moving on to the dormant spears of the next two guards——

Before an outstretched hand fell to his chest and stopped him in his tracks.

The floor seemed to open up beneath him, ready to swallow him whole.

Looking up into the guard's face, Xafiri took in their resolved expression and tried to swallow the wedge in his throat. Nothing on their face offered him any idea of why he'd been stopped. For all he knew, the gig was up, and he was about to have his knees broken by a guard's stiff boot.

Do something, his mind screamed, sweat streaming down his back. *Do something. Do something.*

Anything.

Something.

Something—

"Az-kabza," Xafiri said, with a false confidence that betrayed his very-real fear.

Looking down on him, the old guard studied him for a moment. His face remained stony and cold.

Xafiri bristled.

Oh gods…

A heartbeat passed.

Oh gods please no—

The guard nodded their head, offering a quiet smile to him.

"Az-kabza, *skal,*" they replied, letting their hand fall, opening the route to the gate.

Xafiri gasped and let out a trembling breath.

Shit, that worked?

Realising his luck, Xafiri wasted no time, smiling meekly and striding forward, slipping between the wooden struts of the gate and out into the trees beyond.

As soon as he crossed the threshold of the village perimeter, he stilled the shaking in his hands, looking down the slope to spy the last of the warriors disappearing through the trees just beyond.

By the gods, I made it…

Thanking Kand'u's mercy in all its forms, Xafiri adjusted the collar of his chest-plate and paced slowly down the slope into the trees, disappearing from sight moments later into the deep labyrinth of the forest.

He kept his distance as the warriors moved through the trees, remaining within sight of the older hunters so they didn't perceive him as a threat while also avoiding the younger ones and any unnecessary engagement. It was not a case that Xafiri didn't want to join with them, he knew. In an ideal world, spending time with fellow warriors would have been any Tarrazi boy's dream. Sharing

Fendûrii stories; complaining about their superiors; partaking in unique little games of strength and dexterity. Things that he knew he *should* have been doing at his age, forging the bonds to last a lifetime.

But that isn't how the world works, apparently — or not in my case at least.

He knew his education at the hands of the *Zoltha* meant that a normal life could never be attained, and although he had encountered the thought many times it never made it any easier to swallow. The other young warriors of the tribe had been raised by local knowledge, and Xafiri knew he had been raised instead by the arrogance of a coloniser foe. He had been taught many of the same things – had experienced many of the same problems, too – but the words had come from an Imperial mouth so the similarities drawn up were moot.

And, because of that, the adults of the village made little acknowledgement whenever he was around. In turn their children, fed lies about his allegiances, were made to steer clear of him too. And the warriors, no matter their age or creed, were perhaps the worst of them all: having seen the dangerous effects of Imperial influence on the sympathiser cities in south Tarraz, many of them thought Xafiri was better off dead than a potential agent of the *Zoltha* machine.

They see me as Zoltha-kind in every way, ready to be exploited by our old oppressors the moment the time is right, Xafiri thought, looking through the trees at the warriors just ahead. *They see me as a threat, and a curse, especially now that the Imperials are back in the south.*

If these warriors here were to realise who I was – and how I was really raised many years ago — they would probably hang me from the nearest tree and leave me for the Hounds, using my body as a sacrifice to show the gods that my curse was done.

Ahead of him, another warrior turned back and held his gaze: flinching, Xafiri slipped away and kept his eyes locked to the ground, hoping to avoid any unnecessary attention and the questions that would ultimately follow.

Kand'u is already ashamed of me… let's not make things worse.

With the sun setting fast overhead, and the orange-red glow of the sky coating the world around them like tree-sap, shadows grew under the thin canopies and shrouded the landscape in darkness. All around them, flies buzzed and diced through the air in droves; alongside them, clicking and twittering bats darted through the canopies like ghosts. Somewhere on his left, a larger animal padded away through the bushes, with heavy pads of clawed feet that set Xafiri's heart on edge.

The creatures of the night were all around, watching them and waiting.

But even that wasn't what unsettled him the most in the pervasive, lingering dark.

It's dark… and quiet, he thought, his hand lingering near the spear at his back. The other warriors – *the* actual *warriors* – seemed to sense it too, clutching their waistbands where their knives and daggers lay.

Something about this isn't right. The gods are unsettled. There's a fear in the air, setting with the sun.

Looking ahead to where the warriors drew together, he watched as a whistle went up, and the hunters lifted their fists above their heads, signalling for them to stop.

Xafiri ground to a halt and ducked behind the nearest tree, with a white-knuckled fist clamped across the spear-haft bound across his back. Keeping a close eye on the front of their group, he watched one of the old guards extend a finger and point skyward, whispering something under their breath that got lost in the flushes of wind.

Trying to decipher their words, Xafiri followed their outstretched finger, watching the sky there patiently——

As a murder of crows passed overhead, dicing between each other and squawking in a fearful crush.

Crows, Xafiri swallowed.

So Dal-Guzud walks among us after all.

The birds passed above them and disappeared from sight; up ahead, the old warrior signalled for them to move on, keeping low to the ground.

Xafiri stood slowly and kept his eyes on the sky, watching the clouds there leak with blood.

Night falls, he murmured softly.

And an omen is upon us.

†

Chapter 15

Blood Sky

The omen paced through the desolate trees and sensed the air shift in his lungs. The omen lay in reams of shadow and reams of bloody sky. The omen studied the open canopies above and the quivering roots at his feet. The entire forest shook around him.

The omen did not care.

Bats swooped overhead. Gnats swarmed between the branches. Scorpions the size of rats shifted through the undergrowth.

The omen paid them no heed, swaying between the trunks absently with long, ambling strides. The dusk light danced around him. Bruises alighted over his skin. A chattering voice tapped through his mind like the busted keys of a piano. On and on it droned, with a repetition that would've driven any honest soul mad. But he was no honest soul anymore.

He was not even close to it.

A shiver coursed through his veins and down into the roots at his feet. Worms were drawn to the surface, thrashing about like straggled hair. Somewhere ahead – sensing his presence – a murder of crows took to the skies and squawked their disapproval.

Where lightning quivered in the black, thunderous clouds beyond.

And thunder would shortly follow.

The omen looked down at his arm: the lightning buzzed up his shoulder like a parasite, stabbing across his skin in tiny, needling motions. Waves of it fizzed over his skin. His forearm had started to blacken, matching his charred hands. A stiffness seized in his wrist; his hand twitched and spasmed, radiating electrical energy. The raw power terrified the omen; the omen, in turn, terrified the world. In the palm of his hand, lay so much untapped energy. Untold destruction. The utter, bloody ruin of all things. It was lingering there, tempting him closer. Praying for corruption. Death and madness—

Markus closed his fist with a stifled breath, and let the terror go.

I am in control here.

Repeating the words to himself – in some feigned attempt to silence the whispers that crept through his mind – he carried on through the forest in the rough direction of north, using the setting sun over the distant mountains as a marker.

The night is quiet... things wait in the shadows, he thought, wondering what would entail thereon. The lightning fizzed over his hand again at the tempting thought of bloodshed; gritting his teeth, he dug his fingers into his palm and silenced it. *I hope I don't encounter any Tarrazi out here, in the recesses of this darkness. Their sorrows are already numerous.*

Enough blood has been spilt this day.

A wave of despair overcame his tired body; the voices in his mind silenced for a moment, thinking back to the day before.

They didn't deserve it... none of them did. They were just people... villagers going about their festivities, and I was the intruder who snuck in and stole from them. I took their food and their clothes... I terrified their children. The memory of the boy's face emerged behind his eyes, hovering there for a moment. *They had every right to attack me... every right to kill me, even. But theirs was not a mercy I afforded. Their lives were a mercy taken out of my hands. Death came in a ball of light and the horror of their screams.*

Death came by lightning, and by madness.

Looking to his palm, he watched the muscles tense and bulge as the power tried to prize his fingers apart, hungry to unleash its wrath upon the world once more. Its anguish never ceased. It was insatiable, longing for destruction. He could do little to prevent it, in many ways.

And I fear where this fight will end.

Walking through the gloom and the shadow, melancholy claimed his face, eating away at his stern facade like fungal spores over a tree. He took a few more languished strides – his knees snapping and grinding – before he doubled over with no air in his lungs and realised something was wrong.

What's... happening...

The voices in his head hammered on like nails, dissecting the soft flesh around his temples, forcing him to ply his fingers in there to mitigate the pain—

But nothing worked. Nothing changed. The pain prevailed, mounting to a crescendo against his whim, pressing in against his skull until the bone began to split on both sides—

Markus dragged a shivering breath into his body and sensed something snap in his head. Something taut like a bowstring, relinquishing its hold on his psyche.

The pulsating disappeared. The voices ceased.

Lifting his gaze, looking out through the shadows of the nearest trees, Markus tried to decipher the shapes that lay there.

When his stomach lurched against his ribs, and his eyes narrowed like tiny bullets.

There was a woman there – or what looked like a woman, at least. Their body was distinct and feminine, with the glint of steel at their side. Their hair was dark as night, landing over their shoulders, with steel boots and a steel breast-plate shimmering softly in the dusky light. Their eyes were closed, almost in slumber, with pursed lips that seemed primed to scream.

What...?

Markus puzzled, lifting a hand to rub his eyes. He tilted his head; he frowned deeply. Something about it was distinctly wrong. *Very* distinctly wrong. It was almost too real to be real. The woman was stood too straight — too symmetrically — too still. There was no motion on her body to indicate breathing: no rise and fall of her chest. There were no absent twitches over her fingers, nor pulsing rhythm against her skin. She could've been a statue, for all he knew. Nothing deceived that conclusion.

Am I… imagining this? Markus thought, taking a step to one side. *Is this even real…?*

"Um… *hello?*" he said softly, his voice echoing through the trees, half-expecting the figure before him to simply collapse into dust——

But as the words left his parched lips, resonating across the space between them, the woman's eyes snapped open to reveal two red orbs of blood.

And the shine of a metal plate, embedded in their cheek.

Markus bristled and gasped; the lightning rippled up and down his arm. Disbelief claimed him.

His lips parted.

"…Sav…?"

Opposite him, the woman took a single step forward — blurring out of his vision for a moment like hazy rain — and passed from the shadow of the trees out into the red light of dusk.

And, like a fortune-teller weaving a curse, a different woman appeared in her place: a woman of light and omnipresence, staring right through him.

She had blonde hair braided in a fishtail, spilling over one shoulder. Steel plates were bound across her body, with a military sword at her hip. The ripples of a black-grey liquid swelled in the veins over her hands.

And a white light emanated from her shiny eyes, like two effervescent moons.

What the fuck…

Markus stood back suddenly, lurching away as the shadowy woman became animate and leaned forward with innocent hands, as if she were trying to calm an angry dog ready to tear her apart. Her mouth flexed and opened as if it were talking, but no words came out. The blood-light from the dusky sky above made it seem like she was melting. Markus looked on in wide-eyed shock and resisted the urge to run.

"Who... are you?" he muttered, steadying the power that seized in his hand.

In response, the woman stopped talking almost instantly, and rose to her full height. Something came over her like a ghost, her aura visibly shifting. A horror ripped through Markus' soul, unsure of what he'd done.

Who are you——

"*Markus...*" the woman said – with true, audible words that connected in his ears and triggered the receptors in his brain, so much so that it terrified him beyond any conceivable recognition. "*Markus...*"

"Y-yes?" He took one step forward, blinking, almost with tears in his eyes.

"*Markus...*"

"Yes, yes, I... I hear you... I hear my name..."

"*Markus... you're...*"

He took a step forward; she did too, out of the light and back into the shadow, her hands opened wide and innocent——

When the figment changed and the red eyes reappeared once more, a fanged smile furrowing over the other woman's face like a wolf ready to maim its prey.

Markus stumbled back.

The woman screamed.

"*DIE MARKUS DIE MARKUS DIE MARKUS DIE MARKUS——*"

The figment charged forward, stumbling through light and dark and hell, screaming in hate and pain——

They changed, altered, shifting back and forth between the blonde woman and the maleficent creature, one of innocence and one of horror, battling through the shadows, striding through the dark——

The beautiful white eyes, pleading to his soul——

Beaten back by the red eyes, punctured by malice—
Innocent hands opening out to him—
Killing hands dripping blood—
Fighting, corrupting, on and on—
"DIE MARKUS DIE MARKUS DIE DIE DIE DIE—"
Markus tensed; he froze and shuddered.
The figment's piercing voice grew louder—
The death voice; the hate voice. Taking over—
A sword appeared in her hand.
The red eyes.
The red—
"I'M SORRY DIE MARKUS I'M SORRY DIE MARKUS—"
Markus bellowed; in a frenzy, his hand lifted, and the lightning at his fingertips exploded in a single beam, directed straight through the figment ahead—

He roared; his neck bulged—

The screams tore through the copse of trees—

When the figment collapsed in a mist of shadow, as if it had ceased to be.

Stood swaying, alone in the pitiful dark, Markus sucked air through his lungs and reclaimed what was left of his soul. He was sweating, itching all over, his body heaving with life and reality.

The lightning he had let loose in the moment connected with a tree just beyond, scorching the gnarled boughs right up to the branches where the cessation burned the leaves to ash.

Watching them smoulder, Markus clawed at his chest, lacing his fingers over the stab wound there just beneath his ribs. The figment had been inches from impaling him there: he had seen the shiny edge of the blade glance against the scar.

A scar that had been sealed shut by magical forces that he could never truly understand. A scar showing the place where he had died, and yet was now still living. A scar inflicted by a woman he had once trusted, burned into the base of his skull.

Savanta, he rasped, tears stinging his eyes.

It was you...

A weight took hold of him suddenly and forced him down from his feet; his legs gave way in a trembling mess, coated in reams of bloody sky.

Falling to his knees, with his head in his hands, Markus began to cry.

You were here... you were here again.

And now I'm left with nothing...

†

Chapter 16

Shadows

Night fell, and darkness reigned supreme in the depths of the ancient forest. Stars scattered over the skies above like tiny twinkling candles. The canopies of the trees rustled and whispered to each other. Chirping insects darted between the roots, rubbing their hind legs together rhythmically.

The Tarrazi hunting party had settled in a small clearing to convalesce and refuel, setting watch in the nearby trees to deter any unwanted company. Milled flat-breads and berries wrapped in cloth were handed out to provide sustenance, and a nearby watering-hole had enough filtration through the rocks to make it safe for them to drink. They kept close to the edges of the clearing that night, slipping off to drink from the watering-hole in shifts. No fires were lit, and the lookouts between the trees were only visible under the light of the moon. Their spears glistened like the peaks of mountains, and their eyes were like tiny pearls.

Xafiri positioned himself at the north-most edge of the clearing, looking down on the other fighters from the boughs of a gnarled tree. His nimble frame meant that he could climb through the twisted branches with ease, allowing him the extra protection of being off the ground while also avoiding much contact with the other hunters. He still kept his presence known to them, however, by letting one of his legs dangle in the moonlight like the surreptitious tail of a cat.

That way, should any of the warriors spy him in his roost high above, they would immediately recognise him as a friend, rather than some stalking predator awaiting its prey. Because Xafiri knew such creatures existed in the forests of the Valatuk Hills.

And the screech of a dying bird somewhere off to his left sought to prove that point without question.

Xafiri shuddered and turned his attention back to the clearing, keeping track of the warriors that came and went. The elders were pitched on the south side closest to where the lightning had struck, where they talked amongst themselves and studied the stars overhead, trying to interpret the constellations. There were many of them up there, Xafiri knew: symbols formed from the twinkling stars, depicting the gods and their gifts to the Tarrazi people. There were grasses and bones and spears; trees and animals and skulls. Mantises and deer's and boar and dogs. The tribe held ceremonies to each of them throughout the year, lighting up the night with displays of fire and sparks. It was always quite a spectacle whenever a show was put on, and despite Xafiri's wayward knowledge of the lore, he and his mother could always appreciate their importance to the tribe. An importance that had been handed down for generations past, and would do so for generations to come.

An importance that Xafiri knew very little of, as the Educators had made no mention of it at all.

I don't know what the Zoltha *had against the stars,* Xafiri admitted, adjusting the spear tucked safely between his legs. *Perhaps they just feared its potential: that even though they didn't believe in our gods or our ways, they weren't about to tempt fate and educate any more of us on it. Denying us knowledge of our stars was probably just another thing they sought to control, in the blind hope they could rule over us forever.* Xafiri allowed a smirk.

How wrong they turned out to be.

With his mind drifting, Xafiri's gaze then fell on the group of young warriors nestled beneath him, chattering amongst themselves like birds. They sat together in a flower formation, all facing outwards with their knives between their legs. Whenever they looked around or stared up at the stars, Xafiri saw that their faces were a story of two halves: a mix of youthful exuberance from being out on the hunt, accompanied by the overriding fear of being mauled alive by some night-lurking predator. Watching them closely for a while, Xafiri couldn't help but notice how every tiny noise seemed to draw their attention: be it a rustle in the bushes, or a crackle in the trees, or a particularly strong stream of wind coursing out from the shadows. It seemed to linger with them, setting them on edge – betraying any sense of joy or comradery they claimed to have. The confidence they seemed to have possessed on their journey so far, turned out to be little more than a ruse.

Because there is no confidence in a place like this, Xafiri thought, laying his head back and closing his eyes, letting a gentle warmth wash over him. *There are only those who survive…*

And those who find out too late.

Xafiri awoke to silence, and the pale light of the moon high above him. A light breeze pushed up through the branches and bristled across his skin; the trees whispered amongst themselves with tiny creaks and groans.

In an absent stupor, Xafiri rubbed his eyes and brushed his drowsiness to one side. Creaking his neck, his gaze drifted down to the clearing on his left, wondering how much time had passed since he had drifted off…

To find the clearing was now empty, and his fellow warriors were nowhere in sight.

Xafiri tensed up immediately, clenching his hands. Lifting from the tree branch – hissing at the aggravation in his lower back – he squat down on the balls of his feet and perched like a vulture. Overhead, the moon had crossed its highest point and had begun its slow descent to the west, meaning he had only slept for a couple of hours overall. The darkness around him remained as absolute as before, albeit emptier now that the warriors had disappeared.

The plan was to make camp here and rotate the guards until morning, setting off again at first light, Xafiri thought, feeling suddenly very alone. *No calls went up to indicate danger, or that we were planning to move on prematurely.*

Gods… have I been left behind?

An unrelenting tension rose in his chest at the thought, as the trees leered in around him and the shadows shifted at the corners of his vision.

It can't be, I… I don't know my way back. Or where they've gone. Or how long they've been gone for. How far ahead are they? Where are they? Where am I? Where's the… I can't…

Oh, gods.

Xafiri tried to steady his breathing, but it came to no avail. His skin crawled, as if mites had emerged from the tree bark and burrowed beneath his armour. Air rasped through his pursed lips in vaporous clouds; he looked out over the clearing beyond and blinked slowly.

Something is seriously wrong here.

Adjusting himself closer to the tree's gnarled trunk, he looked down alongside him for his spear, hoping to find comfort with a weapon at his side—

To find it missing, as if it had never existed.

Fuck! Where's it gone?

Looking around him frantically – panic setting in on all fronts – Xafiri considered his options and felt dread build in his soul. He didn't know where he was, or where the others were, or where his weapon had ended up. He didn't know if he was in danger, or if the others were even alive. He bristled with fear, sensing it seize across his body in waves, before his gaze finally landed on the dry earth just beneath him.

And he spied the distinct, angular shape of a spearhead glinting in the moonlight, half buried beneath fallen twigs.

I need to get that. Fast.

Turning his body slowly in preparation for his descent, Xafiri wrapped an arm around the tree-trunk and looked out over the clearing again, praying that it had all been a drowsy mirage and that his fellow warriors were still there with him after all—

When he spied the shadows shift over the roots of the trees opposite, like a pack of animals loping off through the forest.

Xafiri stopped and held his breath.

What was that?

He relinquished his grip on the trunk and lowered back down into a squat, ignoring the rapidity of his pulse as it syphoned through his chest. He kept a close watch on the space opposite where the shadows had moved, his eyes darting between each hallowed bough and the perpetual darkness between them. Misty clouds drifted between the lower branches, like the smoke from a slaver's pipe. The *wesendyri* plants speared out from the gloom like conical fingers, tapping at the wind as if playing a lyre.

Keeping his eyes fixed to the shadows, Xafiri caught the shapes moving again suddenly and traced their progress through the trees. They were low, lumbering things – maybe three or four in total – and if he looked very closely, Xafiri swore he could make out—

Spearheads...

He breathed.

People.

Relief swept through his heart; he gulped it down like pressed berries.

So they are still here, thanks the gods.

But, if they are here... then what are they hiding from?

The tension across his shoulders returned abruptly; Xafiri stooped lower on the branch and kept his breathing to a minimum. He knew certain protocols of the Tarrazi warriors, having learned them from the manuals distributed by the *Zoltha* long ago. Many of his fellow villagers had baulked at just how extensive the Imperial knowledge was of their fighting regimen, and had disregarded the manuals altogether. But Xafiri – making another controversial choice that did him no favours among the tribe – read the entire manual back-to-front, and gauged most of his hunting knowledge from there.

When a danger is perceived by one of the party, the other hunters must be alerted and organised immediately to avoid being caught out by any incoming threats, Xafiri recited. *The utilisation of the surrounding area is paramount to the survival of the party… if a clearing is located, then the more-experienced hunters should organise a perimeter silently and effectively, corralling the threat into the clearing before performing a swift execution.* As Xafiri spied other spearheads glinting between the trees to his left, he assumed that that was what he was witnessing.

A heartbeat later, and he recalled the last line of the manual with a growing sense of dread.

Although, if the enemy is perceived to be too dangerous to execute without potential harm to the other hunters, then the hunt is to be abandoned and the tribesmen must return to the village immediately, or else face catastrophic loss of life…

Xafiri rolled his tongue over his teeth, a burning in his stomach.

Gods, help us…

A silence prevailed for some time thereafter, as fractious movements shifted between the trees and Xafiri adjusted his footing on the branch he called his roost. The chirps of the twilight insects had all but ceased in the clearing; the cold rush of air up his back was unrelenting. The fact his spear lay strewn in the dirt beneath him was a persistent irritation, but Xafiri would not jeopardise the safety of the other hunters in a lame attempt to retrieve his weapon.

They're wary of me as it is, he admitted, rolling his shoulders, *they don't need any more excuses to think I'm not one of them—*

Scraping sounds ripped across the clearing, from somewhere within the trees to the south. Something crashed through the undergrowth there, with no care for how much noise it made, approaching at speed, making for the clearing—

Xafiri sprawled flat against the branch. The spearheads of his fellow hunters disappeared from between the trees. Cold air flushed through the canopies.

And a figure emerged from the south.

In the half-light, they appeared almost like a wraith, with long greying hair and the tiny silver coils of a beard lashed across their face. Their skin lay gaunt; under the moonlight, they appeared almost like a corpse. They wore a pale robe, splattered with dark patches that Xafiri assumed were blood, hiding potential weapons somewhere underneath. There was a distinct absence of motion on one side of their body, too, and it took no time for Xafiri to realise the figure before them only had one arm.

But on the other side of their body – coated in a strange blue light that flashed across their skin in pulses – Xafiri shivered in horror at what seemed to consume the other remaining arm.

It was like nothing he had ever seen before, or had ever read in the tribal texts: here was a wraith-like figure, draped in robes, with spasmodic blue energy erupting over their hand. Its light was powerful enough to illuminate the trees at the edge of the clearing; beneath him, he saw a few of the hunters shift away to avoid being revealed. The figure – stood absently in the clearing – seemed to radiate an ungodly energy, epitomised by the strange energy that fizzed and bubbled across that forsaken arm.

An arm that flinched and twisted of its own accord.

An arm that almost looked like it was coated in——

Lightning.

Xafiri steadied himself with an outstretched hand, his mind running like cogs in a cart wheel.

This thing must have been what caused the lightning blast in the valley yesterday, he concluded, sucking air through his teeth. *Which means the strike was not just a random occurrence or the wrath of the gods…*

It was by the hands of a mortal being.

On the far side of the clearing, the elder warriors – who had no doubt seen a number of horrifying creatures in their time – seemed to realise it too, and slunk back deeper into the shadows of the trees. Beneath Xafiri, the other hunters did likewise, lowering their spears into the bushes and shifting back on their heels. They wanted nothing to do with whatever *thing* had entered the clearing before them. The protection of the tribe came first.

This is not a fight that we can win, no matter the odds in our favour.

From his vantage point, Xafiri watched the figure stop in the centre of the clearing and look up to the moon, letting the light wash over them like reams of cloth. The hollowness of their skin made them seem almost dead.

Dal-Guzud would never have done this. He would never have allowed a being of this power to run rampant in our land. There is no omen here – Dal-Guzud had no part in this being's creation. This was something else.

Something far, far worse.

Glancing for a moment at the tree-trunk next to him – assessing how he could descend safely without being noticed by the figure in the clearing – Xafiri spied a flash of motion between the trees opposite him, and stopped. He looked deeper there for a moment, assessing the percolating shadows—

To spy one of the hunters moving through the shadows, their spearhead glinting like a cat's eye in the dark.

What in the gods' realm do they think they're doing?

Following their path, the hunter stopped within a cluster of *wesendyri* plants to the south, stooping low to the earth with their weapon primed. Before them, the strange figure faced away, staring absently up at the moon still like a wolf preparing to howl.

Xafiri sensed the dread in his heart; it crawled up his spine like a centipede.

Taking a single step forward, the hunter emerged into the low light of the clearing—

And Xafiri realised it was one of the young ones, barely older than him.

What are you doing! Xafiri bellowed through his mind, tensing his grip on the tree at his side. A sense of shock rippled through the air as the other hunters asked the same question, squaring their shoulders and curling their toes and whispering prayers into the gloom.

Why is that hunter moving behind them? What the hell could they be thinking. What are they...

As realisation claimed him, Xafiri's eyes nearly popped out of their sockets.

Oh...

Oh, gods, no, please——

The young hunter stepped out from the bushes, their spear levelled in their hand.

The elders shifted abruptly in the undergrowth, bunching up at the tree-line with outstretched hands——

The young man took another step forward.

The hunters stopped; the air ceased to be.

And Xafiri watched on in horror with his whole world collapsing before him, as the hunter padded over with silent steps and levelled his spear with the figure's back...

†

Chapter 17

Losing Control

Markus gazed up at the pearlescent moon, closing his eyes and pondering over a great many nothings as a cold wind pulled up his spine. The clearing around him was silent, with only the rustle of leaves to break the delicate tedium. There was no birdsong; there were no chirps of tiny crickets echoing out from between the trees. There was only a great nothingness, pervading all sense and thought. It was peaceful, almost.

Not that I can really feel it anymore.

Flexing his hand, the electrical vibrations pulled up and down his arm in short bursts, refusing to keep still at any point.

I am without the stillness I once knew. The voice and the energy keep me occupied, always.

Never letting me go.

He let the moonlight wash over him. Numbness swelled in his chest, tightening like coils.

And yet here, in a clearing in a forest, everything goes silent again. There are no voices; there is no hungry energy demanding blood. There is only open space, and the moon and the trees and the wind. The illusion of peace, lifting its doleful head to greet me.

And the icy coldness of reality ready to pull me back again—

As the thought came, his ear twitched, and the tiny rustles of footsteps echoed out from somewhere behind him. They were heavy boots, padding over soft earth. There was frantic breathing, and muttered prayers. There was fearfulness, as something approached his back and a grunt escaped their lips——

Markus twisted in the middle like a serpent and watched a spear skim past his stomach, directed straight through where his lower back had just been. He looked down on the barbed tip and frowned.

Shit... that was close.

Turning on the aggressor, Markus saw there a young Tarrazi man with four curved talons under his left eye, clasping the spear in both hands with chipped, blackened nails. The face that the young hunter produced was one of shock and horror, realising the magnitude of their mistake as it was too late, trying to recover their balance and pull the spear back to their side——

Markus grappled the haft of the spear and jarred the end up into the young man's crotch, watching him double-over with spit hanging from his mouth.

Adjusting the pole and striking again, Markus smacked the Tarrazi across the side of the head and saw him convulse like a stricken rat, swaying waywardly with a dimness clouding his eyes——

The hunter toppled sidelong and spilled out over the floor, trying to prop himself up on weakened limbs that came to no avail.

Watching him drool and writhe on the floor, Markus found a knot of pity rise in his chest, recognising how young he was and how it was quite possibly his first time out on the hunt.

Let's hope you take this as a warning, then, to not bite off more than you can chew, Markus thought, nodding his head. *Because there are actual monsters in this forest that would make fine things to hunt, but sometimes the monsters of men end up being so much worse——*

Ah! Shit, I... AGH——

A pain erupted over Markus' heart and straddled his capillaries, forcing him to shudder as if he was having a seizure. Blackness filled his eyes suddenly, swamping his vision in torrents.

What the fuck——

A pain rippled up his arm, as lightning detonated over his fingertips entirely against his will. Electrical energy erupted down the spear he was clasping and peeled the wood open in a long trench; a shot of energy fired out from the blunt end and impacted the Tarrazi's shoulder, knocking the young hunter unconscious without even a cry for mercy.

No, no...

Shaking violently, Markus threw the spear to the dirt and shook his hand, hissing at the stinging pains that continued to rifle up his arm and scatter uncontrollably over his chest. The currents fizzed and spat over his skin, like cooking fat over a fire.

What... the fuck... is happening—

Padding feet approached on his right: Markus turned sharply to spy an older Tarrazi hunter closing him down, hefting their spear in preparation for an attack.

The power surged back to life in Markus' hand, sensing the danger of the spear aimed in his direction. He struggled to channel it, tensing his forearm at his side where the pressure nearly snapped his wrist in two.

Above, the moon seemed to possess its own heartbeat, pulsing rapidly in the sky.

Keeping their distance, the old hunter hefted their spear and launched it out towards Markus—

FUCK—

Markus screeched in agony and his arm snapped up in front of his head, unleashing a surge of lightning in a haze of iridescent blue. The bolt quivered down the spear in mid-flight and the weapon exploded in a shower of shrapnel—

Before carrying through the air beyond, igniting over the old hunter's face in a flash of blue and bloody red.

Markus gawped in disbelief, watching the terror unfold: on impact, the hunter's eyes exploded in their sockets, and a fissure cracked open on their scalp to exhume the matter within—

They slumped to the ground on buckled knees alongside the burnt remnants of their spear, toppling sidelong into the dirt in a discarded, aberrant mass.

Markus lowered his hand slowly back to his side, and stared forebodingly at the corpse.

What... is this horror...

As the thought came, more Tarrazi hunters emerged from the trees around him, stooped low with their spears and knives held close to their chests. Almost like wolves circling their prey, they approached cautiously, with the black holes of their pupils gazing sightlessly on. They spared a moment looking over to their two dead comrades who lay strewn haphazardly in the dirt, and a collective fear ran between them at the thought that they might be next.

These can't... be survivors from the village, Markus acknowledged, his vision warping and breaking like the reflection on a lake. *They're... coming from the wrong... direction. This must be a hunting party... from one of the other tribes. They must've set watch over this clearing... to, to see if anything... would pass through...*

And now they're gonna die.

His jaw clicked.

Now they're all gonna die.

The Tarrazi closed in, hoping to overwhelm him with superior numbers.

The hairs on Markus' nape lifted like heckles; he ground his teeth together and tried to steady the electrical bursts in his hand.

I don't want to fight... you people... I don't want... to kill you. I don't want any of this. I have no... quarrel... with the Tarrazi. I want no part in this... this fucking war!

He peered up at the moon, sorrowful and lost.

I don't want anyone else to die.

The voice kicked up in his mind again like drumbeats. His name rattled through his head. Something close to the word *'wrong'* accompanied it, although he wasn't sure what it meant.

So is... is this it? he pleaded, mouthing prayers to no god that would listen. *Am I just... destined to kill and hurt for the rest of my life... in pursuit of... of something that can never bring me the peace I desire? Am I just a hunter... mad and lost... lost in this perpetual fucking cycle of fucking death and death and death and DEATH—*

Running feet surged forward on his left: three of the hunters – younger again than the one he had incapacitated earlier – rushed toward him with spears and knives raised, hoping to shock him into a mistake and score a quick kill.

Markus shook his head, gritting his teeth with black eyes and a half-smile, half-scream, begging and begging with the darkness of his soul to stop—

Please, I don't want to do this—

When a blast of light and energy, strong enough to form its own wind and rattle the trees on either side, surged from his fingertips with a devastating force, striking out toward the three hunters as they made their approach—

The first two Tarrazi seemed to detonate in an incredible flash of light, as the lightning ripped through their bodies and obliterated the very fabric of their being.

A dark, vaporous mist showered the night air; the snap-crackle of charred bones shot off into the foliage just beyond—

The third man, just behind them, leered over to one side in an attempt to escape the horror, but even they could not move fast enough before the lightning struck.

The blast of energy and heat tore their arm from their body, ripping their flank open to expose the intestines shivering gorily beneath. Blood coated their face and mouth as they made to scream; fluids and residue exploded out their stomach in terrifying spurts. They collapsed sideways and lay convulsing in the dirt, clawing up to the skies.

But their death came swiftly thereafter, proving to be a mercy in the end.

Markus lowered his hand and turned to the other hunters, a blackness behind his eyes that refused to let him go.

Please, stop...

His entire body spasmed and twitched in shock. Tears flocked at the corners of his eyes and seemed to burn off of his skin. His shoulder tensed in agony as the lightning tore down his arm.

I'm... losing control...

Ahead of him, out of the darkness, two other Tarrazi appeared like hunting dogs and kept their distance, circling with small steps and the moon glinting overhead. Menacing bronze knives lay outstretched in their hands, allowing better manoeuvrability in response to Markus' attacks. Their approach was slow and orbital, never letting him fall out of their sight.

Markus tensed his hand and tightened his jaw until his teeth rattled. *If I let the lightning... dictate this battle... then all shall die in the end.* He reached down to his side with shuddering fingers and unsheathed his blade.

But perhaps... by the blade... they may yet live.

Sensing a change come over Markus, the two warriors closed in on him at the same time, perhaps believing that his lightning had been expended and he was now only left with a blade.

But as Markus flexed his wrist, and saw the shards of light dart between his fingers, he knew that was very far from the truth indeed.

The Tarrazi hunters attacked him together, cutting in on both sides so he was on the back-foot almost immediately. After several sparring matches alternating between them, Markus found that his two opponents were very adept at fighting, even though they possessed the slim frames of hunters not suited to hand-to-hand combat. Every strike that he gave had a counter ready in reply; every deft turn of his hand was parried aside with unassuming strength.

As the fight escalated, the hunters turned to crafty tricks and made good use of Markus' weak spot: he had to cut through to deflect the Tarrazi knives as they turned in close to the stump of his arm. With his own blade weaving between the two of them, Markus' boots scraped over the dirt, and he hissed with frustration at being pushed back when he had grown so accustomed to winning with ease.

And the echoes of power tensing over his knuckles reminded him of that with every motion.

In a sudden flurry, Markus cut through against the fighter on his right, watching their teeth flash. He managed two more successive strikes – forcing the Tarrazi back – before the fighter on his left came in with their own attacks, driving deep into his circle.

Markus struggled to adjust, manipulating his wrist furiously to slap the knife away. The Tarrazi lurched backwards but recovered just as fast——

Several successive attacks followed, the Tarrazi's knife moving like a blur in their hand, lunging in and pulling out at such impressive speed——

Markus stepped forward with a growl and forced them back; a heartbeat later and the Tarrazi did the same to him——

The knife slid dangerously close to his stump: Markus hissed and carved across, catching the Tarrazi over the chest——

His blade scraped across chitin plates, glancing off again moments later to little effect——

The fighter on his right lunged in while he was distracted; Markus flicked the blade across and parried the weapon, leaning in to make his own fatal strike——

When the fighter on his left stepped in again and punched him in the side, before sliding the knife across his jaw like a dissection.

The blade snapped against Markus' chin and buried deep into his cheek. A cavity opened in his flesh, deep enough to scratch his gums and scrape against his teeth. The knife slipped away just before it pierced his eye socket, flicking a line of blood up onto his scalp.

Markus stumbled backwards, shaking his head and rubbing his eye, tasting iron on his lips. Pulling his hand away, he saw blood coating the charred skin there like wine. The electrical pulses in his hand fizzed over them and burned it onto his flesh. Demanding something of him.

Demanding *more*.

Sensing a change starting to come over him, Markus backed off and shook his head, blackness clouding his eyes and his thoughts and burning the blood in his neck. He railed against it, battering against its cage as the bars closed in all around him——

Giving in, in the end.

Letting the omen take hold…

Harnessing the hungry power surging through his arm, Markus grinned and bellowed at the top of his lungs and carved down toward the warrior on his left——

A scar of lightning ejected from Markus' blade and carved across the man's body, forming an attack with effortless precision without the sword ever even touching them. The energy seemed to tear the warrior's body in two, boiling the flesh from their shoulder to their waist in a horrific, bloody line. The Tarrazi didn't even have a chance to scream, let alone respond: his torso slid off of his legs and doused the floor beneath in blood.

The other fighter dropped his knife and screamed.

Markus could only smile.

Death and death and death and death——

Turning on his heel, the Tarrazi struggled to stay upright as he bolted back towards the trees——

Lifting his hand, Markus held it aloft and saw the light flash between his fingers——

†

Chapter 18

The Deathbringer

Xafiri watched the bolt of energy shoot from the figure's hand, like a falling sun at the end of time coming to obliterate the world. In a perfect line, it fizzed through the air toward the fleeing Tarrazi, illuminating the trees that surrounded them in menacing shades of blue.

The blast hit between the warrior's shoulder-blades with the force of a *Zoltha* cannon. Burning on impact; shredding through armour like paper. Xafiri felt his stomach churn, as the lightning vaporised their chest cavity and bore a perfect hole through their body, exiting out of their sternum in a shower of blue sparks.

The warrior didn't even get a chance to scream. They toppled forwards with the force of the blast and crashed down in a pile of limbs. The sparks that had exploded from their chest set tiny fires at the clearing's edge, where the *wesendyri* plants crackled and popped under the heat.

Xafiri looked on from his roost in the nearby tree – as the reflection of tiny fires danced over his eyes – and found he was unable to breathe.

By the gods... what is this thing?

The figure – whatever it was – stood at the centre of the clearing flexing their hand, watching the *zazkan* flash and pulse over their charred skin. There was a menace there, Xafiri saw: some corrupted, ruinous thing that blackened the soul and wept through the brain. How they stood – how they lurched – how they studied the tree-line and flashed their teeth, wolf-like and feral. Each glint of the figure's eyes passed like a ghost. The very earth they walked upon seemed to tremble in their wake.

Keeping his gaze locked on the enemy, Xafiri adjusted himself around the tree trunk further, until only the end of his foot remained on the branch and he was bracing against the knotted boughs for dear life. He sucked a breath through his lips and shivered violently.

I don't want to die, came the futile thought, trying to stall the trembling in his hands. He looked out on the space behind the figure and saw the bodies of his fellow hunters: mangled corpses, some little more than cinder and bones, sprawled out across the clearing for the gods to bear witness. They had been massacred, and had so little to show for it. Their bodies had been desecrated, and would soon be lost. They could never receive the burials they deserved, at the hands of their loved ones and families.

At least the gods could witness it, Xafiri considered, although even that felt like little consolation to the sheer number of dead who littered the ground that night.

The gods have witnessed our people's deaths...

And yet They do nothing to the enemy who caused it.

As the thought came and went like a whisper of wind, the figure tensed up in the clearing ahead, and Xafiri dug his nails into the tree trunk with a prayer humming on his lips. The blue energy over the figure's hand surged to their fingers suddenly – and like a bear on its haunches, they swung their arm up in anger and hurled a hail of lightning off into the trees.

Xafiri ducked down as it hissed across the dry earth and ignited everything in its path, sending a torrent of fire lashing through the undergrowth in its shameless, ruinous path. It illuminated through the boughs off to his right, and somewhere there he heard a screech of pain and the *thud* of a body hitting the ground—

A sudden blast of firelight enveloped the area where the lightning had struck, glowing bright and ferocious as the warrior was burned alive where he lay.

Birds alighted in the canopies. The trees rustled in terror. Xafiri swallowed bile, as the fire flushed and lurched across the tree-trunks. It seemed to go on forever – the screeching of the dead ringing through Xafiri's ears – until the grove extinguished itself suddenly in a flash of colour, and the forest lay still once again. The warrior had succumbed to the flames, it seemed.

Another is added to our tally this day…

Xafiri felt his heart wrench and let out a shaky exhale, adjusting his grip on the trunk.

So many dead… so many lost for nothing. Are the gods even watching us anymore?

Do They even care?

He knew it was blasphemous to question the gods, and would see him shunned by the tribe if he admitted to it, but some part of him didn't care in that moment. It didn't seem right to care. Death had swept through without mercy, and his own people had suffered in its wake. The Tarrazi had been forsaken that day.

And the gods are blind to our suffering.

He closed his eyes – closed his soul on everything he had ever known – and opened them again slowly, to neglect the gods and look upon the clearing just ahead where the figure stood—

Watching him with blue-black eyes, the lightning twitching in their grasp.

Xafiri stopped breathing, sensing the world about to swallow him whole. He blinked once, and once only.

Oh shit.

He slid his foot from the branch and shifted down the tree-trunk in a frenzy, his heart pounding through his ribcage like the knocker on a skin drum.

Seconds passed like hours.

Sweat lined his forehead.

In the clearing ahead, the figure flexed their hand, setting their face with a grin—

Xafiri gripped the nearest alcove and rested for a moment, staring deep into the monster's soul and reading their intentions there—

Their hand lifted in slow motion; the lightning surged from the fingertips—

Xafiri gasped; his head turned—

He jumped into open air.

An explosion ripped up the tree at his back like thunder. Lightning fizzed through the air, and fire roared all up his spine. His vision as he fell was suddenly awash with oranges and yellows, as if staring into the pit of the sun—

The shockwave of the blast hit him a heartbeat later and sent him spiralling forward, crashing over the dirt and vegetation in a mass of tangled limbs.

His shoulder crunched. His head snapped backwards and he blacked out for a moment, dragged back to reality by the momentum of his fall. The bruises over his body churned. He thought he'd be sick.

Xafiri came to a halt between two serpentine roots, with the massive burning vortex of the tree he had just sheltered in roaring across his vision to the right. Rolling to the side, he dragged his legs up beneath him and stumbled slowly to a stand, propping up against a nearby tree to drag ashen breaths in through his mouth. His skull pounded like splitting stone, and the floor seemed to tilt on an axis. The fire ahead was impossibly bright, and he shielded his eyes from its maw. A hiss pushed its way through his cracked lips, as he looked up through the inferno he had just escaped from—

And saw the figure there just beyond it, watching him patiently.

Silver hair. Hungry eyes. Beige robes. Blood stains.

Hate, and venom.

Corruption.

Death.

Xafiri looked on, his heart exploding out his chest. Sweat lathered his body. Somewhere, something screamed—

He watched the shadows shift in the firelight, merging with the flames and the darkness above the figure's head to reveal something there. Something huge and formidable. Something impossibly vast.

Something dangerous and terrifying, that scarred his very soul.

Gold eyes in the gloom. Twitching ears. Obsidian fur.

An exposed white skull.

Snarling jaws. Slathering lips.

Hatred embodied.

Venom enthralled.

Corruption, until the end——

Death, His mighty.

The figure lifted its hand, conjuring shards of lightning from the air.

Beyond them the figment howled into the night, sending shivers down Xafiri's spine.

This is not the work of Dal-Guzud, he breathed in terror. *This is not the work of an omen. This is hate… this is a curse.*

This is fear itself.

His mouth opened to speak or pray, but no words found his lips.

Here before me stands the Deathbringer, conjured from the pits of the hell-lands. A denizen of monstrous wrath ready to claim the world…

He gasped, looking up to the figment at their back.

And here lies Tazûl, master of all shadows…

The infamous God of Death.

Without another thought, Xafiri turned tail and ran, sprinting off through the trees with whatever strength remained in his legs. Sweat spilled over his body. His soul thundered and cried. Death was a shadow at his back.

The howls echoed on in the dark.

†

Chapter 19

Ruin

Markus watched the young Tarrazi boy skitter off through the trees, disappearing amongst the shadows of night therein. There had been fear in his eyes, Markus knew; he had looked so weak and frail in that moment. To kill him would've been easy. A mercy, almost.

And yet, despite the hungry energy throbbing in his wrist, begging to slaughter the young lamb stumbling off into the dark, Markus clenched his fist and exhaled slowly instead, taking command of his ailing body once more.

I have sated your appetite… now heed my command and silence yourself, he growled, pressing his fingers into his palm until his nails cracked the skin. The power bubbled through his veins vengefully in response — a sensation that almost made him spew across the dirt at his feet — but Markus held strong nonetheless, guiding his mind through the anger, and after a few short breaths the energy seemed to subside altogether, yielding to him like a disorderly child.

He squared his jaw and growled.

You make a monster of me…

With the dissipation of his power, fatigue began to drip through Markus' system, crippling his limbs. His feet melted in their boots; stabbing pains pierced up his thighs and over his knees; his ribs felt like constricting vines, spearing into his organs. The knotted wound over his stomach throbbed intensely.

As the energy pulled back up into his chest, the charred splits over his hand erupted with pain, more intense than he could possibly comprehend. His flesh contorted; the black tissue moved like scales; blood peeled up around the edges and dripped from his broken fingertips. The magnitude of agony exploding across his body — compounded by a headache that seemed to vibrate his entire skull — tore through his heart and shot bile into his mouth and reduced his vision to a hazy mirage. He knew the suffering he endured in that moment was not death — he knew better than most what that was — but it was as close to the long bright passageway as he believed any man could experience.

Tears lined his eyelids.

I've lost… control…

His knees gave way; Markus screamed as he toppled sideways, collapsing like a felled tree.

And just before his head slapped the earth and he was lost to the world once more, a pair of golden eyes shifted through the trees at his side, and an ominous howl caught in the wind.

It sounded almost like mourning…

The depths of his unconscious: limitless, and absolute.

There were no dreams there. No hopes. No lies.

There was sorrow, and silence. There was darkness all around. There was pain there, too. Always there, clawing its way to the surface——

Sheer, unfathomable pain.

The void swallowed him whole…

Even his subconscious could not escape the reality. His mind was screaming, reeling against the pain that racked his body. Ripples of sensation tapped through his nerves, plugging his synapses. Life swam across his vision in flashes: lights and colours, and voices he recalled but never fully understood. His memories seemed broken and half-digested, with little recollection of the past few days. Everything was in pieces; nothing made sense. His mind wandered aimlessly, as the void pulled him deeper and deeper.

The pain became incredulous. It tore through every fibre of his being, and alighted in his mind like serrated knives. There was no escaping it, as there seemed no way of escaping the unconscious prison he had fallen into. He was trapped. A victim of his own fallacy. Of his own deceit. Everything was dark and silent and perpetual all over.

Pain and pain and pain and pain and——

Death and death and death and death——

Markus awoke with a start, and the chirps of crickets in his ears. He lay on his side, with twigs digging into his jaw and a low vibration in his skull. His skin – plastered in dirt and sweat – bristled and twitched introspectively. Every breath felt like a choice.

What's going on…

Groggily, without much thought, Markus dragged his arm out from under his body and rolled onto his back, gazing up into a starlit sky now streaked with reams of red. The twilight was slowly giving way to early morning, as the sun lifted its head over the Icebreaker Sea in the east and illuminated the world again in fleeting, dancing shadows.

Markus lay still for some time, gazing blankly at the sky above, wondering what would come next. The numbness was suffocating, pinning him to the ground and making it impossible to move, but he also knew it was a damn-sight better than the pain he had endured before he blacked out. He recognised that that pain still remained, however, just below the surface: focusing on each individual part of his body, Markus could still feel the bruises and the scars and the bleeds of before, stirring just beneath the skin. The numbness tried its best to hide them away – to save his battered body from the realities it chose to ignore – but there was no escaping the sheer ruin his physical self had undergone.

And there's no telling just how damaged the mental self is, too.

Alongside the chorus of crickets chirping in the undergrowth, and the delicate lashing of wind in his ears, Markus closed his eyes and found the drumming sound had returned, but this time without the accompanying voice of before. Instead – due to his numbness or his fatigue, he wasn't sure – the pulsing in his mind seemed empty or vacant, as if something that usually filled that space was no longer there. It was an absence; it was oddly discomforting, he found, to be without something that had become so normal in his thoughts. Part of him wondered if something had gone wrong, and he had lost part of his power.

Part of him wondered if it was fatal, if he never got it back again.

Fearing the worst, Markus closed his eyes tighter for several moments, trying to pick apart the empty space to see what he could find—

Before lurching backwards suddenly and heaving in a breath, clutching his stomach in pain.

What the hell…

As he had gone to it, deciphering it like an old riddle, the empty space in his mind had reached out for him suddenly, clutching at his head with prying hands in the hope of drawing him in. The world had started spinning on its axis, as if he was falling off a cliff. Light had leeched from the world, dissembling the parameters of his vision. Terror had ignited in his system almost immediately – and, like pulling his head from a freezing river, Markus had torn himself abruptly away before it could pull him in any further.

That was fucking strange.

Free of the impulse, he exhaled gently, rolling his fingertips together. Clouds of red and grey passed overhead. In an absent welt of his overloaded thoughts, he couldn't help but wonder if he was still dreaming—

When a shadow crossed behind his tired eyes, and the drumming in his head seemed to build in frantic jumps.

Whoa—

A single moment later, and something filled the space behind the drumbeats suddenly. Something warm and comforting, and oddly disconnected.

Sensing the change, Markus tensed his shoulders—

"*Markus!*"

The voice returned all of a sudden, clearer again than it had been before. There was a joyful shock to its tone, almost as if it'd been taken by surprise. Exactly who or what it was – or whether it was a *she* as the voice suggested – Markus was still unsure. But whatever had come over him when he had tried to search the void, had clearly alerted the voice to his presence.

Perhaps I woke her up, he joked quietly to himself, *which would make sense I suppose, because it's still early in the morning*—

The humour gave way to a gasp; Markus pushed up on his arm and sat still, pressing a hand to his chest.

I woke them up...

He blinked.

So does that mean the voice is an actual... person?

Markus closed his eyes again, shutting out the gloom and shadow of the forest beyond, and registered the numbness within—

"*Markusss.*"

The voice responded, speaking directly to him, guiding him like a beacon atop a mountain. The vacant space beyond the drumbeats opened out for him again as it had before, this time with something there to accompany him too—

Numbness claimed his limbs. His skin seemed to liquidise. A sensation pulled across his scalp, as if his brain were scattering to the stars.

The trees rustled and leaned in around him. The crickets chirped in the bushes. The wind coiled about his body in tight little pirouettes.

Letting it take over him, Markus breathed deeply, and stepped out into the void that started to claim his soul——

When a biting pain snapped across his hand and fizzed up his arm, tearing him from the trance suddenly like a viper embedding its fangs.

What——

The voice silenced, and the numbness in his head seemed to disappear completely, abandoning him to the dark.

Wait, no——

A flood rocked his system: a sudden, crushing pain swept over his entire body and fell away again in seconds——

Sensation spurned to the surface. The numbness he had felt when he woke up disappeared. In its place, the familiar weight of the electrical energy resurrected in his core and dispelled through his limbs. His blood pumped and his lungs swelled and his neck creaked steadily like an old tree.

No... no no no...

Opening his eyes, he looked down to his arm and saw the blue light returning there, snapping over his charred skin in iridescent rivets. The pulse reignited in his veins; the scale-like tissue fused together once more. His fingers twitched and flexed of their own accord, delighted by the newfound energy that buzzed through them. Everything swarmed back to reality all at once.

Markus felt like crying.

I don't want this... I don't want any of this! he pleaded. *Nothing is worth this pain! Nothing can endure... I can't endure this! Just let me die!*

Please, just let me die...

With his head held low, looking to the dirt at his feet, a single tear traced over Markus' cheek and dripped onto his beige robe.

Just... please...

Let me die——

Snapping twigs echoed off to his right: Markus tensed up and rose to his feet, struggling to stay aloft as he looked through the trees in that direction. The drumbeats surged into the forefront of his mind again, almost as a warning cry, but Markus swatted them aside and let the energy surge over his hand. His skin was alive with activity, suddenly, picking apart the shadows to see what lay within—

To spy a pair of gold eyes there, and a slathering jaw full of teeth, watching him from the gloom.

Markus nearly fell backwards, losing his breath suddenly. The eyes were almost the same height as the tree canopies, and the jaws were as wide as he was tall. The darkness that swelled around them was absolute, defying any chance Markus had to see the creature for what it really was. Instead it just hung there, with snarling teeth and a watchful stare, draped in reams of shadow.

What the fuck are you?

As heartbeats passed, and the night grew still, the eyes in the shadows did not move. The trees around them did not stir even once. The entity simply watched him, assessing him – testing his resolve, perhaps, in the face of such fear. Looming in the canopy at the tree-line, coated in an overwhelming darkness. Silent and still.

What does it want—

Before the question could even form – and before a response could even stipulate in his mind – the eyes in the shadows turned away from him suddenly and disappeared from view. The swollen darkness dispersed with it, slowly fading out between the boughs of the trees, revealing more of the world beyond to Markus' waning eyes...

...where he saw a red light glowing in the distance, hardly recognisable in the gloom.

Pulsing to the same rhythm as his heartbeat.

Markus bristled, then frowned; any fear he felt seemed to slip away.

What is that? He stepped forward, sensing the energy soothe in his hand. *It's strange and strong and it's... it's almost...*

Calling to me...

The drumbeats rose in his head again; the voice hummed his name over and over again with a fearful, fleeting urgency. It battled through his mind, duelling with the electrical energy for control of his being.

But Markus didn't even realise it was happening. He hardly realised his own existence, then. A silence fell over his soul, which pushed out the numbness and the voices and the energy and the lightning. It was deafening, the sheer nothingness that filled his mind in that moment. Focused squarely on the red glow ahead, whispering out through the trees before him…

Markus stepped out into the darkness, letting the voice and the energy battle on through his head. Approaching the red light in the distance.

Lost to the world he'd always known.

Chapter 20

Gods and Heretics

Xafiri broke from the tree-line gasping for air, looking up at the sky as the sun rose in the east. A chill wind whipped up over his face. Red and gold streaked through the clouds like shredded ribbons. The fuzzy shades of blue began to emerge here and there, as night turned to day and light returned and the falsehood of reality came with it.

It was almost like an omen.

I'm running out of time.

Stumbling over a latent root, Xafiri managed to dislodge his shoe and hobbled on the spot for a moment, jamming his foot back into the boot with a frustrated hiss. He picked up speed again, ascending the steep incline toward the village gates where guards stood watching him silently, crow-like faces steeped in shadow with an ugly look of bewilderment.

Xafiri paid them no attention, as he looked over their wary faces and lamented the pains shooting up his legs with each stride. He wasn't sure how long he had run for in the end, through the endless labyrinth of gnarled trees. His pace had been fortuitous through the twilight gloom; stops had been infrequent, and brief at most. One time he had come over in a fit of coughing, and a gobbet of phlegm had spluttered from his mouth to spray the dry earth below. Another time, he had stopped with heaving breaths, awaiting a surge of sickness that never came. Even then, he had pressed on at the same pace regardless, determined to get back to the village and put as much distance as he could between himself and the horrors he had encountered in the valley, banishing the memory but not alleviating the pain that stained his mind like old blood.

The Deathbringer, that preyed upon us with such savagery. The thought sent shivers up his spine, recalling the events that had unravelled in the clearing: the death of his fellow warriors; the blast of lightning that had thrown him from the tree; the explosion of fire at his back, consuming the roost he had hidden away in moments before.

Tazûl, pacing behind the Deathbringer in the shadows, engulfing the world in His hate.

What could have we done, to bring such wrath upon us now?

Xafiri stumbled toward the guards in a daze and looked between them like a starving beggar, hardly keeping his balance as he ascended the dirt path. The guards, in turn, watched him with furrowed brows, their hands tightening around their spears uneasily. They shuffled closer together, setting their jaws, closing the path to the southern gates and the village Xafiri called home.

Recognising their fear, Xafiri slowed up immediately, a wedge forming in his throat that he couldn't swallow down. He lifted his hands above his head in a sign that he meant no harm, opening his eyes up like a young fowl's to look doleful and innocent. It did little to deter the guards at first glance – and a very real fear claimed Xafiri that he wouldn't be allowed in – but a change came over them as he padded a bit closer, and they recognised him as one of their own.

With a misguided sense of relief, Xafiri stopped several paces before them and froze, the foremost guards like two black sentinels against a bloody sky. No light penetrated their dense shadows; it appeared like something out of his nightmares.

An omen, he rasped, swallowing painfully.

Gods, what have we done?

"A… Az-kabza," he spluttered, hiding the anxious shakes in his hands as he conjured up the words he was looking for in Tarrazi.

"*Xu… feduzak…*" He placed a finger against his fake *zaz-gûla*, to indicate he was a warrior like them. "*Zazkan… vedu zazkan…*" Struggling with words, he went for gestures and pointed off to the south – where, much to his relief, thin trails of smoke billowed up through the dawn sky from where the attack had happened. "*Ubentü… Verlunz, zazkan, ubentü…*" He rolled his tongue over the top of his mouth, wrestling with the word '*danger*' and realising how it was pronounced. "*Qu… Qutönûska… vedu qutönûska…*" He tapped his eye again. "*Feduzak? Nedu… nedu feduzak.*"

As a final gesture, he drew his thumb over his throat; the connotations were clearly read, as the two guards before him gasped.

"*Consul… Verlunz. Consul!*" he exclaimed as his parting demand, gesturing incessantly to the gates ahead.

Opposite him, the two guards looked to each other with puzzled and terrified expressions. They opened their mouths to talk, but no words issued from therein. The wedge in Xafiri's throat grew tighter as the heartbeats passed them by.

Please tell me they've understood. His dry throat hitched as he breathed.

Gods… please.

With no other choice, Xafiri stepped forward——

The two guards turned towards him——

He tensed his hands——

As they stood to the side, and one of them signalled for the other guards to open the southern gate.

Trembling gently, Xafiri blew a stream of air between his lips.

I thought I was about to die.

He looked up to the bloody sky and tapped two fingers against his scalp, balancing a silent prayer.

I am not ready to die yet… not when so much is still at stake.

Slipping past the guards, he kept his head low and approached the gates, aware that his luck could turn at any moment and he could be executed on the spot. Wasting no time, he slipped through the gates like a gust of wind, flinching at the sound of grinding gears as they promptly shut again at his back.

On the inner side, several other guards watched him skitter past with harsh glares, their fingers never straying far from their spears. He stumbled between them with nods of acknowledgement, and walked on down the open street with his eyes to the floor. The wedge in his throat swelled; his skin was clammy and prickling. Even when he was clear of danger – several dozen feet down the road without a whisper of dissent – Xafiri could still feel the guards' eyes boring holes in his skull.

They fear that I've been corrupted in some way, by whatever's out there, he thought, holding his side. *They fear what I've seen… because they don't understand it. If they knew that I had witnessed Tazûl, and believed that there was a Deathbringer walking up the valley towards us as we speak… they'd probably bar the gates and leave me out there to die. Seeing the God of Death is a curse unlike any other. It's said to bring untold suffering to any who witness it.*

He sighed.

Not that I haven't seen enough of that suffering already.

Around him, emerging from their homes to go about their morning duties, the villagers watched him skulk past with confused, tremulous expressions. Many of them had probably watched him leave the village the previous day with the hunting party, setting out with the blessing of the gods and the Verlunz' well-wishes. Many of them had likely expected him to return with those same hunters, too, espousing triumphant stories with a butchered carcass or two to show for it.

But to see him then, walking alone down an empty street with repulsion leaking from his skin, spoke more of the truth of what had happened than any words could ever convey. One that left so many devastating questions, never asked for fear of the answers: what had become of the rest of them? What did they find out there in the end?

And why was this lowly Tarrazi boy pacing down the street with the stench of death, alone and afraid with ghosts in his eyes and blood trailing his step?

Because we're all running out of time. Xafiri shook as a gust of wind launched up his back; the smell of cinder caught in his nose, triggering memories he would've rather kept buried.

Because Death approaches, and these people don't even know it.

Stumbling on a loose stone, he put his hands out and nearly passed into the void, the blood-orange sky above swelling across his vision and darkening his periphery like tar. He sucked in a breath and collected himself, acknowledging the state of his body. As he did so, a pang of guilt caught in his chest, unravelling like entrails.

Mother doesn't even know where I am, or where I've been... I imagine she's worried sick. Looking down the street ahead, he almost expected to see her there running toward him, hurling reprimands through a wash of relieved tears. *I have to find her and warn her about all this. I have to get her somewhere safe. Maybe she'll listen... most likely she won't.*

Either way, I have to try.

Xafiri pressed on down the street through the haze of dawn, flinching at the shadows in the corners of his eyes. Ahead of him – at the bend in the road that led to the square – he saw a commotion begin to form suddenly, as villagers and guards circled each other and shouted like rival gangs. The guards waved people away and grimaced, demanding that they disperse; the people, in turn, pointed down the street – pointed at *Xafiri*, he realised – and shouted something in Tarrazi.

And, whatever it was that they were shouting seemed to get the guards' attention, as they turned to him and their eyes widened in their deep, shadowed sockets.

Xafiri's stomach twisted.

This can't be good.

A jostling followed shortly after, as the guards moved the people back from the street and organised them into a line. His fellow villagers wore agonised looks and lowered their heavy heads, kissing their fingers and mumbling to their gods in the hopes it would guard their fates. Meanwhile, Xafiri slowed his progress and tried to ascertain what was going on, and why they were moving people out of the street into a strange curling line—

When the long red robes of the Verlunz manifested from behind the houses, and Xafiri's heart sunk like a stone in the depths of a surging river.

This is really *not good...*

The Verlunz approached the crowd with a sneer and cuffed one of the guards across the shoulder, grumbling in his ear about what the commotion was all about and why they were getting in their way. By means of response, the guard jabbed his finger out to where Xafiri was standing and only managed a frightened mumble in reply, cowering away from the huge chief for fear of further outrage.

But the Verlunz seemed uninterested in dishing out any more reprimands just then: following the guard's outstretched finger, they spied Xafiri down the street and narrowed their eyes, furrowing their brow at the sight of such a young, unimpressive boy.

Oh shit... wait, no...

The Verlunz thanked the guard at their side – smirking as they flinched away – before they clasped their huge hands at their back and paced down the street ahead.

Moving directly towards Xafiri, who could do nothing but stand and watch.

"Az-kabza, *skal...*" the Verlunz thundered, with Xafiri attempting to interpret as his hands twitched furiously at his sides. "There is lot of noise. Lot of talk. What news... you have?"

He swallowed. "*Xu... xu...*"

"You are... hunter?"

"Yes, hunter," he replied.

"You went... with others?"

Xafiri nodded, saving his breath.

"And what did you *vesrrr*——?" the Verlunz thundered, slurring the last word as was common in Tarrazi dialect, leaving it entirely undecipherable for Xafiri.

He blinked.

What? What did he say?

'See'? Did… did he say, 'see'?

Xafiri pointed to his eyes. "*Vesti…?*"

"Yes, *vesti!*" the Verlunz bellowed. "Speak!"

"*Zazkan!*" Xafiri spluttered, feeling as if his mind were sinking into a quagmire. Despite the wind racing across the street, the heat across his head was unbearable. "*Zazkan… vedu zazkan. Visiorga, zazkan.*"

"A lightning *person?*" The Verlunz frowned intensely. "What… you mean? Explain."

"Yes, lightning person. *Visiorga.* Person with lightning hand. Very bad… very bad. Shadows all over. *Pluzrys.* I fear… I fear…"

Xafiri lost his train of thought, staring vacantly at his feet as the memories flooded through his head and threatened to swallow him whole.

The clearing. The bodies. The shadows and the fire.

The Deathbringer.

Tazûl—

The Verlunz placed a fat finger on Xafiri's chin and tilted his head up, locking eyes with an unrelenting intensity that spoke volumes of how they felt inside.

"What… you fear?" they said slowly, patiently, coated in reams of orange light. "What did you… see?"

Stood opposite them, with a solitary tear weaving its way over his cheek, Xafiri ground his teeth together and inhaled deeply.

"No omen. No *ubentü,*" he proclaimed. "Dal-Guzud has done nothing. The *zazkan,* the shadows, the fires: not Him… the other warriors are dead, but not by His hand. They died of another…" Xafiri paused, taking another breath. "The *visiorga…* was a Death-bringer. They were *Yabusto.*"

The soldiers around the Verlunz gasped, their terrified eyes flitting between Xafiri and the wall to the distant south. The Verlunz themself closed their eyes and tapped two fingers on their chest, nodding their head slowly. "If *Yabusto,* that means…"

"Yes." Xafiri shivered; the wind grew suddenly colder. "Yes, I saw *Him*. He walks among us! I saw——"

The Verlunz held a hand up and silenced him, shaking his head. "No names... no names here. Do not bring His... *hate* here." They were silent for several moments, before producing a heavy sigh. "Az-kabza..."

A crack of thunder split the sky off to the south, and tiny florets of lightning flickered over the clouds there. The guards positioned nearby watched it with trembling lips.

Xafiri smelt the burning again.

He's coming for us all...

"You are sure... that you saw?" the Verlunz asked, their eyes fixed on the distant thunder and the bleeding sky high above. "You are sure... you saw *Yabusto?*"

"Az-kabza, yes," Xafiri affirmed, shaking his head and lowering his eyes. "My sorrows to you... bringing these stories. No good, only bad. My sorrows..."

"No sorrows, *skal*." The Verlunz placed a hand on his shoulder, nodding their head once, and once only. "You warn us... you live. You bring honour. The warriors... now mourned. The *Yabusto* comes... we must make *ready*. No sorrows... only time."

There was a defiance in their voice, Xafiri realised: misguided, perhaps, but he found himself nearly crying with relief that they had understood just how serious it was. Perhaps it was the death of so many hunters that rallied the Verlunz' thoughts; perhaps it was staring so deep into Xafiri's eyes and seeing the truth burned there, that convinced them to act. Not acting was tantamount to suicide — and, by some turn of the fates, the great Verlunz saw that too.

It seems we have hope after all, he thought, with a joy filling his chest that he could hardly countenance with words. *The Verlunz understands, and they'll soon prepare. They see the danger for what it is.*

And perhaps we can fight this thing off — or at the very least, we can seal our gates and send them away, praying that Tazûl is merciful on us now He has exacted His toll. Either way, we will be ready.

Perhaps all is not lost.

The Verlunz turned back to the guards to give them orders; Xafiri felt his legs quivering beneath him, overcome with a sudden exhaustion.

I can warn my mother now, and pack our things. We can be ready to evacuate if need be.

I should go and warn her now, just in case——

Like a thunderclap, a booming noise reverberated through his ears suddenly: a shout, off to Xafiri's left, forcing the Verlunz and the guards to form a defensive circle, clutching at their spears.

The wind snapped over their heads. Heat flushed across their backs.

And as Xafiri turned slowly, scanning the street at his side, he saw there a huge figure wearing a heavy snarl.

A sight that tore the breath out of his throat, and broke his soul in two.

"*Zoltha boy!*" *Hajiin* Temusceh roared, spearing a finger at him with all the venom he could muster.

Xafiri blinked; two of the guards turned to him with conspiring glares.

No, no… shit, no!

Temusceh ambled forward with an awkward gait and spittle hanging from his mouth, hurling more insults at Xafiri; the Verlunz, trying to grapple the situation, lifted their hand out to stop him and demanded an explanation.

"*Zoltha… pe'nu Zoltha!*" Temusceh roared, gritting his yellow teeth with his finger still jabbing at Xafiri. "*Vesti*, Verlunz… *vesti…*"

The Verlunz turned to him; their eyes became narrow slits.

Xafiri panicked, realising what was going on.

Oh gods please no…

The Verlunz stood to one side and let the *Hajiin* saunter past, who charged toward Xafiri with a dangerous grin over his face.

Trying to step back, Xafiri cursed the numbness biting through his legs; he lifted his arms above his head——

Temusceh grabbed for him, pulling his arm away and reaching out toward his face with bulbous fingers——

Xafiri squealed and pushed away as his grip got tighter—

The brutish man twisted his wrist and grappled his jaw; Xafiri clawed at his forearm in a desperate attempt to break free—

Behind them, the guards readied their spears—

The Verlunz looked set to intervene—

When Temusceh planted his thumb against Xafiri's nose…

…and wiped the *zaz-gûla* clean from his face.

Pleased with his work, Temusceh shoved him away and Xafiri sprawled out across the floor with a *thud*. The *Hajiin* then turned to the Verlunz, curling his nose up to elucidate his disgust.

"*Desgundy nedu-paraba,*" he grumbled, gesturing to Xafiri and tapping his own head. "*Pe'nu Zoltha.*"

The Verlunz looked from the huge *Hajiin* to Xafiri just beyond, and the look of betrayal in their shimmering black eyes made it seem like the sky was raining blood.

"You… you are the boy from *Fendûrii!*" the Verlunz gasped in Tarrazi, as realisation swept through them. "I saw you. You are *Desgundy nedu-paraba.*" They closed their eyes and sighed weightily. "I should have seen…"

Xafiri held up his hands, shaking violently. "No, no you don't understand! I only went there to… to…"

He lost his words, struggling to speak through the terror that exploded through his body—

And in that same heartbeat, he realised his fatal mistake, as the guards turned their spears on him and Temusceh grinned despicably.

Xafiri's eyes bulged; his feet melted into the floor.

I just spoke… Provencian…

As the words left his lips, Verlunz looked away from him and sneered with disgust: with a flick of their fingers, two guards closed Xafiri down and locked his arms behind his back. He tried for a moment to squirm, struggling in their grasp, but he knew in the end that it was futile. His breath quivered in his throat.

Thunder echoed out over the sky.

Is this it? Am I dead? He could hardly breathe; tears formed in his eyes. *I've committed the worst sin of a Tarrazi. I've fabricated my rite of passage. I left the village limits. I watched true warriors being slaughtered by a Deathbringer in the forest.*

They'll call me a mantugo. *They'll call me a heretic. They'll order me to be killed. They'll execute me, and burn me on a pyre. I'll have spears impaled through my stomach, in front of hundreds of people…*

I'm going to die…

The Verlunz looked between their guards and Xafiri, pursing their lips in anger.

"Barricade the gates," they commanded, their tone like hardened steel. Turning their head, they peered down on Xafiri with disdain.

"And throw this *mantugo* in the cellar…"

Chapter 21

I'm Sorry, Markus

The sky was bleeding, and the world below was dark. Shadows traced under every bough, and seemed to split across the canopy like veins. The roots of the trees – like big arteries pulsing under the soil – were flush with luminescent spores, yellow and white in colour. Capillaries of electrical light flashed through the air, with a static energy that rustled the branches above.

And between the gnarled, spotted trees, a lake appeared in a wide clearing, in a place where no water should have formed but seemed to do so anyway. Soft soil fed out across the clearing from its shoreline, sprouting tiny shoots of dark ivy leaves. Closer to the lake's edge, polyp-like bushes swelled over the ground like tumours, rising to thick reed beds along the far edge where the lake met the trees. The water's surface rippled with the movements of strange, aqueous creatures; skating the air just above, many-legged bugs with purple tendrils flitted about in small clouds. In the harrowing red light of dawn, the water looked almost like a pool of wine.

That, or a pool of blood, drained from the veins of the sinful.

From the southern edge of the clearing – stumbling about in a daze of his own making – Markus emerged out into the red light and bent double as if to be sick, his trembling hands planted flat against his thighs, goggling at the dirt at his feet. The air was thin and cold, prickling through his lungs like needles. Each exhale came with a rasp of vapour that alighted the static around him. His skin — even under the folds of his dirty robe — fuzzed with activity, forming goose-bumps over his pores and igniting his nerve endings like flies.

Steadying himself and rising to his full height, Markus blinked through the haze and looked across to the blood-lake nearby. With no light to reflect off its surface, it looked like a layer of skin over the earth, only occasionally broken by the motions of fish stirring just beneath. It reminded him of something, in a distracted sort of way. Some figment of his imagination, or a memory he couldn't quite place. A lake in a clearing of trees, coated in layers of shadow.

And as he turned his head away, he swore he saw an old house in the trees off to his left…

What is this place? he thought, with no reply forthcoming.

What is this… place…

Markus stumbled over to the lake, and felt his ankles relax against the soft soil. Mud stuck to his boots with every step; water oozed from the ground around his heels. The charismatic *squelch* of nature brought some life back into his soul, as if some normality had returned to the horrifying world at last.

He reached the water's edge and half-collapsed across the mossy ground, his knees submerging in a puddle of ooze and mud. The lake rippled out before him in crimson waves, with the black shadows of night still twisting between the trees beyond. The bugs in the air had all but disappeared, and the reeds lay still on the opposing bank. But without even registering any of that — let alone caring for his own safety — he dug his charred hand into the thick water and splashed it up across his face, listening to the tiny hisses of electric exuding from his palm.

The electrified water — ferociously cold in the depths of night — tingled over his skin with an almost erotic joy, peeling away layers of dirt and sand that had coated his face for weeks. His pores breathed again; his eyes opened without any stinging; the taste of grit finally left his lips, allowing him to roll his tongue over the cracked skin there. His vision and mind cleared with an acuteness that nearly toppled him over, as the headache ceased and the drumbeats returned and sensation swelled over his corpse like a virus.

In that exquisite moment, part of him wanted to throw caution to the wind and cast himself headlong into the lake, cleansing his body of the sins he had witnessed – and committed – over the previous days. To clear the corruption in his soul, and finally open himself up to the light again—

But he knew to do so was a fool's gambit, and not something he should consider lightly. He knew nothing of the dangers that may have been lurking beneath the lake's surface, or the creatures that burrowed through the mud awaiting absent prey to feast upon. Even as he thought it, the murky waters where he had just scooped his hand came alive with the wiggling shapes of leeches, carrying their disease and decay in their tiny, discordant bodies. Further out, larger creatures stirred in the waters, eyeing him up with patient, pale pupils.

This is no place for idle fools to wander into, he deduced, placing his hand flat against his thigh and peering down over the waters below.

Only death awaits those who think otherwise…

Watching as the water drew still beneath him, Markus traced the shadowy outlines of his face and the mad coils of silver hair pulling in at his cheeks. Although exaggerated by the water's motion, he saw there the features of a gaunt and tired man facing impossible realities. A hollowness in his eyes; the broken trenches over his forehead and jaw.

I have been aged in this new life… by the powers I possess, he deduced, glancing at the fissures of lightning darting between his fingers. *It takes from me with every expulsion… takes something I can never have back. It fuels me and feeds me, while also exacting a cost of the one thing I can ever truly control.*

Time.

Studying his reflection again, a wave caused by a disturbance further out distorted the image for a few moments, as water splashed up over the moss at his knees and wetted his dirty beige robe. Markus struggled to keep focus, discerning which shadow was which, but as the water stilled again everything became clear once more.

And he stared down into a face that was not his own.

The face he saw was that of a young man, with short-cropped hair and silver eyes. There was the distinct straight edge of a tunic over their shoulders, as well as the jagged collar of an undershirt. Their lips were still, and they didn't seem to blink once, staring off into the crimson skies absently without a thought in all the world.

Markus squinted and frowned at the image, both recognising it so distinctly and yet knowing nothing of it at all. *Should I know this person?* He searched for an answer somewhere in the silver of their eyes, hoping some revelation would come to him—

When he spied the tiny opening of a pellet wound in their forehead, almost like they'd been killed by a crossbow bolt.

Wait... is that—

But before any recollection could emerge in his mind, a shooting pain lanced through his skull as if he'd been concussed, and he was forced to close his eyes suddenly to mitigate the strain. The energy tingled in his limb; the drumbeats rose and fell in his mind like undulating hills. Rolling his jaw slowly, the pain subsided almost as fast as it had risen, and Markus peered back down into the blood-red waters to spy another face there.

Only this one he remembered all too well.

Much of the face lay hidden beneath the wide, unmistakable brim of a shadowy hat, except for the quill-like point of a smoking pipe jutting out to one side. A faint glow emanated just below where their eyes would have been, and if Markus looked closely, he could almost see them smiling.

The Handler, he remarked, feeling a twitch at his side. *The one who took my arm and threw me into that slave wagon... the one who sent me to fight in the arena for their entertainment and profit. Another face from my past, come to haunt me.*

But... why am I seeing you here?

Squinting, Markus lifted his hand and rubbed his eyes absently, in some feigned attempt to clear his mind and wash any thoughts away. He dug the edge of his palm into his socket and pushed against the skin there, manipulating his eyelid before pulling away again——

To look deep into the eyes of a child, their pupils white like gem-stones.

Who the hell are you? he mused, noting the curvature of the skull and the distinct lack of ears the child possessed. Their entire shadow seemed to ripple and pulse like an active organ, almost as if the child was talking. *I don't know of any Tarrazi... or none that I've acquainted well enough to recall the face of.* He spied a reddish smudge under the boy's left eye, almost like something had been wiped off there. *I don't recognise this child at all. I haven't seen any Tarrazi children up close.*

He looked down to his hand, and followed a thought down a rabbit hole.

Unless that's the point: that I don't recognise the child, because I haven't even met them yet. I can't remember something I haven't seen. The cogs in his mind churned over.

This... vision, or whatever it is, reflecting in the water... may be detailing something in my near future, as it did in my past. Perhaps the power within me has some foresight that I haven't realised yet, guiding me down a certain path. This could be some sign as to what I should look for next.

But leading to what, I don't know.

Markus considered the possibility – laughing, for a moment, at the sheer ridiculousness of the concept that he could see through time – before turning his attention back to the reflection below——

To stare into the golden eyes of a woman, with glinting armour and a fishtail plait.

Markus felt his heart shudder and lurched backwards suddenly, as the golden eyes tracked his movements and the thin white line of their mouth twitched.

Lightning fizzed up his arms; heat surged over his scalp, butchered by cold cuts of wind up his back. The drumbeats launched into another crescendo, matching his rampant breathing.

I... recognise you, he thought after some time, steadying himself and leaning forward once again. *You were in the clearing when I had that last vision… you were saying my name, and trying to reach me.*

Yours is the same voice as the one in my head, came the second thought as he tensed his hand. *I… I could hear you in my mind, even when your mouth couldn't speak. You have some connection to this power I have… some understanding of it that I don't. Maybe you can control it…*

Or maybe it's fighting you, came the final thought, as a bolt of fear ran up his spine. *Maybe something's wrong… or corrupted, or whatever. Maybe there's a blockage somewhere, in me. Because whenever the drumbeats rise, the power becomes numb… and whenever the power surges…*

…your voice goes away.

He rolled his tongue over his gums and sighed.

Something isn't quite right about this. He looked again to his hand, and recalled the pain and destruction it had wrought. *It almost feels like there's an imbalance… like two things are vying for the same power. Two entities, each with one goal, occupying the alcoves in my head. There's the woman of gold, who speaks my name and guides me where it can. And then there's the other one, rotting my soul…*

He let his hand drop; his eyes flicked back to the water—

Red eyes stared back at him.

A woman's face.

Shimmering fangs.

The woman of red…

The face grinned.

"*Savanta…*"

Markus rolled backwards and gasped in fear, scrabbling away from the water's edge, flicking clumps of dirt and moss from the ends of his boots.

Lightning pulsed over the earth and singed the ivy-like plants. His head, like an inflation sac, felt set to explode.

Dragging himself to dry land, he stopped and heaved air through his system, re-establishing some sense of control beyond the drumbeats that rattled in his head.

It's fine, it's… it's just a mirage… just your mind, playing tricks, he wheezed, blinking slowly. *There's nothing really there.*

There's nothing...

...really...

Falling short on his conviction, his eyes locked to the waters ahead, pristine with the colour of arterial blood. There were no fish there to disturb it; no flies buzzing through the air above. It was a completely still surface, devoid of conscience or motion.

With the matted hair and glowing red eyes of a half-submerged head, staring at him from the edge where he had just been.

What the fuck...

Markus shifted his feet beneath him, lifting slowly to a stand—

When the figment emerged from the water as if ascending a stairway, striding forward onto dry land with its black skin dripping like tar. Its hair lay in long, thick clumps; its red eyes shimmered; fangs glistened in its poised mouth; a menacing blade lay coiled in its hand, ready to strike.

Markus went for his own weapon and withdrew the short sword, hunkering down in a fighter's stance as the apparition came to a stop. His entire body shivered and vibrated with unease; his heart lay in his throat, pulsing ferociously. Even the energy – hungry and reckless as it was – seemed to shrink down in the presence of the figment, drawing back into his veins.

What the fuck are you? he thought, clenching his blade tighter.

What the fuck is any *of this...*

In the dull red light of dawn, with shafts of crimson pulling down through the canopies above, the apparition seemed to smile and run its tongue over its pointed teeth. Lifting a sleek hand up to its face, it brushed its fingertips over the hollow shadows of its cheek.

Revealing there a glint of steel, locked against its jaw.

No...

"What... what are you?" Markus bellowed, gritting his teeth. "What is all of this? What the fuck do you want with me!"

The apparition didn't answer: it only stared through him, piercing his shadows.

"This can't be real, this… this isn't real. This is just a projection of my mind, staring back at me. Isn't it? *Isn't it*!" Spittle flew from Markus' mouth like spilt wine, gritting his teeth together. "Answer me! Fucking *answer me!*"

The apparition only grinned, revealing white fangs as long as needles—

"Don't toy with me, you bitch! Don't fucking toy with me! What do you want? What the *fuck* do you *WANT FROM ME*—!"

"*I'm sorry, Markus-us-us-us…*" the figment spluttered, it's voice echoing vacuously like the hiss of a serpent. Its head tilted quizzically to the side, studying him. "*It was the only way-ay-ay-ay…*"

"What are you saying? Why… why are you saying this to me?" he pleaded, reciting the words – *her* words – over and over in his mind. "This isn't real. This… this isn't you. You aren't *her*… you can't possibly be her. This isn't *real*…"

The apparition twitched. "*I'm sorry, Markus-us-us-us…*"

"Stop." He pressed a hand to his ear, grinding his jaw. "Stop it."

"*It was the only way-ay-ay—*"

"Stop it, don't… don't say these things… don't—"

"*Markus-us-us, Markus-us-us—*"

He cowered. "Stop, *stop*—"

"*I'm sorry, Markus—*"

"Stop *talking*, stop—"

"*I'm sorry—*"

"*YOU WERE NEVER FUCKING SORRY, SAV!*" he roared, an unbreakable tide that swept out over the clearing like a violent flood. Opposite him, the apparition seemed to shy away, drawing its arms in closer to its chest. "You've never been fucking *sorry*! It's always been the same with you! Determination, dedication… and so many fucking *lies*…"

Looking into the hollow dead of the figment's eyes, Markus felt his heart turn inside-out, unravelling memories and pain from where he'd buried them long ago.

The rise in his chest returned; the pulse, along with the electrical current in his arm, intensified. An amalgamation of wrath surged to the surface like a noose, tightening around his neck.

His eyes swam in the haze of red. The option was there to push it all down again.

Except this time, he didn't. This time, he didn't fight it.

Instead, he set it free.

"You never cared for what you *stood for*," Markus spat, gritting his teeth. "Everything was fleeting for you: like an arrow in the wind, never quite meeting the target. Everything was a means to a fucking end – the company, that you dedicated yourself to for *years*, was just an idle profession to keep your mind occupied as the reality sunk in. That sheer, brutal reality… that at the flick of a match, every single little *fucking* thing you had in your life could go up in flames, and you would have nothing to show for it but your ignorant sorrow and your sudden lack of *direction*." His nostrils flared. "How *sad* for you, Sav, that your pretty little way of life was ruined, that you so callously threw away. How fucking *sad* for you, that you caused the deaths of so many innocent people, burned alive in a forest because you didn't have it in you to make an *honest* decision. And how *fucking sad* for you… that that stupid metal plate in your cheek was the only real damage you *GOT FROM IT!*"

Spittle flew from his mouth. A tear rolled down his cheek. The electric seized over the hilt of his blade as the apparition watched on in silence.

"I watched you *suffer*, Sav: sat in that chamber, with stitches all over your fucking face… I watched you *suffer*. I watched you wallow in grief, and lose yourself over what had happened to the company… and despite everything – despite my own feelings, and my own grief – I didn't blame you *once* for it. Because I didn't think it was right to. I saw the pain written across your skin, and accepted that for what it was. But that was the coward in me talking, I realise now: the coward who shied away from the truth…" He ground his teeth, shaking his head. "Because the truth is… you didn't give a *shit* about them. About *any* of them. Provencian, Tarrazi, mother, child… it was all the same to you. All meaningless – all a *means to an end*. You never cried over their deaths. You never cried because you *cared*. You cried, because you lost your *direction*, and you cried because you had no fucking way of *fixing it*."

He jabbed a finger out toward the figment, which rippled and pulsed like a cyst in the red light.

"So you did the only thing you thought you could, when faced with such odds. The only thing that felt right in your absent, violent little mind. You found someone to blame, far away in a great walled citadel that was impossible to reach… and you decided you would *kill them*. You decided the best medicine for your grief, was *blood*. No matter what it cost; no matter how hard it was…" – the scar burned on his chest – "…and no matter who would have to *die* for you to achieve it."

The apparition blinked; recognition crossed its face blindly. The dead orbs of its eyes pierced the darkness like a demon's.

"Markus-us-us-us, I'm sorry——"

"You're a *LIAR!*" Markus bellowed, the electrical pulses pulling across his shoulder and melting the fibres of his robe. "You're a self-absorbed, reckless, ignorant fucking *liar*." He ran his finger back and forth across his chest, where the scar from the fighting arena throbbed angrily. "'*I'm sorry*' doesn't explain this. '*I'm sorry*' doesn't explain the people you've murdered, or the lives you've ruined, in pursuit of your own foul fucking *destiny*. In your miserable, suicidal pursuit of an enemy you don't even know and can't even comprehend. It's pathetic. It cost you *everything* you've ever known, or pretended to care about, and *FOR WHAT!*"

Markus ground his jaw, feeling the tears burst out from his eyes; his breathing became shallow and thoughtful, like the beating wings of a songbird. The electric hummed quietly at his side, thinking on the sins of his past.

Thinking of the sinner stood before him, marked by reams of shadow.

"I loved you, Sav," he spluttered, unravelling himself. "As a comrade, as a hunter, as a fighter… as a friend, I loved you. You were the one person in this tiresome fucking life that I would stand beside and defend no matter what – that I would listen to, take orders from, and follow to the ends of the known world if you asked me to. I saw the good in you – your promise and hope, as a mercenary and as a woman – and I believed it. I fucking *believed* it, every single day…" He shook his head; anger flared to the surface. "And then… in that arena with a blade hanging over my chest, watching my time in this world slip away… I saw the *real* you. I saw what you had become in your own absence. I saw the covetous, deceitful *bitch* that you had released from its cage, and I was *disgusted* that I had ever believed in you at all…"

The apparition quivered; the fangs flared over its face. Something shifted over its amorphous body, tensing under the blood-sky above.

"I loved you, Sav… and I would've done anything for you," he said, staring deep into its red eyes. "But in the end, your apologies mean nothing. Your sorrow, and the hurt you feel inside… it's all false. You're a liar, and a treacherous snake. A ruinous fucking woman with no heart in her chest. You will bring ruin to everything in your path, until there's nothing left but your pain and the hundreds of dead bodies in your wake." Markus inhaled gently. "And I *cannot* let that happen. I cannot let you destroy this world and everything in it. I am the only one who knows it, and the only one that can stop it."

He levelled his blade against his chest.

"So know that I am alive, Savanta, and that I am coming for you. I will hunt you down, and I will bleed every vessel in your body… because you are not the woman I once believed in, and once called a friend…"

The apparition glared at him and screeched.

Markus roared.

"You're just a *fucking monster*…"

The figment charged forward, its entire mass bubbling and breaking at the seams, its sword dripping with black-red liquid, screaming through the gloom.

Markus dragged his foot through the mud and exhaled slowly, before curving his blade up and stopping the apparition in its tracks. Their blades chimed; the crimson sky glistened over Markus' sword like an omen.

They pulled apart moments later and he carved down again, forcing the figment back a step. It growled, almost moaning with frustration, and counter-attacked just as fast, striking down toward his shoulder.

Markus saw the attack coming long before it landed, and brought his sword up to slap it away and come in with a quick lunge straight after. The blade glanced across the apparition's stomach, flinging a slick of black ooze out over the sodden earth beyond. Its red eyes seemed to bulge with disbelief, as its fangs flared and twitched like needles. Markus stood back and lowered into his stance again, flashing his own teeth with spittle over his gums.

You mean nothing to me anymore, Sav.

The electrical pulses accelerated up his arm. Spasms of light lurched toward his blade over and over but refused to ignite, channelling over his shoulders and stomach instead, harnessing his physical power. It embodied him, surging through every sinew and muscle in his body. There was none of the hunger or recklessness of before; none of the wanton destruction waiting to be unleashed at his expense. There was a tameness there, instead, as it flashed and rippled over his chest, awaiting the thunder before the lightning struck. Awaiting his commands, almost.

I am the master of my own journey... even death could not deny me that.

Markus cleared his mind and strode forward, carving down in terrifying arcs with a blue glow in his eye. The apparition screeched – begging and pleading in a voice that was hers, but not quite hers – trying to hold its ground. Its body fizzled and cracked, like lancing a boil and watching the pus fly. Markus pushed on with his onslaught, staring deep into its death-red eyes and seeing the sorrow and ruin therein. The corrupting, venomous malice that embodied its every motion. *Her* every motion.

You're a monster, Sav… there's no saving you now.

Only death remains.

He drew a hot breath into his lungs and stepped into the apparition's circle, carving the sword up from his waist. The blade dug deep across its blackened body, sluicing the oily skin apart from the stomach to the throat.

Ruptures formed over its body; the screeching tore through Markus' ears, as its red eyes nearly popped from its malformed head.

It stumbled backwards, caught in a frenzy, pulling at the wound down its middle with its hands. Tearing at its matted hair and hollowed face. Clawing at the white-red mark over its cheek where the metal plate would have been.

The waters of the lake thrashed at its back. Waves pulled up over the moss and seemed to cut through its ankles. The reeds at the far side bristled and tensed.

To death… a deed is done.

Markus sheathed his sword and closed his eyes, letting a numbness unravel within him. The air hollowed in response, emptying from his lungs; cold winds whispered over his face. A crackle of thunder tore through the distant skies.

And lightning was sure to follow.

With a growl, Markus opened his hand out and lifted it like a priest at an altar, professing the sins of the masses. As soon as his hand rose above his head, a burst of light claimed the red skies above, and lightning snapped down into the clearing. It tore through the air at impossible speed, obliterating the shadows in its path—

It connected with his hand and seized over his arm, the pressure billowing out over the trees to either side—

Markus ground his teeth and stood firm in the face of its power, harnessing nature itself and bending it to his whim. Energy surged through his system, coiling about his heart – igniting a welt in his chest that he had never felt before, at the dead centre where his soul resided. It seemed to feed on the energy, harnessing it with effortless grace. Markus could feel it shudder through his very bones.

A tiny smile licked across his face.

Beyond the light, Markus saw the apparition lift an aqueous hand up to its face, as if shying away from its light. Its screeches had quietened to delicate whimpers. The look it gave him, in the wake of such power, suggested mercy.

And Markus, in turn, suggested no such thing.

"You… are a *rot* on this world, Sav!" Markus bellowed, lowering the lightning to his side with immense strain, the muscles in his neck bulging. "You are… a traitor… and a *liar*…"

He looked between his hand and the apparition; thunder cracked the skies above.

"You are the… *ruin*… you are the… *pain*…"

Markus brought his fingers together, sensing the power erupt.

The apparition stared through him.

"I am the blade…"

A scream.

"And your death… is *mine!*"

An orb of lightning snapped across his hand and erupted in a beam of pure light.

Spinning off into the trees, it tore through the apparition's chest, burning over its liquefied skin.

Torturous noises escaped the figment's lips, as it's body began to boil like fat——

Markus held strong, bellowing with agony as his muscles seized and snapped. The power fed out from his soul and the sky, reloading the blast over and over, using his arm as a conduit. The apparition opposite him was lost in a haze of energy, it's smouldering body popping and hissing as if scalding hands had come to drag it back to hell. Markus felt his skull rupture with power, fizzing out behind his eyes.

The gods witnessed him.

The world witnessed him.

Sorrow and anger.

Grief and pain.
Destruction.
Lightning.
Death.
The lightning surge gave a final blast and snapped from his finger-tips like a crossbow bolt.

The apparition exploded, detonating over the clearing in a mess of watery ooze, its screams snuffed out by the effortless certainty of a violent and exacting death.

Markus brought his hand back to his side, balling it into a fist as the muscles contorted and cramped. His skin crawled with activity; air pulled up his spine. Bones creaked in his back. The entire world seemed to spin on its axis—

And then, all was silent again.

The sky opened out, revealing streaks of orange and yellow with the delicate waves of blue in the east. The shadows, haunting the clearing like a ghost, dissipated entirely, revealing sunlight between the trees and over the plush mosses underfoot. The ground dried up beneath, and the tiny lake receded from its banks, lapping delicately with the motions of a gentle wind until it was little more than a swollen puddle.

Markus gazed out on the world beyond, and sensed his vision clearing. The rancour and desperation in his mind became little more than an echo. Looking down over his body, he realised that the lighting blast had burned the robe from his shoulders, and it now lay in a smouldering heap at his feet as if he had shed his skin. In its place, the metal stomach-guard remained, as well as the chitin pauldron on his shoulder, but the skin extending out from his arm was now coated in blue spiralling marks, like some ancient cave painting or the native tattoos of his kin.

And then, as his eyes traced over his arm down to the hand below, he realised just to what extent the lightning had altered him and transformed him into one of its own.

His arm was no longer black, and all the way down to his wrist the skin had fused back together in hardened lumps. Blue veins ran between them, where the energy fizzed and danced like migratory fish swimming upstream, revelling in their new home. Black marks and dots coated his elbow, and spread across his forearm down to his knuckles, which could now move with the same freedom he recalled from his previous life.

Holy hell...

Markus looked upon the changes quizzically, and marvelled at how *healed* he looked. *This is remarkable, I feel...*

Reborn.

The energy – or whatever power it was that had taken residence in his soul – had done nothing but take from him since he crawled from the rot-pits in Val Darbesh. It had drawn life from his body with each use, tearing through his system. It had weathered his face and broken his bones and tightened remorselessly on his mind. The fear of an early death under its strain had plagued his mind throughout – thinking back on it, he was surprised he had survived the ordeal at all.

And yet, studying his arm then, and feeling the clarity enveloping his conscience, it seemed that the original toll the energy had exacted had been all but reversed. Instead of taking from him and ruining his body, the lightning coursing through his veins seemed to provide him with a new lease of life.

It seems this is not the power it once was, Markus acknowledged, flexing the joints in his hand.

And I am not the man that I used to be.

Looking off to the skies above – inhaling properly, without a weight over his shoulders at last – he spied a thin trail of smoke to the north, disappearing through the clouds. There must have been another village there somewhere, not too far away – likely the one that sent out the hunting party that had intercepted him that night.

Glancing through the trees in that direction, Markus nodded his head. *I think I'll pay them a visit, and see what I can find,* he decided. Maybe *they'll have some good information on a suitable path out of these hills to the north.*

He opened his palm, and felt the lightning there almost imme-diately.

And I'm sure a bit of persuasion wouldn't go amiss, if they prove to be unwilling...

Closing it again, he gazed down on the ground just ahead of him, and the dark stains that marked the earth there. Reminding him of just how much he had been through; reminding him of his true purpose, on the long and dangerous road ahead.

Even though I have overcome, the task remains the same, he proclaimed, squaring his jaw. *Savanta must die still, and I must be the one to do it. No-one else will stand in my way.*

Not even her memory — not anymore.

Markus turned his attention north and stepped out into the trees, disappearing amongst the shadows and making off toward the village on the hillside.

A village that knew he was on the way.

The Deathbringer himself.

‡

INTERLUDE

Something bad has happened… something serious." She pressed her hands against her scalp as a headache pulsed to life. "I still don't quite know what exactly, but it just feels… ominous."

"I sensed a disturbance, in my early stirrings from sleep," they replied. Their shadow loomed large against the dawn light spilling in from the attic window. "What did you feel exactly?"

"I felt… I don't even know what I felt. I was awoken by a presence — like some ghost was in the room with me — and as I reached out to see what it was, the Rapture seemed to drag me in, like I was being… swallowed." She shuddered at the thought.

"What happened when you entered the Rapture fully?"

"There was darkness, and emptiness, and… it's hard to describe. The void looked bloated, as if it were set to burst. There was something very wrong about it all. Something… damaged, almost." She paused. "That, and they were also there, too."

"Who?"

"That Markus person. Mother Katastro's heir. They were there when I entered… they occupied the same bloated void as me."

"I see." They said nothing more for some time, as their face hardened like chiselled stone. "And what happened from there? Were you able to communicate with them?"

"No… no I didn't even get close. I only caught a glimpse of them, like a brief flash, before my presence ruptured the void entirely."

"What do you mean by that?"

"It's the only way I can explain it. As soon as I entered the void, Markus screamed in terror and... and he was sucked through the floor. Consumed, almost. Spat out of his own subconscious before I could even get to him." She recalled the memory and scoffed. "I mean, if I'd known any better, I'd have said that their Rapture did it... almost like it was——"

"Coveting them."

Their words echoed out through the room and danced with the shadows; she furrowed her brow in response.

"I was gonna say 'avoiding' me," she said quietly, "but what do you mean by 'coveting'?"

"Did anything else happen after that?" they replied, avoiding the question she had asked.

"Well... yea, things just went back to how they've been over the past week: I enter the void; I shout their name; they register but don't respond; I shout louder; they close me off. I still can't get through to them, or even get a response... and their hold on the Rapture is still negligible at best."

"I see." They nodded. "Now, I understand that that's what happens normally... but, when it occurred this morning, was anything different? Were any of the sensations different? I need you to remember for me."

She narrowed her eyes. "I mean... maybe? I was cut off quite abruptly when they did finally swat me aside, I admit, and that was only after they made some feigned attempt at entering the Rapture again. After that I was only able to sense the rhythms of their heartbeat... I have no idea why, though."

"They cut you off after trying to enter the Rapture again?"

She looked deep into the hollows of their eyes, and a shudder ran through her. "Yea... like I said, it was quite abrupt."

"And your connection after that was nearly completely gone?"

"More or less so, yes." They stood straighter suddenly. The hollows of their cheeks darkened.

She bristled, as her heart raced faster in her chest. The Rapture bubbled between them, frightful and unwieldy. "I need you to tell me whatever the hell is going on... now," she said.

In response, the figure opposite her let out a delicate sigh. "I didn't think it were possible," they muttered slowly. "Probable, yes, but only in theory. And yet, based on what you're describing... I can think of no other explanation."

"What? What is it?"

"Their Rapture has been corrupted, and their connection has been frayed by some malignant presence in their mind. Something has attached to them, clinging onto them... and, as I said to you, it's now coveting them as its own." They paused. "It's feeding off their Rapture like a parasite..."

Her stomach dropped to the floor as the words left their mouth. Her skin crawled thinking about it. "How... how is that even possible?"

"Without assessing them fully, I have no way of knowing the truth behind their affliction. The exact causes cannot be known to us without seeing them in the flesh. But, what I do know is that it would explain why you cannot access them, and they cannot access you: because this corruption in their mind has grown across their Rapture like a tumour... and although they may attempt to fight or weaken it, it will still remain there nonetheless."

"And that's why the void felt so bloated and rotten when I entered it: because it quite literally was bloated and rotting."

"Precisely so... and very badly, by how you described it."

She pursed her lips. "So, what does that mean for Markus? How does that affect him? Is it just in the void, or in his physical body as well?"

"It will likely be a combination of both: I can only guess as to the severity, but I imagine it can become quite intense. Visions, voices, whispers, screams... seeing apparitions, perhaps... losing the function in his limbs... blacking out... seizures..." The air around them became heavier. "Worse, even, if it's left untreated."

"So... so what do we do?" she spluttered, her heart in her throat. "What can we do? We need to help them... we need to get through to them. If they're fighting this thing in their mind, we need to be there to fight it too. If a Mother's—no, no, if a person's soul is in danger, then we have to do something. We have to try no matter what. We have to... to..."

Placing a hand on her shoulder, they knelt down before her and nodded their head. "We will, don't worry," they said. "We will reach them, and we will fight whatever it is that haunts them, and we will win. The odds are stacked against us, it's true, but they always have been. And I know you will do whatever you can to save them, regardless of who they are." They managed an awkward smile. "I would expect nothing less from the All-Mother's champion, after all."

She smiled back to him, wiping at her cheek. "Thank you, truly. I just want to ease the suffering in this world, before it's consumed by our violence, and this... well, this feels like a good way of doing that."

"Agreed, Successor. I could not have said it better myself."

"Thank you." She nodded contemplatively. "So... what should we do now?"

"I would advise we carry on as we are, and you continue to act as legate for the upcoming elections here in the City — that's where our efforts are best served, and where our diplomacy is most needed." They rose to full height and brushed their robes down. "Beyond that, we shall continue to monitor the wavelengths of the Rapture and see when this Markus person comes close to connecting with their void again. When that happens, we must try and reach them as quickly as possible, and attempt to bridge the gap that the corruption is currently blocking."

"I guess we'll meet a lot of resistance doing that."

"Most likely so, yes. Whatever it is that's currently corrupting his mind will want to retain hold over it with an iron grip — and we, as intruders, will bear the brunt of its reprisals."

"Is there anything we can do to, y'know... mitigate that?" She held out her hands. "I mean, if we're treating this corruption like an entity in of itself, then that sounds like it can be manipulated, or maybe weakened?"

They considered. "The corruption can be weakened, yes... but not by our hand, or anything that we can do from here," they explained. "We are coming at it as outsiders — thieves of the mind, almost — so our abilities to help are very much limited as it stands." They shook their head. "Which means that the only person who can actively weaken the corruption, or fight against the darkness... is Markus himself. He alone has the power — the sheer, unfathomable power that seems to break the Rapture at its seams whenever its used — to fight it and weaken it enough for us to intervene. That is the only way forward with this, beyond whatever small contact we can make as we are."

"I see." She rolled her fingers together. "I guess we'll just have to wait and see... and pray nothing bad happens."

"We should be okay, Successor... do not fear. If this Markus is half as sane as we hope he is, then he will most likely be going about his life as normal and keeping far from any danger. With these powers he seems to possess, and the constant droning of noise in his mind, I imagine he's quite scared and closed off, just waiting for some answers."

"Yea... I just hope that when we do try and give those answers, that he doesn't freak out and it makes things worse."

"It is a concern, yes... but I believe our chances of success are quite high so long as we can fight this corruption with him." They paced over to the window and looked out on the city beyond. "That, and he keeps himself out of danger for the time being."

"Very true," she replied. "I mean, I dread to think of what he'd be like if he was in the middle of Tarraz right now, fending off hordes of angry blackcoats with only his wits to spare. Imagine being foolish enough to do that."

"Yes indeed," they muttered, tracing a finger along the windowsill. "Imagine..."

†

Chapter 22

Mantugo

The cellar that they had thrown him in was located in the basement of an old storehouse, formed by a natural opening in the rock like an abscess. It had been used as a hideout against Imperial administrators once upon a time, he knew, when the Occupation was in full-swing and legions of foot-soldiers had swarmed over the Hills like ants. Whenever they had arrived at the village walls, the Ritualists – those who spoke directly with the gods on matters of life and tribe – had taken shelter in the subterranean chamber Xafiri now found himself in, and prayed to the gods from their candlelit shrines for the *Zoltha's* swift undoing – that, or their equally-swift demise, in a burning and fiery hell.

Even then, looking over the glossy grey walls of the cellar around him, Xafiri could still make out the Ritualists' markings across each wall, faded from several long months of disuse. There were red spirals and tall towering columns; depictions of skulls and trees, with dots lining their edges. There was even what appeared to be a drake on the opposite wall to him, with huge fangs and prodigious-looking talons, that the Ritualists had hoped to summon to run the *Zoltha* from their lands once and for all. Although even that had failed to come to fruition in the end.

They probably would've hunted it for sport, anyway, Xafiri thought with a scoff, *knowing what the Zoltha-kind are like.*

He adjusted slightly, finding another equally-uncomfortable ridge to sit on, and looked over to the wall on his right. A single wooden staircase ascended up the outer wall, with the thick panels of the storehouse floor jutting out just above it. At the apex of the stairs, the folded doors of a locked hatch lay ominously closed, with the shadows of guards passing just beyond.

No way of escaping, Xafiri acknowledged soberly. *No way of getting out of here, except on the long walk to my execution.* He sighed with exhaustion.

And that's something that seems all but inevitable now.

The echoes of Temusceh's heinous laugh still rang in his ears, after he had been apprehended by the guards and dragged off to the cellar. The huge *Hajiin* had been overzealous with the result of his efforts, and had tried to haggle with the Verlunz over a reward of some kind.

But the Verlunz had not shared Temusceh's zeal at calling out Xafiri for his sins: their face had been grave and stony, like an old soldier looking upon an infected wound. Xafiri recalled how they had turned and paced away from the scene in silence, disregarding the great *Hajiin* altogether. The sky had darkened over their head as they had departed, and a chill wind seemed to cross the square around them like the ebbs of a coming storm.

There is nothing to celebrate, and the Verlunz knows that... even if Temusceh doesn't. Xafiri clenched his fist, recalling the fat man's glee at his arrest. *Catching me, and revealing my ruse, does nothing to change the fact that there's a very dangerous enemy coming from the south as we speak, intent on our destruction. Whatever sin I've committed doesn't change that.*

And we're still running out of time.

Looking up to the locked hatch in the apex of the roof, Xafiri considered going up there and trying to prize the latch open, making his desperate escape. He was a dead man anyway: if his escape failed, that inevitability would only be brought closer. Nothing would really change.

Or maybe he could convince the guards to listen to him. Maybe they would let him out under armed guard, trailing at his heels, so he could actually go and see his mother and tell her how much danger she was in—

Xafiri laughed, shaking his head. *Who in the gods am I kidding? The guards don't care about me or my mother. I'm a full outcast now – a* mantugo *in blood and name. They wouldn't listen to me even if I tried.*

His head dropped slowly, inch-by-inch, until he was staring down at the bare rock beneath his feet.

I have no hope anymore…

He wasn't sure how much time had passed before the cellar hatch finally reopened, and light spilled out over the grey stone like reams of woven silk. Time was endless, down in the subterranean abode, and without the pulse of his heart or the rhythmic intake of breath, Xafiri almost forgot he was still alive. Everything was still and everything was silent, and the shadows crawled along the rocky edges of the room like prying fingers in the night.

So when the hatch did finally fly open, and dull sunlight spilled down into the cellar, Xafiri lifted a hand over his eyes and winced at the pains in his head, longing for the darkness again where he could be numb and reserved in his sorrow.

Squinting up, he spied three sets of boots at the top of the wooden staircase, descending slowly into the recesses below. The two boots at the back were coated in chitin plates, and were quite obviously those of the guards' who had apprehended him before – but the third pair, at the forefront of their trio, were different. They were simple leather slip-ons with a cord-like strap, which made almost no noise as they descended the rickety steps. They were familiar – concordant, almost – and if his memory hadn't failed him, they were also almost exactly like the ones his mother—

"*Ma?*" Xafiri spluttered, lifting to a stand with an aggravated *click* of his knees. "Is that… *you?*"

The person in question descended the stairway slowly, turning their head as they dipped below the ceiling to—

"Xafi!" his mother gasped, charging down the last few steps and hurtling over to him at speed. They locked arms and embraced tightly, as warm tears spilled over Xafiri's cheeks and splattered against the auburn folds of her robes. She smelt of cinnamon and dashka flowers.

She smelt just like home.

"Thank gods you safe," his mother said, stifling her tears. "Thank gods... praise them..."

"I am okay, ma... I am all okay." He held her closer for a moment, before she drifted back and held his shoulders, frowning at him intensely all of a sudden.

"What happen to your face? Are you hurt?" she inquired, lifting a hand toward his smudgy eye—

Xafiri knocked it aside and forced a smile. "Is nothing, ma. Is nothing. No pain. No problem."

"Okay... okay, good." She bristled for a moment, and looked behind her to spy the guards lurking at the base of the stairs. Their earless, orb-like heads were unreadable in the shadows of the cellar. "The guards... they say... tell me that you are bad... you are in trouble. Is it true? What happened? Where did you go?"

"I would not believe everything they say, ma," he evaded. "Not always true."

"But what happened? You were gone overnight."

"I was busy, was all."

"With what?"

"I don't really—"

"*Xafi*." She levelled her gaze with him. "Just say... tell truth. Please."

In response, Xafiri went to open his mouth – to espouse another condescending remark about how she '*didn't need to worry*' – but, as he looked deeper into the wells of his mother's eyes, he stopped himself and sighed. There was no use lying to her, or evading the questions. There was no use hiding from what had really happened. He had the opportunity to tell her the truth, there and then, and he knew it would be daft to not take that chance.

Otherwise others will tell the story for me, he thought with a grimace, *and theirs will be far more flexible with the truth.*

He peeled her hands off of his shoulders, and held them in his own. "I went outside," he said, looking to the floor. "I went... outside the walls. With the *feduzak*. I... followed them."

"You went with them!" his mother spluttered in disbelief. "You went out... into danger! But, why? How... how did you..." Her words tapered off slowly, and her lips grew still—

And her eyes yawned open, as she looked closer at the black smudge under his eyelid, and her jaw fell aghast like a trapdoor.

"Xafi... did you—?"

"I'm sorry, ma," Xafiri muttered in reply, flinching at the disappointment in her tone. "I'm sorry—"

"Why you do something so stupid! Don't you know how bad is for tribe? For you? Why did you do!"

"I understand, yes... I understand. But it was important—"

"*Import-tant?* Why was it import-tant? Doing something so *stupid!*" An anger flashed across her wrinkled face, alongside the shine of fresh tears. "Put yourself in danger! Went out with them... in the dark... could have died! Dangerous, Xafi, dangerous!"

"I knew the risks, ma," he said levelly, trying to hide the emotion that boiled over in his stomach. "I knew what I was doing. I knew it was *wrong*... and I know what the consequences are now. But you don't get it, because I *had* to—"

"Had to what?" she snapped. "Had to what? I was scared for you. For my Xafi... I was scared. Worried you were okay. And then I find you... here, in *gugol*... locked away like dead-thing, because you went *out the walls!*"

He bit his tongue. "Ma, you don't understand—"

"Under...stand what, Xafi? What I not know?"

"Please, ma—"

"How could you do it!"

"Because I——"

"Xafi, why——"

"Because I had no other choice!" he bellowed, snarling with his teeth and fists clenched. Torrents of vitriol lashed at him like whips as his heart thundered in his chest.

Opposite him, his mother shied away like a reprimanded pup; the guards behind her tightened their grip on their spears, taking a step forward.

Watching them, Xafiri sensed the emotion waver within him, relenting against their fear and demanding to be brought down once more.

Only this time, he didn't bury it.

Instead, he set it free.

"I had no other choice… because I was fucking *scared,* ma," Xafiri said thunderously, releasing his fists. "I had no choice… because we had *no* idea what was out there, and *no* idea what we were up against. The Ritualists didn't know; the gods, in all their splendour, couldn't give us any answers. We were *alone,* up against something we have never seen in this world before… and I didn't know what to do. I didn't even know if we'd *survive…*"

He gulped, grinding his teeth together. "So I made my choice: I went out there and I followed the *feduzak,* and I found my answers. I found *our* answers, which may just help this village survive what's coming for us. My sacrifice in that outcome, means nothing… I don't *care* what they do to me now, or the fate I now face. Because it was never really a choice for me in the end. That was a reality that I had to face long ago, off the back of another choice that I had no say in. A choice made at the hands of the *Zoltha* and their Educators, forcing my hand and driving a rift between us all. Making me an outcast… making me a *disappointment* to all of you… leading to that fateful, terrible day when *pa* looked me dead in the eyes and… and…"

And never came back.

The knot unravelled, like a serpent in his soul. The dam breached, and a flood claimed his chest that threatened to topple him over. It all came spilling out – his father's face, over and over again – until it seemed to hang in the shadows of the room like statues. Looming there, watching him, his voice in Xafiri's head.

'*You no son of mine…*'

'*You no Tarrazi…*'

'*You* mantugo…'

'Zoltha, *just like all the rest of them…*'

Xafiri reached out and clasped his mother's hands again, holding them tight in his own with tears streaming down his cheeks in silence.

"I made a choice, long ago, that I didn't even know I was making… and I lost the only man in my life that I thought I could trust to be there for me," he said. "So when I saw the *zazkan* in the south, and I saw the *Feduzak* depart… there was no choice to it in the end. I *had* to go, and I *had* to be certain of what we were up against…" He sobbed, and looked deep into the pools of his mother's eyes. "Because I couldn't bear the thought of losing you as well… and making a choice that could've cost you your *life*…"

He lowered his head and wept quietly, letting the flood wash over him with no means of letting go. His hands trembled at his sides. His pulse was but a tiny tapping in his chest. His mother's hands felt so delicate in his own.

Until, after several numb moments that seemed to stretch on for an eternity, Xafiri felt a hand against the underside of his chin, lifting his head up from the floor.

He looked up and saw the beautiful black orbs of his mother's eyes peering back at him, smiling in a soft way that reminded him of flowers. Her pristine face and the innocence of age curling at the corners of her mouth. She didn't speak for some time – stroking his jaw with the end of her thumb with the tenderness of a baby– until her lips finally parted.

"I love you, Xafi," she said with a smile. "You're no *mantugo* to me."

She pulled him in close, placing his head on her shoulder, and brushed his hair with her thin fingers like the bristles of a comb.

Xafiri wrapped his arms around her, sobbing, and pressed his palms flat against her back. His heartbeat rustled to life, matching her pulse; the voice in his head grew quieter and quieter.

His lungs seemed to expand with each breath he took. His numb legs, quivering beneath him, found some foundation once more.

"I love you too, ma..." he muttered, tight in her arms.

I love you always...

They parted again after several moments, looking at each other in a way only a mother and child could. Xafiri sucked in deep breaths and tried to smile; his mother, rubbing his shoulders, nodded gently, agreeing with whatever unsaid sentiments passed between them. The tension waned in the air; everything seemed a touch brighter for a moment.

When her head turned suddenly to the open hatch above them, where the two guards were also staring.

Xafiri, in something of a daze, took a while to register what it was that had caught their attention — but as sensation prickled in his ears, realisation followed, and the darkness swelled in the corners of the room.

Stomping boots above... and running feet.

A shiver ran through his heart.

Something's happened—

A thunder-like *boom* sounded from somewhere in the village above, and shook the spacious cellar around them. Dust lifted from the tiny alcoves in the ceiling; a few loose stones dislodged from the walls. The guards tensed up and their eyes bulged, looking between the open hatch and the prisoner they were supposed to be keeping an eye on.

His mother turned back to him and stared, reaching out for support as another tremor rocked the cellar.

"Xafi, is it—"

"We have to leave, *now*," he commanded, as the guards opposite grappled their spears and launched up the staircase. "We have to go..."

Another shudder rocked the ground at their feet.

Xafiri held his breath.

It's here.

†

Chapter 23

Storm-Clouds

The forest lay in darkness, at the base of the small hill leading south from the village gates. The broken stone path meandered down from the high walls, honeycombed by shadows, before slipping between the gnarled tree roots and disappearing altogether. The trees above offered nothing but silence; their rustling branches diced together in the wind. Tiny swarms of purple flies buzzed through the air like clouds of sparks. Thunder whispered over the distant mountains to the west.

They didn't even see it coming.

The guards – a dozen of them, pressed up against the gates of the place they called their home – tensed their hands about their spears and jumped at the whispers in the dark. The murmurs in the trees; the lilting tones of the wind. A palpable tension lay in the air, which pulled up their backs and flinched across their shoulders. Waiting for something. Waiting for nothing.

An enemy was approaching from the south.

A crack of thunder bellowed out from somewhere above the village, startling the guards. Ironclad clouds rolled off the mountains and blocked out the sun, bringing a dull misery to the landscape below. Shadows swelled between the branches all around them, undulating like great black fish, surfacing at the scent of desperation and exalting with the taste of fear.

Rain splashed over the guards' hands suddenly, fizzing through the air like static. The ground at their feet absorbed the rain greedily, churning the clay mud. Energy swam through the air around them, filling their lungs with an icy coldness that stirred the bile in their stomachs.

Looking out to the trees below them, as the unnatural rain grew suddenly heavier, the guards struggled to pick apart the shadows beyond the haze——

As death stepped out from the tree-line like a ghost, setting his sights on the gates above.

The guards saw him manifest there beyond the deluge: a pale figure of silver and black, pulsing like a heart between the trees. Coated in rainwater; coated in spirals and intricate marks. They were at their spears in moments, blinking through the storm. The sentinels above the gate bellowed a warning, as another ripple of thunder boomed overhead.

The figure did nothing, and gave nothing in response. He stood there, with floods of rain coating his exposed torso, and stared up at the gates expectantly. The sky brightened and darkened overhead in waves, illuminating the rain like tiny arrowheads.

The guards watched on, pulling in closer to the gates – watching as a flash of blue appeared in the figure's hand suddenly, forming an orb that hissed like ignition powder. It flushed and spat and glowed as bright as the sun, consuming all things in the clearing beyond.

The shouts that followed were never heard; the sentinels' cries above them were lost in the blasts of thunder.

As Markus lifted his blackened arm, summoning the wrath of the storm, and the lightning shot from his hand in a single stream, exploding across the gates behind——

The blast detonated in a shimmering orb of light and electrical fuzz, expanding outwards as the gates blew open on its hinges.

The guards scattered; their disoriented bodies were thrown out into the trees.

Rain hissed like fat on a fire; wood shrapnel exploded outwards and crippled the surrounding walls.

The struts that held the sentinel platform aloft snapped in several places, and the guards' terrified screams were the last sound to be heard before lightning cracked the sky above and the platform toppled sidelong into the mud.

Markus let the rain wash over his body, bathing in the steam that rose steadily from his arm as the platform collapsed ahead of him. The grey and black clouds overhead tossed and turned in their rage, swamping the distant mountains in a dying golden glow. Shadows crept through the corners of his vision, lurking like ghoulish fingers.

Out in the shadows of the beyond, a wolf began to howl.

Wasting no time, Markus ascended the stone path to the remains of the village gates and surveyed the carnage that had ensued. The guards that had been caught by the initial blast lay unconscious in the dirt nearby, straddled across the roots of the trees in awkward, misshapen piles. Smoke rose from the impact zone ahead, where a small crater had formed and toppled part of the surrounding wall. The rain had already started filling it like a reservoir, and the stone path at his feet was laced with tiny rivers that tickled out into the forest beyond. There were a number of voices somewhere ahead, too: the commands of authoritative figures, merged with the screams of the hapless villagers. Reacting to the sudden explosion that had rocked the walls of their home, no doubt.

And the perpetrator who now stepped past the remains, entering into the village-proper.

Markus assessed the world around him through a haze of smoke and rainwater, deciphering the shapes and sounds with the crater now at his back. There were domed houses to either side, like those he had seen in the village to the south; there were cobbled streets, and many paths leading off them like a rabbit's warren; there were villagers in coloured garbs, fleeing the scene with horror on their lips and prayers beaten back by the storm.

Embracing the chaos, Markus inhaled lengthily and looked up to the sky, watching the lightning crack and fizz as another wave of thunder boomed. The rain had altered the landscape completely: what had once been dusted, dry earth now lay in thick layers of mud, which tore the street out from under his feet and churned the stones from their sockets. The air was lighter; his skin crawled as icy wind diced up his back. No sound could penetrate his ears beyond the driving maelstrom above.

And this is but the beginning, Markus mused.

Let the storm come.

Looking left, he saw the collapsed platform sprawled out over the mud in several pieces, its struts like mangled limbs thrashing out against the dirt. It had been well-constructed, Markus acknowledged, and had been held together strong interlocking pieces – but he also knew that even that was no match for the full force of a lightning blast.

Broken apart… never to be whole again. Markus clicked his tongue against the roof of his mouth. In an absent part of his mind, he wondered whether either of the sentinels had survived the fall from the platform, or whether they had suffered some grievous injury from which they would never recover—

When an arm emerged from behind one of the collapsed panels, followed by a sharp intake of breath.

Markus raised an eyebrow and tilted his head.

Resilient types, these Tarrazi.

He paced towards the collapsed platform, gliding through the rain like a wraith with his ragged hair plastered to his scalp. The vomiting storm overhead muted the squelching of his boots, and the tap-tap of tiny droplets against his chitin armour. But as he drew closer to the wreckage, the panicked sound of the sentinel's breathing prickled in his ears alongside them, rising to a crescendo as he drew suddenly closer.

Closing the man down, Markus watched the sentinel flip onto their back and scream, the black pools of their eyes goggling out their head like a lizard.

Markus lifted his hand, settling down onto one knee next to them, and shook his head.

"I'm not gonna hurt you," he said slowly.

The sentinel – despite their best reservations – seemed to catch his meaning, as they stopped screaming and stared out at him with delicate trembles in their hands. They looked immensely pale in the low light – and, despite there being no sign of blood or exposed wounds over their body, Markus couldn't help but notice how their knee buckled at an awkward angle.

Broken their leg, he thought. *Was probably hoping to crawl away and see out the attack from a hiding place. Wise move.*

Terrible execution, though.

They muttered something to him in Tarrazi – some half-garbled sentiment addled by the shock of the blast – before a sad whimper escaped their lips and more rain surged down from the clouds above. Markus paid them no attention, picking away at his memory to try and locate the word he was looking for.

"Where is... *Ver-loons?*" he spluttered, rolling his tongue like a slippery leech.

The sentinel flinched as he spoke – some perverse recognition crossing their gaze – and their mouth drew together in a thin line. They didn't bother with a verbal response: instead, they lifted their arm out to one side, and pointed off down the road heading north.

Markus bowed his head slowly. "Thank you."

The sentinel blinked in reply.

Looking down the road to where they had pointed, Markus spied the shapes of other Tarrazi warriors approaching, manifesting in the gloom with their bronze armour and cutting knives. They hadn't spotted him yet, and were spending most of their time scouring the nearest houses to try and evacuate civilians, but he knew it was only a matter of time.

Turning back to the sentinel, Markus saw the fear in their eyes and let out a consolatory breath. Reaching out toward them with an outstretched hand, the sentinel flinched as Markus placed a finger on their forehead—

And they slumped down into the mud, as an electrical pulse knocked them unconscious.

Rest easy, innocent one, Markus proclaimed. *My quarrel is not with you. My goals are far greater than the life of one Tarrazi.*

He looked back down the street, hearing the warrior's cry as they finally spotted him. A smirk curled over his face.

One, or a dozen.

He rose to his full height and inhaled until his chest felt like bursting, as rapturous thunder and callous lightning boomed and flickered across the sky overhead. His skin crawled with energy; the light fizzed up and down his arm like the legs of a millipede. The well in his soul drew its power once more.

The warriors charged forward with weapons raised.

Markus lifted his hand and fired.

†

Chapter 24

Forsaken Gods

Xafiri stepped out the storehouse door and felt the surging rains sting his scalp, looking up into the storm-clouds above as they swirled and convulsed like a vortex.

What the hell is going on...

"Xafi!" his mother cried behind him, pressing against the door-frame and gasping at the world outside. Her voice was little more than a murmur beneath the howling winds. "What... what happening!"

"I don't know, ma!" he replied, lifting a hand to his face as a strike of thunder tore through the clouds above them. "Whatever it is... is not good."

"What we do, Xafi? Are we... is there danger?"

Danger doesn't even begin to cover it, came a thought that never left his mouth, as he furrowed his brow and pursed his lips. "We must get to safety. If we find Verlunz... we have protection. Verlunz will protect us. We go to the square... pray all is okay."

"Yes... yes, pray. Pray to gods. Pray..." His mother whispered a few words under her breath and put two fingers to her ear.

Xafiri scowled and shook his head.

Good luck getting anything from Them, ma. They don't care. We're alone out here. The gods have forsaken our people this day...

And Tazûl has come for us all.

Another crack of thunder split the grey clouds overhead; Xafiri turned left and paced along the storehouse wall, wiping the sheen of water from his eyes. His mother trailed close behind, flinching at the angry sky and the occasional *boom* of lightning somewhere off to their far left.

It was an unnatural noise, Xafiri found: even above the rancour of the storm, there was something hollow about the blasts as they rang out in his ears. Something unwieldy and rotten. They were too close – too low – too violent to be anything natural. Zesmu, God of the Wilds, would never have willed it; the storm that raged all around them, equally, could not have been Her doing. Something had broken the back of the world – something foul and furious – and they, the Tarrazi of the Valatuk Hills, were the ones witnessing it.

Xafiri shivered and peered around the nearest house.

Let's hope this will not be our undoing.

Scanning over the houses to the south – picking apart the rooftops in the grey gloom – Xafiri saw chaotic flashes of blue in the distance, accompanied by a delayed rumble that rippled over the puddles at his feet. They were like *Zoltha* cannons, echoing out through the streets in sudden bursts, accompanied by the bellows of Tarrazi warriors.

And the screams of their dying kin.

Xafiri held out his hand, holding his mother behind him as another blast shook the houses around them.

"What? What that sound?" she inquired, peering past him with an inquisitive fear.

"The enemy… the *Yabusto*," Xafiri replied, as a stab of cold air lanced up his back. "They are in village… the noise, is *zazkan*."

"Where? How… far?"

He lifted a finger off to the south-west, where another flash of blue eclipsed the domed dwellings. High above, through the torrential rain, the sky swirled and pulsed like tangling eels.

"Over there, on far side," he explained. "Still some distance."

"It not found the Verlunz yet?"

"I do not think so, no. Verlunz safe." *For now.*

"We should go there. Find them. Gods will help us."

Xafiri drew his tongue across his front teeth. "We will go there, ma, yes. We will go and see the gods…"

He turned to the nearest path and grimaced.

And hope that our prayers are reckoned with…

As he set off down the next side-street, the clouds seemed to swell and bellow unnaturally overhead, like a bloated stomach on the verge of being sick. The rain lashed down harder again, streaming off the walls of the domed houses around him, churning with the thick mud underfoot until it was almost impossible to walk. His boots were filled with a thick, gunky ooze; his clothes lay plastered across his skin, making every step an arduous task. Cold lashings of air whipped up over his face and blinded him momentarily; he wiped them away with an absent hand and he pressed on deeper into the storm.

This is fordüra, he thought, thinking of the decrepit cess-pits where all forsaken Tarrazi were said to go. *This is the terror that wipes us from this world. Nature shall revolt against us, and rip the land up from beneath our feet. We will be hopeless, in the end, as the gods pass Their judgement, and we are handed our sentence to death. Nothing shall survive Their reckoning: be it in the fire that burns deep in the earth…*

He gazed up; a strike of lightning crackled across the clouds.

…or the thunder that bellows out in the sky.

"The weather's got bad, Xafi!" his mother shouted at his back. Her hand clamped tight around his shoulder. "We really… we really need to—"

A blast of thunder, loud enough to ring in Xafiri's ears, quaked over the skyline above their heads.

A shudder ripped through him, as his mother suppressed a scream at his back—

Light flooded his eyes suddenly, consuming all sensation as a blast of lightning surged down across the earth in front of them and detonated—

Xafiri shielded his eyes; the shockwave threw him backwards, dragging him off of his feet—

He slapped down hard against the earth—

Grass lined his gums; wave of mud and grit splashed over his skin, coating him like a death-mask—

A scream echoed out behind him—

The air left his lungs in a sad wheeze, like a dying man's breath on the cusp of oblivion. The sky swam overhead, as if in its death-throws—

And had he the care to look, he could almost call it an omen.

Lifting his head again slowly – spitting the sod from his mouth in thick, viscous clumps – Xafiri blinked a few times and re-engaged with the world around him. His head spun; his stomach quivered and lurched like a landed fish. Water continued to flood from the clouds in an unrelenting wall, stinging his eyes and beating him down like thousands of tiny fists. The shadows swam all around, with the hollow light of the sun just visible over the distant mountains to the west. The furrows of mud and the pools of rainwater dissected the earth like trenches, weaving their way around the lofty clay domes until finally reaching—

"Ma!" Xafiri gasped, launching up from the mud toward the still form of his mother, sprawled out in the dirt nearby like the snapped bough of a tree. She didn't move at the sound of his voice; she didn't stir, as he stumbled shakily over to her and dropped down into the mud at her side.

"Ma!" Xafiri bellowed, feeling his heart in his throat.

Oh gods please no…

"Ma! *Ma!*"

A tear laced down his cheek; he placed a hand on her shoulder—

When she rolled out of the mud and coughed suddenly, looking up at him with bleary eyes and residue coating her lips.

"Hi Xafi, I… I'm okay," she muttered, reaching an arm over to clutch at her side.

"Oh gods… oh thank the gods…" Xafiri said softly, pulling her up from the saturated ground and wrapping his arms around her shoulders. "Thank the gods…"

Pulling away, his mother managed a weak smile and stroked his wrinkled face. "I thought you would get no answer, if you try to do talking to gods?" she said facetiously, smirking with a glow like stardust.

Xafiri smiled back, stifling a relieved laugh. "You're alive, ma…" – he touched two fingers to his head – "and that's all the answer I need."

They shared a few moments in silence, as the rain eased off slightly around them and the sky seemed to brighten overhead. It was fleeting, and fragile, but held them close like a delicate embrace. A moment shared between them, where fear no longer held sway.

But before long, the thunder bellowed out overhead, and the flash and crackle of blue lightning echoed off to their left once more. It was much closer this time around: perhaps only a few streets away. Meaning the Deathbringer was still very much alive.

And they're approaching the village square.

"What we do now?" his mother asked, flinching at the noise. "The *Yabusto*… it gets close. What we do?"

Xafiri sensed the static in the air around him, fizzing over the raindrops as they fell from the sky. A sigh escaped his lips. "I don't know, ma," he said quietly. "The *Yabusto* is getting close to the square – they'll be here, soon, if something isn't done. The Verlunz is in danger, and… and I'm the only one who knows what we're facing. The only one who can help the Verlunz survive. Because if the Deathbringer gets to them, then… then I don't know what will happen. Tazûl will end them: He'll clamp down with His jaws and tear them limb from limb. He'll do it, just like out on the hunt when we release the… the…"

Xafiri stopped himself, his eyes nearly popping from his sockets. A thought overcame his mind, circumnavigating all of his fear.

The Hounds.

He blinked once; his mouth fell agape.

Of course…

His mother held his arm. "What, Xafi? What is it?"

"Get yourself to the edge of the village, and find a place to hide," Xafiri commanded. "I'll head toward the *gat'unsk* where the Verlunz is, before the *Yabusto* gets there."

"But Xafi, the danger! What will you do?"

His mother's eyes spoke of a thousand tiny fears that she could never fully relay to him.

And in that moment, taking one look at her, Xafiri nodded his head, answering every one of them in a way that only a child ever could.

"I have a plan, ma… trust me," he replied, looking off to the sky to the west. "I'll head for the *gat'unsk* as fast as I can…"

And I'll let the Hounds do the rest.

†

Chapter 25

Mercy

ercy, like death, was a fickle mistress, and never strayed far from one's mind. To some, it was borne an illusion: the idea that any one individual could hold such sway over another's life, and choose to spare them, was ridiculous. Mercy was therefore fanciful, whereas death was altogether more meticulous. The path to killing a man was shorter, and far simpler; the path to killing was plain, and violent. Wrath was the great deceiver, and also man's best friend. It came for all, eventually, if one waited long enough.

So when Markus looked down into the Tarrazi's hollow eyes, as they lay sprawled out in the mud with a burn mark over their right shoulder, he saw there the fine line between the two: the balance between mercy and death, held precariously in his hand. Fizzing there; rupturing over his skin in beautiful blue light. The clouds rumbled overhead, and lashings of rain whipped up over his face, but that didn't seem to matter to Markus when lost in the eyes of his victim. He saw a million tiny thoughts flicker beneath the black orbs of their gaze, and in return a million tiny battles raged in his mind in response to them. Morality. Truth. Life. Sacrifice. Sanctity. Mercy.

Death.

Markus blinked once, washing the rainwater from his eyes, and felt the energy twinge between his fingertips. The Tarrazi beneath him, half-blinded by the storm, clenched the sodden earth tightly at their sides.

Mercy and death, Markus thought, *death… and mercy.*

To death a deed is done…

He ground his jaw; he curled his fist up.

But I'm done making deeds.

A single punch, flying through the air like a cannon, connected with the Tarrazi's forehead.

Their head snapped backwards; their entire body shook.

They fell unconscious almost immediately, sprawled out in the mud looking off to the stars.

Markus lifted to a stand and pulled the strands of wet hair from his face, pulling his finger through the salty coils of his beard. The pulses in his hand seemed to rebel against him – against his answer of mercy – as tiny shockwaves twinged over his scalp and zapped across his chest. The black, swirling marks on his skin seemed to spin and morph through each other like a pool of eels; lowering his hand to his side, Markus dug his fingers into his palm and dispelled the power in an instant, reprimanding the stubbornness that the energy seemed to exude.

This is no time for insubordination, he mused, inhaling the cold air that prickled through his lungs. *This is the time to find balance, and chart a path ahead. I am here for answers, above all else.*

And a means of getting what I want at the end——

"Markusss…"

He jolted, almost like he'd been shot with an arrow. The rain seemed to fade momentarily around him, as a wave of numbness swept through his mind and dispersed again seconds later.

You're still here? he puzzled, looking up into the maelstrom above. *But I thought you'd be gone… I thought what happened at the lake was the end——*

"Markusss…"

"What do you want from me?" he exclaimed aloud, panic coursing through his veins.

A silence was all that answered him, ticking by for several moments.

Then, the voice in his head seemed to smile.

"On... your left..."

Markus blinked; he frowned and turned—

Lifting his hand suddenly, he jabbed his fingers into a Tarrazi's throat looming next to his ear, just before they could rally the courage to plunge a knife up into his chest.

The Tarrazi coughed and spluttered, their pale skin bulging as they struggled for air, stumbling back and reaching up for their neck—

A squelch of mud to Markus' rear, and he pivoted on the spot with a sharp intake of breath, narrowly avoiding a spear-point as it thrust into the space where his stomach had been. The barbed ends of the spear-head glistened in the half light of the storm beneath him; Markus gritted his teeth and swung through with a meaty fist, using his instincts to assess where the enemy was—

His punch connected at the dead-centre of the Tarrazi's bare chest, throwing them backwards with a shockwave as a fuzz of energy detonated from his hand. Markus felt bone crack beneath his knuckles; the Tarrazi wheezed as they fell, slapping down against the mud like a landed fish.

The fuckers snuck up on me, Markus considered with a growl.

The gods bellowed and laughed high above.

Turning back to the other fighter, Markus lurched backwards suddenly as their knife speared up towards his head, the glistening point like a needle against the marbled sky. The Tarrazi behind it grinned arrogantly, a touch of malice in their eyes.

Sensing an opening when the knife recoiled, Markus extended a finger and a tiny burst of lightning shot from the tip, arcing along the knife-blade and up into the Tarrazi's hand—

Shocking them; the Tarrazi dropped the knife with a yelp and shook their hand, assessing for damage to their skin—

As Markus stepped in and punched them in the guts, with a burst of raw energy that crippled the Tarrazi's legs and sent them sprawling over the mud.

A bellow of thunder rippled across the sky overhead; anguish lambasted the village around him, reverberating from the domes of their ramshackle houses.

Looking down to the drooling body at his feet, Markus admired his merciful handiwork, and turned to face the other fighter—

When an agony tore across his side suddenly, forcing a growl of anger through his lips.

Following the pain, he looked down and saw the barbed spear-head dragging across his flank, shredding his flesh as it recoiled with his blood dripping from its end.

Snarling, Markus rounded on the perpetrator, and found there the other fighter who he had sent to the mud moments before. They had returned to a stand, swaying in the deluge like a lofty tree, with a devilish – but slightly terrified – grin lining their face.

"You were meant to stay down for longer," Markus muttered, flexing his hand. "No matter though, I suppose…"

I'll just have to make sure of it this time.

The spear-man panicked and lunged at him again, their adrenaline completely taking over—

Markus let the spear-haft glide past him, before wrapping his arm around it and grappling it tightly, breaking it from the Tarrazi's hand.

The fighter, now dispossessed, looked at him dumbly—

As he swung across his body and caught the fighter across the jaw, impacting like a ballista and splitting their mouth in two.

With a string of spit and bloody gore launching from their lips, the Tarrazi toppled sideways and lay wheezing in the mud, the energy entirely lost in their wayward limbs.

Victorious, Markus threw the spear down next to them and scoffed at the two unconscious fighters.

So close you were to victory, Markus thought with a callous grin.

And yet, in the end, you are still so very far.

Turning back to the street ahead – with the scourging rain forming a wall at his periphery — Markus took in the dour-looking domes along the outskirts of the village, and sensed the voice resurface in his mind.

Like the fine strings of a harp, it came to him in repetitions, gliding effortlessly forward through the empty vacuum of his skull. For a moment, he entertained it; in the next, he longed to blot it out. But before either eventuality could take hold, his eyes became affixed to something in the street ahead of him, and the breath flooded out of his lungs.

"*Markus*," the voice echoed through his mind.

"I see you…" he replied.

Looking her in the eyes.

Golden hair, shimmering like sunlight. Pale skin. Ruby lips. Eyes as bright as diamonds, gleaming in their sockets. Steel armour. A sword at her side. Delicate hands that twitched like piano keys.

I see you… by the gods…

The rain seemed to relinquish its furore for a moment, as the ground cleared between them. Markus found himself fixed to the spot, unable to move — unable to think, even, as the figure before him seemed to glow and radiate with glorious light, and tides of numbness swept over him again and again.

"*Markus,*" it said again, and its lips visibly moved with the words.

Expression filled its face; a humanity resonated in Markus' mind that warmed his very soul.

"I see you, I… I *see you…*"

No pain alighted in his body. No thought elapsed in his head. The energy — the power that so feverishly demanded his attention — simply ceased to be. He stood there, in the pattering rain and the churning mud, looking upon a being a light and splendour, the likes of which he could hardly comprehend and could never truly know.

"*Markus,*" it said a third time, softly echoing in his ears.

And, like the threads of a spider's-web caught in the high winds of autumn, Markus latched on to a single word in his mind, and let his lips part. It was so fleeting in its embrace; so unassuming in its passage. A single word, glistening like stardust.

"*Cavara…*"

Something warm enveloped his soul as he spoke, dispelling through his veins in tiny ripples until slowly drawing still again.

The figure before him seemed to glow suddenly brighter, consumed in a blinding light before fading away in a shower of dust.

Light spilled out through a crack in the storm high above, and the road before him lay coated in reams of gold.

Markus, feeling suddenly overwhelmed, let a solitary tear spill down his cheek and nestle in the curls of his beard, letting out a long breath in the shadows of his sorrow.

So I was right… you are real, he thought, sensing the numbness flutter through his mind. *And you have a name, too.*

How about that.

He looked out over the sunlit street ahead, and out to the village square just beyond, following the traces of the voice through his mind as it jousted with the power for his interest. Following it, like one follows the bends of the river out to sea, his wandering eyes drifted weakly into the distance…

…where he saw the golden glow of a small figure slip between two houses, and disappear down a slope at the far side of the village square.

Markus stepped forward, the energy in his hand snapping like broken strings. The rain overhead returned, as the crack of light in the sky sealed over and the thunderous clouds bellowed their commands. A weight shifted inside of him, as subconscious memories flooded back through his mind.

Who was that? he pondered, craning his neck in the hopes of seeing them again. *They glowed like that woman did. Like… like Cavara did.*

The numbness in his mind alighted at the mention of her name, dancing through his head joyously.

Is that person someone I should know? Is it someone that she *knows?* He placed a hand against his cheek, and let the electrical pulses fuzz against his skin. *But I don't know any Tarrazi——*

A memory breached suddenly; he gasped.

Except I do: the face I saw in the lake, Markus recalled. *That was a Tarrazi boy... they had no ears, and they had marks under their eye. I thought it was something to do with my future, because of how I didn't recognise them.*

But perhaps this whole escapade into these hills — and my time spent travelling from village to village — led me to that lake to see that vision...

...and then onto this village, to find this boy.

His gaze drifted back to the village square ahead, where he swore he saw a golden glow just over the crest at the far side.

Maybe he's the one with the answers I seek.

Pulling his legs from the mud, Markus flexed his fingers and paced off toward the village square.

Maybe he can get me to Azbann...

†

Chapter 26

Nobody's Hero

It's here... it watches me.

Xafiri drew his hand along the curved wall of the nearest dome, tracing his fingers over the grooves in the clay like the furrows of a ploughed field. He kept low to the ground, almost in a stoop, padding over the sodden earth as delicately as he could. The mud squelched and oozed underfoot, where pools of rainwater glistened like the scales of a fish. To his left, the flat stone slabs that formed the village square were slick and shiny: tiny islands with rivers running between them, reflecting the storm high above. A storm that continued to churn in on itself unnaturally, insatiable in its appetite for chaos, hailing torrents of rain down on the poor Tarrazi beneath who just prayed they'd get through the ordeal alive.

Pulling a shallow breath into his body, Xafiri shivered at the chill winds sweeping over the village square and clenched his jaw. The rain made every movement an arduous task – and, with a certain amount of urgency needed in the face of such significant danger, it was enough to make Xafiri scream.

Time's running out, he acknowledged, darting to the next house over, keeping clear of the open square to his left. *There's only one chance at stopping this thing, and I'm the only one who knows how to do it. I just have to pray it'll be enough to fight them off.*

And pray I'm not too late already.

Staring through the grey smog that embodied the landscape beneath the storm, Xafiri spied the interlocking trunks and polished clay walls of the *gat'unsk* just ahead, manifesting in the gloom. In the low light, it looked like the spine of some great sand-serpent: gnarled trees locked together with thick walls of clay, painted with depictions of ancient Tarrazi stories and the spiralling patterns of *zaz-gûla*. Massive wooden plates lined the lower edges, coloured using the dyes of local flowers, weaving their way up the sides of the building to the pointed ceiling high above.

As he approached, and the *gat'unsk* became clearer, Xafiri saw how the rain seemed to corrupt the images painted across its walls: every hollow face looked as if it were melting; every spear-point appeared to be dripping blood; the *zaz-gûla* peeled away delicately like tears. The entire structure seemed to sag under the weight of the storm, pulled down by the corrupting nature that swam through the air like a cancer. Xafiri looked upon its hallowed halls with a look of awe and despair, focusing in on one tiny image closest to him, where a man stood alone with a knife blade in his hand, fighting against—

He gasped and looked away suddenly, steadying himself against the side of the nearest dome.

Fighting against a great wolf... with half of its skull missing.
Xafiri blinked.

Tazûl...

A swamping sensation took hold in his chest suddenly, threatening to drag him to the floor. Fire alighted in the back of his head, nearly knocking him unconscious. Numbness revolved over his fingers, tracing through his joints. His skin crawled, not just from the rain, but from the sheer weight of everything around him. Of *everything,* and yet also nothing at all.

I need to stay strong, he muttered, taking a few stumbling steps forward, moving past the last house that bordered the *gat'unsk. I need to do this, to... to save people. My people.* He ambled forward, reaching out with his hands like a sightless person, looking down the slope to his right where streams of water spilled off the plateau of the village square.

I'm almost there. He managed half a smile, looking back down the path he had taken, and across to the square on his left.

I'm almost—

His eyes swelled like galls on the branches of diseased trees; his heart, beating with an anxious consistency, kicked into overdrive. A coil in his stomach unknotted, shooting bile into his throat.

Opposite him, down the street on the far side, he saw a figure of grey emerge from the shadows, with the blue flash of lightning in their hand and the rallying thunder above their head. He saw there a figure of darkness, and deceit; a figure wrought from the bowels of *hellos.*

A figure, which was also staring right at him.

"*Yabusto,*" Xafiri breathed, stumbling backwards with pallid skin and a hollowness in his heart—

Losing his footing suddenly; weightlessness rising—

Squealing, as his back foot slipped and the sky spun overhead, and he toppled down the muddy slope in a bundle of limbs and rain.

His voice – his scream – was swept up by the winds and lost in a crackle of lightning.

He slapped against the wet earth, knocking any air from his chest in an instant.

His head crashed down in a puddle of ooze, splashing up over his mouth.

Instinctively, he wedged his hands down beside him, stopping the roll down the hillside—

He skidded; the mud gave way beneath him and—

He started sliding, caught in the tributaries of water that streamed off the village square above, losing all traction in the momentum of the fall.

Shit… shit!

He dug his heels in but found no purchase. He pushed his hands deeper into the sludge at his sides, but found nothing to grab hold of.

Roots slid through his fingertips; the wriggling bodies of worms slithered in his grasp. The ground levelled out several feet ahead, coated in shadows as he hurtled towards it——

Something wedged against the end of his foot and crunched his toes together.

He screamed again, as he rolled head-over-heels and nearly snapped his knees apart.

The ground seemed to rise to meet him, as he landed heavily on his back and embedded in the mud like a footprint, his hands splayed out alongside him like a blood-sacrifice to the gods. The sky swam overhead: drab colours and swirling shapes he could hardly comprehend, blinking through the pain and exhaustion that suddenly racked his body. The rain lashed across his face, pooling in the pits of his deep, cold eyes.

His fingers plied in the mud like the legs of a spider. The mud was cool and mellow to the touch. He lay there for several moments trying to make sense of anything, like a baby that had waddled outside and realised how terrible the world really was.

Above, a rumble of thunder echoed through the clouds, followed by the blue flash of lightning.

And he sight of it snapped him back to life, trembling deep in the pits of his soul.

Xafiri rolled out of the mud and hissed at the aches in his joints, managing to get up onto one knee before his body began to rebel. The mud, slick across his back, began to slide off his body at the whim of the rainstorm. His skin cleared, and with it came an abrupt clarity of mind. He was on the north-most side of the village square, just shy of the *gat'unsk* looming high above. He was down a slope, adjacent to the home of the Verlunz, near the training fields where the Tarrazi warriors practiced their fighting forms. Looking around to get his bearings – imagining the world beyond the bellows of the storm – he deduced from there that he was——

Oh.

His eyes locked to the space ahead of him, as he lifted to a stand

and studied the scene.

Where a tired, but ultimately relieved smile graced his forlorn face.

I'm exactly where I need to be.

Ahead of him, through a clearing in the storm, he saw a canopy suspended on heavy bronze poles, planted in a huge slab of rock. The canopy itself – made only of woven cloth – sagged under the weight of the rain, billowing occasionally in the dicing winds to send a spray of water skyward.

Beneath the canopy, bolted onto the slab of rock by huge bronze hooks, stood three vast cages with thick-set barred gates. They were at least as tall as Xafiri was, and despite the powerful storm-front surging all around, they remained completely still under the battered canopy, like the caverns of a shallow cave.

But that wasn't what drew Xafiri's eye: he cared little for the technical prowess or the sturdiness of the cages.

Because within each cage, in the dark hollows behind the bars, matted muzzles and piercing white eyes stared back at him, snarling and slathering patiently with a hunger that was never satisfied.

And here we are, Xafiri acknowledged, a bubble caught in his throat that he couldn't quite swallow down.

Here lie the Hounds.

He approached slowly, keeping locked on the white eyes and the twisted, fang-like teeth. Wherever he looked, he spied their noses sensing the air – sensing him and his fear, no doubt, trying to ascertain what would come next.

One of them pressed their muzzle up to the bars and produced a low, undulating growl.

There is nothing to fear, Xafiri thought tepidly. *They are animals, just like any other. They are Kazbak Hounds, trained by Tarrazi to never hunt Tarrazi.*

As he passed beneath the cloth canopy, one of them snapped their jaws together and let out another growl.

Xafiri tensed up.

Or at least I fucking hope so.

Studying their cages again – keeping his distance from the bars – he discovered a long rod along the top edge of the cages, connected to heavy bronze hooks on each gate. As his gaze then followed the rod along to the left-most edge, he spied a coil of rope and an odd mechanism, latched onto the cage at an unusual angle.

What is that? he pondered – and, almost sensing his thoughts, the Hounds seemed to twitch excitedly in their cages, looking up to the mechanism with joy in their weird eyes.

It must be a locking thing, to keep the gates closed. The coil of rope attached to it must be what their handler uses to adjust the hooks. He shivered. *And that must also be why the Hounds are so excited.*

Because when that mechanism is released, it's time for the Hounds to go hunting.

Trying to ignore their bloodthirsty rumbles, Xafiri walked to the far end of their cages and took in a deep breath, looking between their thick metal bars and the slope to the village square just ahead. No blue light emanated from over the top edge; there was so sign of any disturbance beyond the storm. But something in him told Xafiri that the *Yabusto* was still there nonetheless, prowling about like a monster of the dark at the bidding of a greater horror.

I know you're stalking among the shadows, Tazûl, he challenged, as another roar of thunder clipped the sky. *I know this is your doing. I know you have come to harm us, and reap your ruin on the world.*

He lifted a hand to the coil of rope and laced it around his fingers; the Hounds in their cages slathered and snapped with glee.

But I defy you, Tazûl: you and your Deathbringer have no place here. The gods have chosen Their path, and we stand alone in our time of need. But even then, we shall stand against you.

Our time is here, and our time is now.

Wrenching down, he pulled the cord.

And you shall never conquer us.

The metal rod quivered; the mechanism switched. The hooks snapped open and released the shutters on the gates.

And a heartbeat later, as the metal bars swung away, three massive Hounds surged out of the darkness, charging up the slope towards the village square in a savage, merciless glee.

Xafiri looked upon the violence he had unleashed, and watched lightning scar the sky high above.

We defy you, Tazûl, he thought with a smile.

You shall not conquer us.

†

Chapter 27

Where Hounds Make Slaughter

He thought it was a dream — or a nightmare, perhaps, in the fractured recesses of his mind. Like the echoes of the past, fomenting chaos; sounds that came back to haunt him. Memories and recollections from what felt like a lifetime ago, where he still had an arm and something resembling an honest soul, surviving day by day with no guarantee of what came next. Facing up against impossible odds, against impossible foes. Their gnashing and slathering and howling, sending shivers up his spine even then.

So he thought it was a dream, stood in the square of the Tarrazi village, when the howls echoed out into the sky.

Until reality dawned in Markus' eyes suddenly…

…and the Hounds became flesh once again.

There were three of them, clambering up the slope onto the cobbled square ahead of him: big ugly creatures with matted tufts of fur and large, mangled claws. Their eyes blinked unnervingly with twisted gums and tumorous muzzles, shaking their thin coats and sensing the air with each breath. They were smaller than the ones Markus had encountered at the lake-house: with shorter legs and thinner bodies, they almost resembled large dogs rather than their wolf-like counterparts. Their ribs pushed out against the flesh on their flanks, and the wilting skin around their jaws showed signs of malnourishment. When they flashed their fangs, the soreness around

231

their gums indicated a poor diet of offcuts and scraps. They were in poor condition, it seemed, compared to the great beasts of the Kazbak Hills.

But that's the point, Markus acknowledged, stooping into a fighter's stance with his outstretched fingers flexing. *These are hunting Hounds, designed to lope through the trees at high speed and kill anything they find. Far faster and more lethal than any other Hounds I've seen.*

And much fuckin' hungrier, too.

As the thought came and went with another flash of lightning, the Hound at the centre locked eyes with him and drew a pink-ish tongue over its lips. The other two spread out slightly and did likewise, snapping their jaws together with an audible *clack* of bones.

Markus tensed the muscles along his back and noticed how the rain surged suddenly, eating away at every sensation with the lashing volleys of the storm. Vortexes of cloud circled above the square; shards of lightning shattered like glass across the skyline. A mad drumming accelerated in his head suddenly, matching the incessant rhythms of his heart.

"Markus… Markus… Markus-us-us…"

He shook his head, blinking through the rainfall as the Hounds spread out in front of him.

"Markus… time… kill…"

The voice morphed and shuddered like static — he clawed at his ear, at the sounds burrowing into his skull——

"Markus… KILL!"

Two of the Hounds launched forward, lurching over the stone with great, loping strides.

Conjuring electrical energy in his palm, Markus sent a quivering bolt toward the Hound on his left, rupturing the air in its passage and turning the rain into steam.

Skidding on the wet stone slabs underfoot, the Hound narrowly dodged the attack, scrabbling on its claws to stay upright——

As the other Hound entered into Markus' circle and lowered its head in a charge, connecting with his stomach before he had any chance to react——

The huge skull snapped across his ribs and knocked the air from his lungs, pulling his legs out from underneath him so he collapsed onto his back.

His head bounced off the floor, sending sparks of light across his vision. He used his outstretched hand to steady himself as the Hound passed above him, carried forward by its own sheer momentum——

Kicking out for purchase, the beast dug a claw into his shoulder and punctured the flesh like a sinkhole. An arc of blood spurted from the wound, and a coil of sick pulled up Markus' throat in response.

Bastard!

He hissed, anger boiling in his skull as he made to turn and gut the Hound that had just knocked him on his arse——

When a searing pain erupted across his leg, burning fire and blood all over.

Tension clamped across his shin. The all-too-familiar phantom pains echoed across the stump of his arm, conjuring memories he had buried deep. Memories of violence and broken bones.

Memories of jaws, and savagery.

Markus craned his neck and looked down the length of his body, bellowing at the sudden pain and the warm flow of blood across his foot——

To spy the other Hound with its teeth clamped on his calf, staring at him with hungry white eyes.

A moment passed between them, with howling winds and furious rain blanching the skyline above, before the Hound yanked his leg away and he skidded over the stones.

Rivets in the rock scraped across his bare skin; his flesh tore, tearing through the ligaments in his leg. A moment of fate and horror followed, where energy siphoned into Markus' hand with a ferocity unlike any other.

Markus lifted his other leg and kicked the Hound in the stomach, forcing it to stop dragging him and stay still for a second——

Gritting his teeth in a venomous snarl, Markus lifted his palm to the Hound—

"Not again, you *bitch*."

The lightning blast crossed the clearing between them in a heart-beat, meeting its mark perfectly across the Hound's jaw.

Its eyes popped, as its entire face seemed to explode in a gore of teeth and skin. Its skull flayed open entirely like a blooming flower, relinquishing any grip the Hound held on his leg. Its broken jaw came away and snapped blindly, rolling like a door-hinge, before the legs gave in and it slumped to the floor with blood pooling over the stone slabs beneath.

Markus exhaled and pushed up to a stand, steadying the pulses that shot up and down his forearm with an erratic intensity. He swallowed through a bubble in his throat—

When a growl sounded behind him suddenly, echoing and regurgitating in the gloom of the storm—

Markus hissed and turned—

A snarl pierced his ears—

He lifted his hand—

Teeth and eyes—

The other Hound lunged up for his head, all savage and lethal—

Markus rammed his forearm into the beast's rash-covered throat, holding its snapping skull inches from his head.

The world shrunk around him. Lightning clipped the sky. The Hound clacked its teeth together over and over, the stench of rotten fish crawling out of its gullet.

Markus strained, sweating, teeth clenching, rain soaked and tired and so furiously *alive,* pushing back against the gnashing fangs and the maw that waited to consume him.

C'mon! C'mon!

Spittle splashed across his face like mud.

He bellowed at the top of his lungs.

The beast's front legs reached forward to claw at him—

Turning his elbow, Markus redirected the attack before it came, throwing the Hound off with a grunt of exertion.

The beast landed on all fours and clawed at the ground to steady itself—

It turned and lunged again almost immediately, its jaws opened wide—

Markus clenched a fist and punched the Hound in the cheek, crunching his knuckles as he did so.

Electric spat out from the impact point. The hairs on its mouth singed and blackened. The shock of the blast stunned the beast for a few moments, forcing it to retreat awkwardly away with the ugly stump of its tail tucked between its legs. The creature hobbled and blundered about, tripping over itself as it teetered sideways. The pining noises that slipped from its lips offered a small victory, even beneath the rancour of the surging rain.

Death awaits, creature, Markus snarled, centring himself on his prey. Defiant against the odds, he took a single step towards the beast with his hand flaring blue—

When another bubble of sickness ballooned in his throat, and a fresh agony pulled up his lower leg, as the third Hound made its attack and snapped through his wounded calf.

Markus hissed, conjuring lightning in his fist—

The Hound slipped away, retreating back from danger—

Gods, that hurts!

Revolting against the pain, Markus turned his attention back to the wound on his leg: at least seven punctures marked his calf and shin, soaking his foot in a torrent of blood that showed no sign of stopping. Muddy, gangrenous marks surrounded them, inviting infection almost immediately. Applying any pressure to his leg was excruciating; the idea of walking on it seemed impossible. Frozen to the spot – following the Hound as it circled him through the storm – Markus considered his options and came up with nothing to spare.

Maybe I… maybe I need to—

"Markus-us-us."

He flinched; another bellow of thunder eclipsed the sky.

What do you want—

"*Markus… power… heal…*"

Registering its words, he looked down to the wound again – and, in the half-haze of light drifting through the dead-clouds above, he saw the iridescent shades of blue beneath the crimson tide of blood, working furiously to stem its flow and seal the wound up once more.

The lightning heals… of course it does. Like it did when the spear hit me. He opened his palm out, and the energy appeared like a dutiful dog, ready to be used at his whim.

So if it's trying to heal itself without any help, then maybe some more direct power could help seal the——

"*Markus-us-us…*"

He flinched at the disruption, looking out into the rain.

And from somewhere behind him, a low growl echoed out.

"*Behind you——*"

Markus only managed half a turn – pivoting on his damaged leg like the wooden anchor-point of a ship – before a weight collided against his back and shoved him suddenly to the ground.

Claws raked against his shoulder-blades, cutting deep; he thudded against the floor with a wheeze of breath, bashing his nose into the stone slabs. An explosion of pain rocked his system, like a galleon hitting rocks, and he felt his vision fade for a few moments.

Until a set of heavy claws *clack*ed against the stones next to his head, and reality pirouetted in his mind like a broken dam: there were talons pinning his lower back; padding feet approaching from somewhere ahead of him; the warm, disgusting breath of an animal looming just above his neck——

Markus' eyes bulged.

Oh fuck——

Like a startled horse, he kicked out suddenly and caught the Hound's hind leg with his boot——

A horrific *snap* sounded in his eardrums, followed by a whimper of fear, as the Hound's leg broke and its jaws clamped shut inches from the nape of his neck——

Seizing the moment, Markus swung his heel across and took out the other back leg, feeling the weight of the beast slide inelegantly to one side—

Conjuring strength in his arm, he pushed up and flung the Hound off of him, using the momentum to continue his roll with seismic shifts of energy coursing over his hand—

The beast landed on its back and howled, attempting to right itself—

Markus flipped over and grabbed the Hound's throat—

The storm howled above—

Lashing rain pummelled his back—

The Hound whined and lunged with its claws, reaching for him desperately—

As a terrifying pulse exploded from his hand, and killed the beast where it lay.

The skin blackened under his grip; the Hound's entire body shuddered and seized. Bruising bloomed under the surface of its pale, malformed skin, as the energy pulsed up its sagging neck and obliterated its brain cavity therein.

The legs buckled at the knees. The gross pink tongue rolled from its mouth and drooled a line of blood. The Hound's attack had lasted mere moments in the end.

But its death had followed in a matter of heartbeats, too.

Pushing up on his hand, Markus dragged his wounded leg up beneath him and eased slowly to a stand, scrunching his face up at the new pains echoing across his back. His skull pounded like a drum, full of incomprehensible noise he longed to dispel. Interconnected strands of light coated his chest, sending shockwaves over his body as it tried to fix him. Somewhere above, the storm shuddered at the will of its master.

And somewhere ahead, another low growl reverberated through the gloom.

Markus gritted his teeth and looked through the maelstrom ahead. His hair lay strapped against his skull, pearlescent in the half-light. Water spilled from his bare chest, hissing like steam as it made contact with the shards of lightning, blanketing his body and igniting over his forearm with a deadly intensity.

He had summoned a storm, by his own hand, and he had broken the very earth they walked upon.

And in its maw, grappling with fate and death, all Markus found he could do was smile.

"I am a monster, and I am a saviour," he proclaimed to the world, following the path of the Hound as it circled slowly ahead of him. "The stench of death haunts me like a ghost… I am the thing the living fear and the dead despise. I am in defiance of the natural order, as the natural order defies me. None shall stop me in my path… and *none* shall stand against me."

Markus lifted his hand to his head and placed two of his fingers together – opposite him, the Hound stopped its pacing and snarled with hallowed eyes.

"I am the ultimatum of all mortal things!"

The beast hunkered down on its front legs; somewhere in the beyond, a golden light glowed softly.

"I am the mercy of gods and sinners…"

Markus grinned; the Hound started running.

"I am the knife of sorrows…"

The beast hurtled forward, driving forward on muscular legs over the wet stone slabs of the square, its teeth gnashing and flaring like a hundred tiny arrowheads, ready to tear him to shreds—

When Markus snapped his fingers.

A bolt of lightning surged down from the skies overhead: a broken, twisted thing of raw energy, breaking from the vortex. It erupted across the sky-line, consuming everything momentarily in a glorious, horrifying light—

Before connecting with the loping back of the Hound, and burning it to cinders in seconds.

The charred corpse evaporated into oblivion. The shockwave rippled across the village square. A metamorphic power had expelled from the world, bleeding it's wound dry.

Light bloomed and light flowed. Rain rasped and rain billowed. The gods looked on and pleaded softly.

Everything was done.

Markus lowered his hand with a trembling sigh, as the rain that had surged down from the clouds above suddenly ceased to be. A faint light returned to the world, illuminating a shadowy land that had been lost in the furore of the storm. Silence followed in trickling intervals, ringing out in his ears with an effortless glee.

Markus held still for a moment, closing his eyes and letting the light wash over him, and found that the wounds he had sustained in the fight had all but disappeared. The punctures on his back had stopped weeping; the claw-mark on his shoulder was little more than a scar. Even the damage done to his lower leg had eased, and allowed him to stand straighter without complaint.

A resolved sensation overcame his mind, settling with the power in his chest. The tension in the air, and in his heart, exhaled softly from his soul. Time seemed suddenly obsolete.

Now peace had finally come.

Markus let his eyes roll open slowly, taking in the square before him, acknowledging the puddles and the sloping houses there—

And the small boy, stood at the north-west corner of the square, watching from where the Hounds had emerged from with a golden aura over his skin.

Markus had no idea who the boy was. He had no idea what he symbolised. He had no inkling as to what connection there was between them and the voice in his head. But all he did know, is that whatever came next, the boy would provide his answer.

The golden child from the lake in the trees.

Markus started walking.

†

Chapter 28

The Choice

The rain ceased. The thunder stilled. The clouds overhead lost their dour greyness, folding in on each other like blankets. Shards of sunlight drifted down from high above. The domes of the Tarrazi houses peeled back from the shadows. Light shimmered over the stone slabs of the village square like fish-scales.

And the *Yabusto* stood at the centre of it all, staring at him intently.

Xafiri stood frozen to the spot, saturated by rainwater with shivers pulling up his spine. Mud plastered his legs, and hardened across his hands like a death-mask. His skin crawled with sensation, as the static in the air dissipated in the winds. He was alone, a wayward ship on an open sea, staring into the eyes of an enemy he could hardly even fathom.

An enemy that knew who he was, and knew what he had done.

The Hounds should've stopped them, Xafiri thought, moving back toward the hillside inch-by-precious-inch, trying to swallow through a knot in his throat. *The Hounds are born and bred to be hunters. To be killers. Nothing survives them. Not even the* Zoltha *can withstand their attacks. The Hounds should've stopped the* Yabusto, *and they... they should've...*

Oh, gods.

A wave of dread overcame him, swallowing him, gazing into the raw, dead eyes of the *Yabusto* stood at the centre of the square. They

240

were like a statue, gaunt and hollow, lashed by the rain and broken by the storm, with the bodies of the dead Hounds littering the ground around them like ornaments to Tazûl.

That was our only chance, Xafiri rasped. *That was all we had left. The Hounds were meant to save us.*

We can't fight this thing. We can't survive whatever power it exudes. Countless have died already.

The *Yabusto* took a single step forward.

Xafiri flinched.

And I fear I may be next.

He didn't bother seeing what happened next – didn't bother watching death approach slowly from the south. Xafiri skidded on his heel and spun around, struggling with his footing as he descended the muddy slope again, using the clefts produced by the running Hounds to guide his path back to the bottom.

Anxious adrenaline fed through his body. His breath matched the rhythm of his heart, rapid and uncontrollable as his eyes bulged and his skin tingled and the presence of the enemy pressed down against his back—

His foot slipped out from beneath him and he threw his hands out suddenly, balancing his weight like a lame puppet and just managing to stay upright. Looking about, the mud around him seemed to slide and ooze, with rivers of water streaming down towards the distant trees. The entire hillside seemed to shift, as the yellowish mud twisted and flowed. In an absent part of his mind, Xafiri thought briefly of his mother, and wondered if she had escaped the storm okay.

Hopefully she has, and I can see her again soon, he thought with a pain in his heart. *Hopefully she's got herself far away from here, and I can see her again once this* thing *has gone—*

Gasping suddenly, Xafiri's foot slipped again, and he collapsed forward with his hands outstretched and catapulted down into the mud.

Sod splattered over his face; slimy residue coated his chest. In desperation, he clawed at wedges of thick mud, trying to scrabble away quickly—

As crackles echoed in his ears and his heart stopped; he turned over and looked back toward the slope—

To find the *Yabusto* already there, stood over him with menace, its features wrought like broken daggers in the low, eclipsing light.

Grey hair stuck to its scalp. Patterns marked its chest. Lightning cavorted up its arm, binding wounds over its stomach and neck.

Bile burned Xafiri's oesophagus. Faintness pulled at his skin.

He lifted a hand in perilous fear.

"Please don't..."

†

"...kill me."

The words left the small boy's lips – little more than a croak in the end – and Markus thought for a moment that he was hearing things. That maybe the voices in his head, chattering like birds, had distorted the sound, and he'd completely missed what the boy had actually been trying to say.

He speaks in common tongue? Markus deduced, his brow furrowing like a landslide. *But if that's the case, then... how does he know that?*

"I don't know if you... if you understand," the boy whimpered, the first spots of tears fresh in his eyes, "but... but please... please don't hurt me... *please*—"

"I'm not going to hurt you," Markus replied – and he watched as the boy's eyes expanded exponentially in their sockets, hearing the words leave his mouth.

"You..." The boy sat up suddenly, all fear lost in his voice. "How do you speak Provencian?"

"It's where I'm from, where I used to live." He shifted his hand behind his back, hoping the young boy wouldn't notice. "But the bigger question is: how do *you* know Provencian?"

"I learned it, from... from the Educators, during the Occupation.

I was one of the children put on their… programme." His words were soft, almost embarrassed: Markus sensed that it had not been easy. "I… I can *understand* you."

"And I can understand you."

The boy raised his brows. "But, if you're from the south then… then are you not a *Yabusto?*"

"A *what?*"

"A *Yabusto,* a… a Deathbringer."

"I… no?"

The boy shook his head. "Tazûl is said to work in deceit, in order to claim His victims…"

Markus scoffed. "Look, lad… I have *no* idea what you're talking about. I don't know who this… '*Ta-zool*'… is, and I am certainly not a *Yabusto* or whatever it was that you said. I'm neither of those things, okay?"

The boy seemed to consider, looking up at him with a terrified, blank expression, like a deer moments before it's hit with an arrow. *He's weighing up if I'm telling the truth or not,* Markus deduced. *This Ta-zool, or whatever it is, must be of great danger to them. They think I'm one of their enemy.*

A flicker of energy pulsed in his hand.

And it's probably because of that.

"How do I know?" the boy asked suddenly.

"Know… what?"

"That you aren't working for Tazûl."

"Well, other than the fact that I don't know who that is, or what they would want with me… I don't have any answers. I am not '*working*' for anyone at all."

The boy was silent again for a few moments, rolling through possibilities in their head – before consigning to defeat, knowing they had no other choice but to believe. "I still don't understand, though… because if you're not *Yabusto,* and you're not from around here, then… why are you *here,* in the Hills? What has brought you here?" A glint of uneasiness crossed his eyes. "Are you here to… *hurt* us?"

"I am not here to hurt you, no," Markus replied, matter-of-factly. "That is never my intention."

"But what about the others... the ones that you killed..."

"No-one in the village has died today, I... I made sure of it."

"And what about the ones in the forest, in the clearing?"

Markus flinched — *how does he know about that?* — before a realisation struck him like a crossbow bolt, and he lowered down to a crouch.

"You're the boy who was sat in that tree, aren't you?" he said softly, levelling his gaze. "You were there when I was ambushed. You... I let you live. I let you run as the forest burned..."

"Yes, I ran away. I ran from *Yabusto*."

"Yes, yes..." Markus nodded, putting the pieces together. "And I *let* you run away and survive... because I need you *now*. That's why the power didn't kill you in the clearing..."

"Power?" he interrupted suddenly, his head on a swivel. "What... what power?"

Reluctantly, Markus pulled his hand from behind his back and placed it on his kneecap. "This," he said, as a flicker of lightning dashed over his knuckles and fizzled out of existence.

The boy opposite recoiled almost immediately, pulling himself back through the mud. He stared at the lightning like it were some accursed thing, left in the trees to fend off demons. And, considering what kind of destruction the lightning had unleashed on his fellow warriors the previous night, Markus was unsurprised by the fearful response.

"It won't hurt you, don't... don't worry." Markus spoke softly, opening his palm out for him to see.

"Wha... what?"

"You're safe, I assure you. I am in control of it——"

"Then why did you kill them?" the boy bellowed, a flash of anger and grief crossing his complexion. Wrinkles formed over his face, almost in a snarl. "Why did you do it? Why did you kill the *feduzak* in the forest!"

Markus opened his mouth to respond – to ask the boy to calm down, and stop drawing attention to them – when the thought passed on a gust of wind and all he could manage was a sigh. There was no use in trying to reprimand the boy. Markus was hardly in a position to tell the boy to watch his anger.

I know I've never been very good at watching mine.

"I... I didn't mean to kill them." He stopped, grinding his jaw. "Well, I *did* mean to... but I didn't have a way of choosing. I didn't have a choice as to whether they lived or died." He lifted his hand and studied it for a moment. "This power... has a mind of its own. It is sometimes calm, and sometimes angry. And it can do nasty things to people, if I don't control it. Really nasty things..." He looked deep into the black orbs of the Tarrazi boy's eyes, and saw an understanding there. The anger had gone; he was listening.

"I don't always have a choice to control it," Markus continued. "It was not my choice to have it in the first place. It was vested in me, when I..." – he snorted – "...for reasons I can't *explain*. And it has been with me ever since then, and sometimes I can decide how to use it, and how much power to give... but other times I cannot. Other times... *it* controls *me*."

He sighed, nodding slowly. "I'm sorry that I killed your people in the clearing... I'm sorry that you had to witness the power at its worst. I was not in control... and I had no choice." He pointed out behind him. "But everyone here in the village – every warrior I encountered in this place – they are all still alive. They are unconscious... or *'sleeping'*, as you might understand it, but they are all very much alive too." He returned his hand to his side. "Because here, and now, I have control over this power... over *this,* that you see here on my hand. It is safe, because I understand it. It will not hurt you – *I* will not hurt you. I just want to talk, and I want to control this power... even though I never wanted it..."

†

"…in the first place."

Staring into the *Yabusto's — no, the person's —* eyes as he finished speaking, Xafiri processed what he had said and saw the layers of mystery peel away, revealing beneath the dark shadows a deep and very lost soul.

He was a Provencian who spoke a language Xafiri understood, with words he could comprehend. He was a being of flesh and blood, with scraggly hair and scars and piercing eyes. He was, at the crucial juncture, just another man: a man who had undergone a change that he had no choice in, and could not revert from now, with *zazkan* in his soul that he struggled to control, affecting those around him in terrible ways. He was a corrupted, tired, dislocated man, regretful of his past and terrified of his future. A man who had stumbled down a dark path and lost his place in the world.

A man just like me.

Xafiri sat up and stilled the shaking in his hands, breathing deeply. *This is nothing to do with Tazûl,* he thought. *I don't know who this man is, or why they're here with us… but this is not a Deathbringer before me.*

This is something very different.

"You have power you can't control… you feel lost on your path ahead," Xafiri said softly.

"Yes," the man boomed in reply, their voice crackling like cinder. "Something like that."

"Well, I… I know that feeling too." He felt his stomach churn at the memory, but swallowed it down. "When the Educators came, I didn't have a choice to take part or not. I was selected, and I agreed, and they taught me everything I know… but I was shunned by my people for doing it. For even *talking* to the *Zoltha.* They thought I was a demon, and a worker of the enemy… and I couldn't even argue against it, because… well, because I never even learned my own language to *try.*"

Xafiri didn't understand why he was telling the man his story, or what instigated him to be so honest — but something about the depths of the man's eyes connected with him, and seemed to draw the essence out of his soul. It was a golden light, almost like a reflection, which lay across the man's vision in hazy colours. It tempered a warmth in Xafiri's soul, as he looked deeper and unpicked the shadows, and saw what was really lost there. An unseen, buried element, glowing like a tiny star.

The truth... our truth.

The things that make us who we are.

"Ever since the day that my tribe found out how I was educated... I have been shunned and dismissed at every turn, and I seem to have no way out," Xafiri continued. "The path forward is not open for me, and it never will be again. I will never be a true member of the tribe; I will never pass my *Fendûrii*. I am condemned to be an outsider for as long as I live here... a *mantugo,* forevermore." Xafiri scoffed morbidly, his mind trailing off. "I mean, I'll probably be condemned to death anyway, just for being here and talking to you. They'll never let me explain my reasons, whatever happens – I'll never get to explain that you're more than just a monster from our legends. I've never even had the chance to explain *myself*... so as soon as they see me talking to you" – he gazed up to the plateau behind the man, and saw a few cautious faces peering over the edge – "it won't even matter anyway. None of it will. Because they'll arrest me once you've gone, and take me away..."

†

"...and come morning, I'll be dead."

Markus saw the boy look down to his feet like he was being condemned to hang, and was surprised by just how frank his perspective was on his rapidly approaching death. The boy didn't seem afraid, or even unsettled: in announcing his execution, he was stating a matter of fact, clear for all to see without a shadow of doubt. He knew he would die come morning, and that was where his story would end. In his eyes – so dark and vast – there was no changing that.

Poor lad… I know how that feels.

In the ebbing silence that followed, with more people appearing in the periphery of his vision, Markus saw the golden aura around the boy recede and expand like the tide, wrestling with emotions and a frightening reality over and over again. He saw conflict and concern, and a greater duty just beyond that seemed to bridge the two.

And, in the black orbs of the boy's eyes, Markus saw his own reflection there, too, feeling the exact same thing. Neither of them knew what it meant, or what would happen next. Neither of them knew what the path forward would entail. The past had been a place of hurt; the future was somewhere that they could hardly contemplate.

But what Markus did know, by the whim of the voices in his mind, was that whatever happened next on his long journey ahead, he would not be doing it alone.

Which leaves me with one choice…

"Come… with me," Markus said bluntly, commandingly, confused by his own words for a moment. "Or rather, I mean—"

"Come with you where?" the boy replied, with a mix of fear and intrigue.

"Well I… I'm heading north into the Wastelands, on my way to… *Val Azbann.*" He winced at the word, and the boy seemed to frown at him in disbelief. "But I know the path there is dangerous, and your people are numerous across this land… and I fear I may never reach that city if I go at this alone, without knowing the safest paths forward. So I came to this village, and came into these hills… in the hopes of finding someone who could take me through the Wastelands and help me reach Azbann's walls." His lips became a thin line for a moment. "And I admit, I was expecting to use coercion to do so, and drag someone with me at knife-point… but now that we're here, and I've found *you*… I wanted to offer it to you as a choice instead."

Cautiously, with half a smile etched onto his face, Markus opened his hand out and extended it toward the boy, who watched the tiny shards of lightning dance over it like fish.

"I know you don't know who I am, or fully understand why I'm here… but I'm giving you the choice, here and now, to trust me," Markus explained. "If I go north alone, I will likely not make it out of there alive. If you stay here once I've gone, you will be executed as a heretic by your own people. You need a way out, and I need a guide who knows the ways of the Tarrazi. *We* need each other, if we're going to make it out of this alive… so I offer you a chance now, to save yourself from death, and come with me to Azbann." Markus twitched his fingers. "The choice, is yours."

Crouched there in the mud, with villagers watching them from the safety of their clay walls, Markus saw a thousand tiny thoughts dart behind the boy's eyes, as he weighed up the momentous choice laid out before him. The choice between betrayal, and certain death. Between duty, and survival. Between love, and hope.

Between fate, and sin.

Markus breathed deeply, sensing the air tense around them, and watched the young boy's hand lift from his side. Time seemed to slow down, as the boy reached out and his fingertips extended, edging his hand closer and closer—

Until a wail sounded from somewhere off to their side, and the wet slap of running caught in Markus' ear—

†

"*Xafi!*"

Xafiri recognised the voice almost immediately – recognised the panic as if it were his own – and a wave of horror overcame him, as he watched the grey man tense up opposite him with the *zazkan* flickering over their palm.

With little time to react, Xafiri turned to his left and stepped forward, shifting between the grey man and the approaching figure who charged over the mud towards them. A figure with mud splatters and rust-coloured robes, and eyes like glossy moons.

A figure he knew better than anyone else, who he was so glad to see still alive.

"Ma!" Xafiri cried, opening his arms out and bundling her up before she could take another step closer to the man. "Ma, stop, it's okay! It's okay…"

Overcoming her sudden panic, his mother looked up to him with a quivering lip and wrapped her arms around him, breaking down in fearful tears, sobbing against his chest. Her hands clawed against his back, almost as if he were fading away.

"You okay…" she spluttered, "you okay… you okay…"

"Yes, ma, I am okay." Xafiri placed his cheek against the top of her head, stroking her back gently. "I'm okay."

"Are you safe?" she asked suddenly, stepping back and glancing behind him at the grey man. "Did it… did it hurt you?"

"I'm safe ma, do not worry. The man was just talking to me, that's all."

"The man?" She paused, frowning. "But, *Yabusto…?*"

"He is not *Yabusto*, ma, he is not. He is a man, from the south, very far away. He is lost. Needs help."

She opened her mouth to say something – glancing past Xafiri again to observe the newcomer – and he saw her throat visibly close up.

"The *zazkan,* Xafi… I see it, he *holds* it…"

"It is a power that he has, ma, yes. He tries to control it. He controls it now. We are safe, I promise you. He will not hurt anyone."

She looked to her left, up over the ridge of the slope. "All the other people, though, Xafi…"

"They sleep, ma. He put them to sleep, like a *redeza* flower. They will wake up soon. He has not killed anyone."

Her eyes shone. "They are all… alive?"

"Yes, all alive."

Colour returned to her cheeks, as a wave of relief washed over her. The dusted orange coils of her hair fluttered in the gentle wind.

"That is good," she said eventually. "That is good. I am glad, I was… worried."

"It is good, yes, of course. It's… yea."

"What is it, Xafi?" she asked, sensing his uncertainty. "Is something wrong?"

"Oh no, I… well, I…"

Xafiri looked up to the clouds above and sighed, squinting his eyes shut. For a brief moment, he turned back to the grey man who bowed his head slowly, acknowledging what Xafiri had to do next, and what he had to say.

The truth that I now have to obey, he thought uneasily, turning back to his mother.

Now that I've nowhere left to hide.

"Ma, I… I can't stay here anymore," he said quietly, fighting the wave of emotion ballooning in his chest.

She puzzled at him, silent and still. "What… you mean?"

"I can't stay in the village anymore, ma, I… I can't live here. I have to go. If I stay, they will call me a *Yabusto*, and I will be killed. I am already in trouble for going out with the *feduzak* yesterday, and I fear that, if I stay, and this man leaves… they will kill me, and I won't get a chance to explain to them what's really going on, and that it wasn't my fault. I have no other choice."

He placed his hands on her shoulders, watching her process his words with the glint of tears in her eyes.

"I know… I know you may not understand, but the man has offered me a chance to go with him… to go north, through the Wasteland," Xafiri explained, holding his own tears back. "As I speak his language, and I've studied the land, I'm the best person for what he needs. I can go with him, and not face the fate waiting for me if I stay here. I can live, and *survive*, and even come back here one day, maybe… but I have to go now, if that's to happen. I have to go and get away from here. I can't stay ma, I can't… I'm so *sorry*, I'm *so*…"

His voice broke, as a bubble burst in his throat and the pain swelled through his body with incomprehensible force. His voice and breath stuttered, looking deep into the heartbroken wells of his mother's gentle eyes. The world crumbled around him, piece by piece, as the sorrow claimed his heart and the choice became clearest.

"I… I don't want to leave you, *ma*…"

Xafiri held her shoulders tightly, his hands trembling, the strength leaving his knees with each outward breath.

His mother stood opposite watching him, her face a contortion of pain and fortitude, reciting his words over in her head. The wrinkles and rivets in her skin made her appear far older, far weaker than he had ever remembered. Her tears seemed like tiny crystals, shining in the low light.

After what felt like a millennia, his mother pulled his hands off of her shoulders and held them in her own. Her eyes met his — a desperate kinship passing between them — and she managed a tiny smile, curling at the edge of her cheeks.

"You must go, Xafi… you must," she said, breathing deeply. "I will be okay here. I will be safe. But you must go… you must live. If this… man, has way of keeping you alive, then go. You must. And I will be here when you come back." She gulped, squeezing his hands. "I will *always* be here, Xafi. Wherever you go, whatever you do… always be here. Always."

Xafiri pulled her in close and hugged her again — for the last time, for what could have been forever — stilling the trembles in his hands and the sobs that echoed out his throat.

She pulled in close, brushing a hand up and down his back before parting again, looking up at him with glassy eyes.

Two fingers touched her chest, and circled around her heart.

"I will always love you, Xafi," she said.

Xafiri placed two fingers on his chest, swallowing through tears.

"I love you too, ma… I'll return one day, I promise."

"I know you will, Xafi… I know you will."

He managed one final smile, clenching his jaw tight until his teeth hurt, before turning from her and wiping a lone tear from his eye.

On shaky legs, he returned to the grey man, who had risen to a stand with his hand against his chest, almost in mourning. As Xafiri approached, the man opened his hand out again to him with tired, haunted eyes.

"So… are you ready?" they said softly, like a wingbeat.

Xafiri drew in a long breath, with the gods' gazing down from high above, and took his hand.

"I am ready… let's go."

†

Epilogue

The Knife of Sorrows

The entire village had gathered to watch them depart, forming a narrow channel to the northern gatehouse lined with the points of spears. The guards wore snarls that oozed with malice; those stood behind them stared wide-eyed as they passed, with fear and anger worn heavy over their shoulders. None of them could quite comprehend what had happened, and many were terrified of what would come next. They turned to their gods for answers, only to find none were forthcoming. They were alone, in the end, wondering what could be done.

Knowing life would never be the same again.

Markus and Xafiri walked side-by-side, shoulder-to-shoulder, wearing grave expressions that spoke of the toll they had suffered. Their boots sunk deep in the wet mud beneath them; a haze of flies followed behind, as if trailing a corpse of the dead. Xafiri, with his eyes red raw and his hands still trembling, looked upon the gatehouse ahead with a sense of dread. Markus, with his hand placed warily on Xafiri's shoulder, looked upon the distant hills past the gates with a sense of relief, knowing his first task was complete. He had found the child, and they had agreed to help him in his journey north to Azbann. The wheels of fate were in motion again.

The question was: what came next?

Looking to the crowds who had gathered around them, beyond

the shimmering spear-points of the guards, Xafiri saw faces he recognised, that he would never see again. Young children with their families, looking on with such intrigue, with their *Fendûrii* on the near horizon; Ritualists and old warriors, curling their faces up with disgust, muttering wards to protect themselves whenever Xafiri caught their gaze; young hunters, who had recently become Proven, smirking with glee as the foolish outcast was marched from their walls, condemned for his sins at last. He spied the *Hajiin* Temusceh and his son among their number, too, staring through him with an ugly smugness, trying to avoid the terrifying gaze of the man at his side.

And then, toward the end of the long corridor of people, Xafiri caught the dark speckled robes and golden necklaces of the Verlunz, surrounded by their entourage of guards. They stood at the end of the line, with a huge number of spears crisscrossing the space in front of them. They bowed their head in sorrow and prayer, but to which gods Xafiri wasn't sure.

As he approached, the Verlunz lifted their head and looked between the two outcasts, meeting their eyes exactingly without any fear or unease. There was no disdain there, for what the grey man had done; there was no disgust with Xafiri, for going with him then. The Verlunz looked upon them both only with a quiet acceptance, as if their fate had been foretold all along.

Knowing they would never return again, to the place neither of them could call home.

Markus drew in a deep breath and felt Xafiri tense beneath his hand. The gatehouse loomed above them, the sentinels gazing down like crows. A lone guardsman pulled the gate ajar, shuffling back behind the line of spears to allow them space to pass. The electrical energy rolled and churned in his stomach, sensing the tension in the air like tendrils.

Xafiri didn't allow himself to look back. He refused to acknowledge the truth as it happened. Placing a hand on the opened gate, he pushed away from Markus' reach and stepped out into the trees beyond, only releasing his breath when the grey man stepped through behind him and the gates slammed shut forevermore.

Ahead, beyond the gnarled wooden wall of the village perimeter, trees and shadows dominated the world. There were pale boughs and rotten branches, with tiny buds of green leaves and algae-like growths across the roots. There were bugs that swarmed through the air, brought out by the deluge that had swept through the village. There was mud at their feet, as thick as quicksand, meandering between the trees in stodgy paths. Somewhere in the distance, the highest peaks of the western mountains poked out between the canopies, marking the impassable edge of the known world.

Markus looked down on Xafiri, as the boy looked up at him, with a worn look on his face that spoke of fate and fear. Markus put his hand on the boy's arm, and tried meekly to smile.

"My name is Markus," he said gently. "What's your name?"

"Xafiri," the boy replied, his eyes flitting like a dragonfly.

"Well, Xafiri, from hereon the path is completely yours. Get me through the land ahead, and on to the walls of Azbann, and I will protect you every step of the way and guard you with my life." His face turned suddenly sinister, flickering with deadly shadows. "But if you choose to betray me, or lead me into the maw of the enemy... then there will be nowhere you can hide from my blade, or the consequences of my wrath. Do you understand?"

Xafiri didn't respond to the threat; he hardly responded to his words at all. Grief coated his face, and it refused to let go.

"Understood," he mumbled quietly, opening a hand out to the trees. "This way, if you will."

Xafiri turned from him, his heart in his stomach, and traipsed off into the shadows beyond.

Markus stood watching him in silence, uncertain of the boy he now had in his company. They were similar in so many ways: ground under the wheels of fortune, and spat out by the anguish of others; motivated and resolved, but never truly trusting; ready to lend their hand to help those in need, but also waiting to let it go.

The boy was a force of nature; he was nature, by force.

Offering a sigh, Markus allowed his hand to slip from the boy's shoulder—

And hissed, as a pain snapped across his palm, where he looked down suddenly to see—

A dash of gold lightning pass between his fingertips and disappear a heartbeat later, pulling back up into his arm as if it had never been there at all.

Markus' heart thundered; Xafiri turned back to acknowledge him, before shrugging and walking on.

What… was that…

Markus closed his hand, balling it up into a fist, and clamped his jaw together. The energy pulsed and flushed for several moments before finally laying still. His skin crawled with activity, pulling up through his veins as he tried to bury the truth about what he had seen.

The gold…

He shook his head and blinked into the sun.

Just the light, that's all: the light playing tricks…

Looking ahead, he saw the boy slip between the first pair of trees, out into the shadows beyond.

Markus looked down at his hand one more time, tracing the black marks over his knuckles, before scoffing and following behind. Out into the forests of the Valatuk Hills.

Onwards, to Val Azbann.

A GLOSSARY OF TARRAZI

- *Az-Kabza* – a traditional greeting or expression used among all Tarrazi cultures, meaning 'blood or death'
- *Kal-Vak'tun* – the God of the Hunt, depicted as a legged serpent in green robes
- *Va'javesti* – a mark of comradeship, meaning 'brother' or 'friend'
- *Verlunz* – a chief or warrior of a Tarrazi tribe, elected for their prowess in verse, combat or diplomacy [they are often referred to as 'princes' by Provenci scholars, although this is a grossly-appropriated reference]
- *Scolgul* – 'patience'
- *Zoltharyya* [Zol-thar-ya] – the term given to the Provenci military occupation of Tarraz after the Collapse fifty years prior; it is used as an insulting, derogatory term, translating literally to 'invaders with knives'
- *Zoltha* – a name used among the southern- and middle-tribes of Tarrazi when referring to a Provencian person; it is also used as an insulting, derogatory term, meaning 'invader'
- *Tarmun* – an insult, meaning 'fool' or 'idiot'
- *Zaz-gûla* [zaz-goo-la] – the ceremonial markings inked onto a Tarrazi's face, as part of their initiation into adulthood [known as becoming 'Proven' among the tribe]; they reflect a distinct connection to a specific natural element or diety, unique to every individual

- *Skal-thüm* [skal-thoum] – meaning 'young soul', it is used in both a literal and derogative sense to indicate a young or naïve person
- *Ras'gandû* [raz-gan-doo] – the God of the Skirmish, depicted as a mantis coated in metal scales
- *Mantugo* – translates literally as 'other', describing an object or person with a foreign or distasteful nature [more recently, it has also been used to describe young Tarrazi people schooled by Provencian 'Educators' during the Occupation]
- *Desgundy paraba* – loosely translated as 'Proven', it is an honorific title given to young Tarrazi who undergo their rite-of-passage, which usual occurs after fourteen- to sixteen-winters; once they become 'Proven', a Tarrazi is given their first *zaz-gûla* and there is celebration among their close family
- *Desgundy nedu-paraba* – a term for an 'Unproven' of the tribe, although the phrase is often only used as an insult to those who have failed to achieve their rite-of-passage [as opposed to the word *skal,* which is more commonly used and translates to 'youngling']
- *Fendûrii* [fen-doo-rey-ee] – 'rite-of-passage'
- *Marzedna* – translations of the term are poor, but it is commonly ascribed to the word 'mother' or 'matriarch', and usually describes a respected female among the tribe and/or family
- *Hajiin* – a 'herbalist' [often referred to by Provencian scholars as an 'alchemist']
- *Nedu* – a broad, negative term meaning 'no' or 'nothing more'
- *Bujanti* – translated literally as 'enough'
- *Ful-Vankyra* – the God of the Feast, depicted as a hound made from reams of red cloth
- *Vas-gal* – a ceremonial statement, meaning 'you are seen'

- *Dügër'ma* [doo-je-ra-ma] — an incredibly-sacred term, only used by a tribe's Verlunz or appointed official during ceremonial occasions; in a direct translation, it means 'God-spoken', proclaiming the superiority of the Tarrazi people and their right to prosper and expand [during the Occupation, Provencian propaganda and scare-mongering tactics sparked an outright ban of the phrase for nearly thirty years, as it was viewed by Imperial administrators as a 'provocative term inciting violence', due to its reference to expansion]
- *Zazkan Stor'oma* — 'lightning reigns'
- *Dal-Guzud* — the God of Omens, depicted as a black scorpion with gold claws to represent darkness and the end times
- *Oruma* — translates to 'prayer', and is typically used in a religious/pious context
- *Ubentü* [uh-ben-too] — translates literally as 'omen' or 'fate-marked'
- *Kand'u* — God of the Warrior, depicted as an eagle with black eyes and tassels for wings
- *Wesendyri* [wes-en-dear-ee] — a native Tarrazi plant, found in arid or semi-deciduous regions, with multi-pronged, conical branches and a complex root system — they store water within their branches, which is then absorbed by a thin membrane on the inner wall during extreme dry seasons
- *Tazûl* [ta-zool] — the God of Death, the most feared of all the gods in Tarrazi scripture — they are depicted as a giant wolf with gold eyes and half its skull exposed. Seeing them is considered a curse.
- *Feduzak* — a new word meaning 'warrior', adopted in several Tarrazi tribes to accommodate for the broader vocabulary utilised by the Provencian military during the Occupation

- *Qutönûska* [Que-town-oo-sk-ah] — translates literally as 'danger' or 'threat'
- *Vedu* — an exemplifier, meaning 'very' or 'much'
- *Consul* — a verb that is by chance very similar to the Provencian word: to 'consult'
- *Vesti* — a Tarrazi verb, meaning 'to see'
- *Visiorga* [vis-ee-or-gah] — taken from a wide diaspora of terms, *visiorga* refers to a 'person' or 'mortal being', but it also has other connotations: when describing a sacred object, it can be referred to as *visiorga* to accentuate its spiritual qualities — equally, it can be used to describe a collective group of people with similar social or hierarchical standing within a tribe, like hunters or herbalists
- *Pluzrys* [ploo-zer-iss] — meaning 'shadow', it can also be used to describe 'darkness' or, in a metaphorical sense common in Tarrazi scripture, 'absence'
- *Yabusto* — a cursed word rarely used outside of Tarrazi folklore, it implies an agent or denizen of Tazûl that roams the land as a mortal and kills people in Tazûl's name, which has been translated by Provenci scholars as meaning 'Death-bringer' — there have been three recorded *Yabusto* in Tarrazi scripture, with each symbolising the coming of the end times and the dawn of a new era, involving massive loss of life for the Tarrazi tribes across their lands
- *Zesmu* — the God of the Wilds; they are depicted as a deer with glass antlers, and the eyes of fallen stars
- *Fordiira* [for-doo-ra] — definitions are inconclusive, but it is believed that the word is a cultural term used to describe a form of underworld or spiritual 'dark place', similar to the word '*hellos*' [or '*hell*'] in Provencian — for Tarrazi people, this 'hell' is a transient space that people can experience and endure in life as well as death, as their soul transitions back to the gods; it is often described as a cesspit or an 'ooze', similar to a bog, where foul creatures reside and people are

plagued with nightmares of their former lives
- 	*Gat'unsk* — a Tarrazi village hall, constructed using inter-locking tree-trunks and branches with a reinforced clay 'skin' over the top; it is typically used as a communal dining hall and is the residence of the local Verlunz
- 	*Redeza* — a native purple Tarrazi flower with sleep-inducing properties, found in high altitude regions

ACKNOWLEDGEMENTS

This book started out as a short-story project, that would feature in a collection published when the *Blood and Steel Saga* was completed. It then became a novella, bridging an important gap for Markus between book 2 and book 3, focusing on his rise and fall in grief.

So, to see it here as a full length interconnected-standalone novel, is as much a surprise to you, the reader, as it was to me writing it. But when I tell you this was the most fun I've ever had writing a book, know that I mean it — and I hope that translates over into your experience reading it for the first time.

So, I want to offer my thanks, in no particular order, to those who have done the most to help on this weird and wonderful journey:

First, a thanks to Diego Spezzoni, for once again producing a fantastic cover and continuing to be the most excellent illustrator around.

Second, a thanks to Jog Brogzin, for creating another beautiful map to perfectly encapsulate Markus and Xafiri's journey.

To my ARC team, for your wonderful support in the promotion and release of this title.

And to you, the reader, for sticking with this series so far, and

giving a young writer a chance with his debut series. Without your continued support and encouragement, none of this would be possible, and I could not be more honoured to have such a wonderful and engaged community around me.
You are all friends, always.

And, as a final note, I hope you have enjoyed this story of Markus and Xafiri, and look forward to their return in Book 3 of the *Blood and Steel Saga*. Expect naval battles, sieges, conspiracy plots, blossoming relationships and so much more in the next instalment, which looks to be the biggest and bloodiest yet.

I wish you all the best, and as always…

Happy Adventures!

THE HONOURS LIST

Giving a massive thanks to:

Jennifer Sutton
Ross MacBaisey
Henry Sinclair
Glenn Dove
Ganesh Subramanian Alwarappa
Jake Wilson
Joseph McLachlan
Sean Doty
Claudia May
Joanne & Nick Guy
Rebecca King
Chris Fisher
&
Charlotte Macbean

For their support and contributions to the production and publication of this book and my future projects.
You are remarkable people, and have made a young man's dream come true.

I hope to do you proud.

www.ingramcontent.com/pod-product-compliance
Lightning Source LLC
Chambersburg PA
CBHW072257130726
47910CB00012B/2068